Meeting Stasio explained a lot about Nikos....

In fact, what Rachel had learned tonight explained Nikos in a way nothing else could have done. It had made her realize that Stasio and his younger brother were leagues apart, unless Nikos had changed a great deal.

The Nikos of six years ago hadn't been made of the same stuff as his brother, or he would never have rejected her so cruelly. Would never have damaged her friendship with his sister...

Stasio said, "It'll be good for Stella to have you back in her life. You couldn't have shown up at my office at a more propitious moment."

That sounded cryptic. She sensed there were things he hadn't told her. Private things. She discovered she wanted to know everything about him....

Her hands clung to the arms of the chair. "Stasio? I—I don't know how long I'll be able to stay in Greece." *I don't know how long I can be around you and pretend your nearness doesn't affect me.*

A new tension crackled between them. "I thought you wanted to be with Stella."

I did. I do. I planned everything so I could be with my best friend and get Nikos to fall in love and marry me. What I hadn't counted on was meeting you.

Dear Reader,

As you can imagine, I'm a reader as well as a writer. In my teens, one of my favorite books was Alexandre Dumas's classic story of revenge, *The Count of Monte Cristo*.

I can remember how excited I felt when Edmond Dantes finally dealt with his enemies who, of course, deserved everything they got.

Yet, all the time I was rooting for him, I cringed because his revenge was so perfect, so exquisitely precise and cruel. By the time I finished the book, I discovered I was horrified by what he'd done.

Regardless of the fact that he'd been an innocent man who was kept from the woman he loved, an innocent man confined to prison in the prime of his life—regardless of the fact that his enemies deserved to be punished for their crimes against him—I felt as empty as Dantes, who discovered too late the hollowness of his victory.

Oh, yes, he'd wreaked his revenge, but in doing so, he lost his soul.

In *If He Could See Me Now,* my heroine, Rachel Maynard, wants revenge. As you begin reading, I think you'll understand her pain and you'll cheer her on.

But I'll leave it to you to find out what happens to Rachel's soul as she travels down that lonely and precarious path to victory.

Happy reading!

Rebecca Winters

IF HE COULD SEE ME NOW
Rebecca Winters

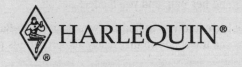

TORONTO • NEW YORK • LONDON
AMSTERDAM • PARIS • SYDNEY • HAMBURG
STOCKHOLM • ATHENS • TOKYO • MILAN • MADRID
PRAGUE • WARSAW • BUDAPEST • AUCKLAND

ISBN 0-373-70840-8

IF HE COULD SEE ME NOW

Copyright © 1999 by Rebecca Winters.

This edition published by arrangement with Harlequin Books S.A.

® and TM are trademarks of the publisher. Trademarks indicated with
® are registered in the United States Patent and Trademark Office, the
Canadian Trade Marks Office and in other countries.

Look us up on-line at: http://www.romance.net

Printed in U.S.A.

IF HE COULD
SEE ME NOW

CHAPTER ONE

"BY THE YEAR 2000, I PLAN TO become Mrs. Nikos Athas!"

A collective gasp escaped the twelve women assembled in the meeting room of the Michelangelo Institute of Philadelphia, Pennsylvania.

The middle-aged director, who had introduced herself only as Erica, put on her glasses and rose to her feet.

"Thank you, Rachel. Now that each of you has told the group the goal you wrote down on the application before it was sent to us, we'll get to work making those dreams come true. Open your folders and read the mission statement."

Twenty-six-year-old Rachel Maynard followed Erica's bidding, although she already knew what was printed inside the front cover. She'd scanned the contents while the others shared their ultimate dreams with the class.

Perfection needs no improvement, only illumination.

Michelangelo's genius was rooted in the belief that perfection lay inside the cold, unyielding marble. His job was to chisel away the unnecessary elements until the masterpiece appeared intact, a perfect whole.

Like the statue inside the stone, there is a beautiful, desirable woman inside of you waiting to emerge, a woman who is physically, mentally and emotionally healthy, a woman unafraid to reach out for her destiny.

The Michelangelo Institute for Women will teach you techniques for your illumination. Our goal is to free you from the prison of your own making. We will enable you to open the door and walk out the confident, beautiful person you were meant to be, a woman in control of her own future, a woman who can make her wildest dreams come true.

Everyone's dreams were wild all right, Rachel thought wryly. Not one of them sounded attainable—particularly not hers. She knew she'd shocked the others; in fact, she was well aware that her goal had to be the most preposterous and outrageous of them all. But the institute, after approving and in some cases modifying each woman's goal, had promised results—results, furthermore, that were completely legal and would never hurt anyone.

"As you can imagine," Erica said, "illumination doesn't happen overnight." For the next while she expounded on the philosophy behind the institute's program.

"In conclusion, Michelangelo's is expensive, and the program is spread out over a six-to-thirty-six-month period, depending on your particular requirements.

"However, no graduate of ours has ever questioned the amount of time and money invested *once* she achieved her goal. The list of our famous alumnae would astound you, but those names are kept confidential.''

If Rachel was careful with the money her father had left her, she could afford to be enrolled for six months and invest the remainder to secure her future—regardless of what happened.

''Now then, you've each been given a different bedroom on the third floor. You will also see that a schedule has been made up to suit your individual needs. You will report to the room assigned when I dismiss you. Take a good look at each other now, because you won't be meeting as a group again. When you leave this room, your new life begins. Your activities will be known only to you and your advisors.''

The institute, housed in an historic three-floor colonial mansion, had to be Philadelphia's best-kept secret. For four years, Rachel had attended university here and had never heard of it. Michelangelo's didn't advertise.

In order for a woman to become a temporary resident, she had to be referred by someone of whom the institute approved and used as its initial screening process.

In Rachel's case, her general physician, Dr. Rich, had been the person to inform her of its existence, giving her entrée. During her college experience, he'd become a good friend. She'd first gone to see him because of some minor medical problems that had arisen, and afterward, she'd stayed in touch with him and his wife. Dr. and Mrs. Rich took an almost parental interest in her; Rachel valued their support and had occasionally turned to them for advice.

After college, she'd returned to Nevada, where she had lived with her father until his death. Losing him so suddenly had turned her world upside down. She couldn't sleep, constantly replaying past regrets and present fears. Finally, in desperation, she'd phoned Dr. Rich for help, even though he was several thousand miles away.

That was when he'd told her about the Michelangelo Institute and the miracles it performed.

She would definitely need one....

Following the instructions on the schedule, she exited the meeting hall with the others and made her way to Room Twenty on the second floor for her very first appointment.

A short fatherly figure with salt-and-pepper hair, wearing a tailored suit and tie, sat at a large mahogany desk with state-of-the-art electronic equipment in front of him. He waved her inside and told her to shut the door.

She approached and sat down in a comfortable upholstered chair. The tall ceiling and ornate cornices hinted that his office had once been a luxurious bedroom. But space-age technology had intruded to make the setup incongruous.

"Ms. Maynard, I'm Carl Gordon." He extended his hand, which she shook.

"Hello, Mr. Gordon."

"Mind if I call you Rachel?"

"Of course not."

"Good. Then please call me Carl. Since I'm the counselor who was assigned to your case several weeks ago, I feel I know you already and would prefer dispensing with the formalities right away."

She eyed him frankly. "I'm a case, all right. Forty pounds too heavy, as you can well see. I've been depressed—not sleeping, eating too much. Dr. Rich, who referred me to Michelangelo's, didn't say as much, but

I initially assumed the institute must be a glorified diet clinic.''

At first sight, she'd thought this counselor rather benign and jovial looking. But his shrewd regard revealed another aspect of his nature and seemed to challenge her statement.

''This institute can be anything you want it to be. If it's weight you need to put on or lose, we can help you accomplish that goal. But life's more complex than that, as you well know. If you'll put yourself in my hands, I'll help you take charge of your life.'' He chuckled. ''Sounds contradictory, I know, but I can show you the way. Teach you techniques to increase your confidence, organize yourself, get what you want.''

''Well—'' she flashed him a brief smile ''—I know you're not my fairy godfather, but it's obvious I'm here to be made over.''

''You didn't read the mission statement?''

''Yes, I did. It said there's a whole, beautiful person inside me waiting to emerge, and the institute is going to help that process along.''

''But you don't believe it.''

''Let's put it this way. I'd *like* to believe it. But the truth is, my doctor knew I was depressed. Perhaps he thought that some time spent in here losing weight would pull me out of it.''

''Depression masks anger. You're a very angry young woman, Rachel. Obviously you're angry enough to spend a good deal of money embarking on a new journey. Let's make the most of this opportunity.''

Unlike Erica, Carl Gordon didn't sugarcoat his words. His astute observation sent the heat rushing to her cheeks, yet she admired him for his blunt speaking. Instinctively she felt he was someone she could trust.

She removed her glasses, which she only used for reading and had forgotten to take off. "How much do you know about me, anyway?"

"I already know more than you'd probably want me to know." He pressed a switch and sat back in his chair. Suddenly the room was filled with the sound of her voice.

"By the year 2000, I plan to become Mrs. Nikos Athas!"

He shut off the tape and sat forward. "That, Rachel, is the sound of anger. This—" He picked up the lengthy application Dr. Rich had given her to fill out before he sent it in to Michelangelo's. "This tells me that from the ages of fourteen to nineteen, you were at boarding school in Montreux, Switzerland.

"A quick search of the school's records by the institute's legal department confirms that Stella Athas, daughter of the late Paul Athas, a prominent and wealthy Greek businessman turned high government official, was a student at the same school during your last year."

Shocked by the amount of private information Carl already knew, she realized she'd completely underestimated what the Michelangelo Institute was all about.

"Nikos Athas, her dashing older brother, is always big news. He was Greece's winter Olympic silver medalist in the downhill in Chamonix, France, and since his thirty-second birthday has been touted the jet set's most desirable bachelor. The tabloids have proclaimed him to be a great womanizer, much to his father's chagrin."

Rachel sat there stunned as Carl continued to peel

away the layers of her past that linked her with the
Athas family. She felt...exposed. "And you were a
vulnerable teenager who lost her mother to cancer at
thirteen. You were placed in a foreign boarding school
while your Air Force father worked for the space program. You had to learn the hard way that the Nikos
types of this world trample little girls' hearts. He tram-
pled your heart, didn't he, Rachel?"

Good heavens. She lowered her head. "Yes."

"You want revenge. Satisfaction."

"Yes." *But I want that revenge to end in marriage
to him.*

"Tell me what he said or did that changed your
world."

Rachel's thoughts flew back to those years in Switzerland. "I was something of a loner and didn't make
friends easily. Madame, the headmistress, promised me
I could have a room of my own during my last year at
school.

"Of course, she reneged on that promise when a
Greek girl, Stella Athas, arrived at the school. She was
obviously someone important, otherwise Madame
wouldn't have accepted her when the school was already filled to capacity. There was only one bed left—
in my room.

"By some miracle, Stella and I took to each other
immediately. It was just one of those things—" Rachel
shrugged. "We felt we'd known each other in another
life or something. She was always very kind to me,
even more so when she learned about my mother's
death. Stella had lost her mother in a ferry accident. I
think that was why she always seemed so sad. We had
those losses in common, so it didn't take long for us

to become best friends. I'd never had a best friend before.''

She stared down at her clasped hands. ''The first time Stella showed me pictures of Nikos, I developed a huge crush on him. She had dozens of snapshots of her family in her wallet. Every time he came to the school during the year—to take her skiing or travel around on weekend trips—I fell more in love with him.

''But Madame didn't like Stella leaving on these little excursions. She warned her that she'd fail if she missed too many classes. I thought Madame was too hard on her, so I always offered to do Stella's homework while she was gone with Nikos. He smiled and praised me for being such a loyal roommate. That attention won me over completely.

''As for Stella, she told me that no friend of hers had ever done anything so unselfish for her before. She promised I could go with her on winter break to watch Nikos train for the Olympics. She knew how crazy I was about her brother.''

''Did she keep her promise?''

''Oh, yes. We stayed in their family-owned chalet in Chamonix. The idea of being around him all the time absolutely thrilled me. This was the most exciting thing that had ever happened to me.

''Those ten days were heaven. I didn't see a lot of Nikos during the day because he was out skiing. But when he came back to the chalet at night, he kidded and teased us and I never wanted to go to bed. I wrote in my diary that he was the man I would love all my life.

''But then it was our last night before we had to return to school. I overheard him talking to Stella while I was in the bathroom. At the time I thought he couldn't have known I was in there. With hindsight I can see how naive I was back then. He wanted me to hear every word—so I'd leave Stella alone.''

''What did he say?''

Her head came up. '''Now that you're going back to Switzerland, Stella, we have to talk. How come out of all the girls at school, you had to bring along that short, fat, funny-looking American Army brat?' That's exactly what he said. Stella got upset with him. She defended me, said I wasn't an Army brat. She explained that my father was a pilot working in the American space program. I remember she practically yelled out that I was *not* funny looking, and five feet four wasn't that short, except to the men in their family!''

Rachel recalled the rest of that interchange, almost word for word. ''Come on, Stella,'' Nikos had said. ''With that orange hair, she belongs in the circus. She totally ruins your style.''

''Her hair is not orange. It's red! You're being mean.''

''And you're being a fool. I'm going to tell you something, little sister. Pretty as you are, if you let *her* hang around you, the guys are going to take one look at her and run in the other direction. You, of all people, can't afford to let that happen.''

''But I love her, Nikos! How can you be so cruel when you know yourself that she's the reason I'm not failing at school right now? Rachel's a true friend, and she doesn't have her mother anymore, either. I hate you for saying those awful things!''

''Hate me all you want, but when you get back to school you'd better get rid of her before Stasio finds out you've been running around with that kind of American military trash.''

"Stasio would understand!"

"Are you sure about that? He has eyes and ears everywhere, Stella. It would better to end your relationship with her now. Otherwise, you could find yourself back in New York or Greece under big brother's thumb again. After what happened last year, you more than anyone should know what that means. Stasio will allow you even less freedom than before. Why risk it?

"Besides, you're growing into a real beauty. Believe me, you don't want to be associated with some plump ugly duckling trying to pretend she's something else."

Rachel had stopped crying over that dark moment years ago. His brutal remarks no longer brought her pain. But she was human, and she'd never forgotten those words.

Clearing her throat, she said, "I loved Stella for defending me. But when we returned to school, I told Madame I'd rather room with another American. She demanded to know why, so I told her what Nikos had said.

"Madame listened, then agreed that it might be better not to do anything to upset the Athas family, so she moved Stella to the second floor and put another American in with me.

"Stella never knew the change came about because of me. Very slowly I turned to other girls for friendship. Little by little, I weaned myself away from her to save her the trouble of having to drop me."

"Didn't she attempt to fight for your friendship?"

"Yes, even more than I would have imagined. I think now that what I did to her hurt her much more than anything Nikos did to me. But at the time, I felt I had no choice."

"Have you had any contact with her since?"

"No. The day I left Switzerland and flew here to Philadelphia to attend college, I told the headmistress not to give my address to anyone. Stella never knew where to reach me.

"A few months after I left Switzerland, the headmistress mailed me a letter Stella had sent me in care of the school.

"I tore it up without reading it, because all those memories hurt too much. I've never seen her or Nikos since, except in newspapers and magazines, and of course on those celebrity TV shows."

Carl sat back looking extremely satisfied, his palms together beneath his chin. "With the institute's help, you'll not only be seeing him again, you'll make him take back those words." Her counselor's eyes actually twinkled with mischief.

She could almost believe him. A smile broke the corners of her mouth. "I certainly hope so."

Rachel felt she needed to keep things light in front of her counselor. He could have no idea how vital it was to get Nikos to fall in love with her.

"Some men don't mind the extra weight and many of them would find you attractive the way you are right now." Rachel knew that. Her ex-boss, Manny, loved her just the way she was. "But since Nikos Athas is your quarry, I made a study of the types of women he likes to be seen with in public. They're all anorexic-looking Hollywood-type blondes."

"I know. So it means I've got to lose fifty pounds and dye my hair a champagne color."

"Wrong. He's still a playboy, because none of those women has managed to capture his heart. It's going to take a *real* woman with natural beauty and no artifice—

someone like his mother or sister—to make this man shed his bachelorhood.''

''You've seen pictures of Stella and her mom?''

''As soon as I was assigned your case, I made it my business to learn everything possible about Nikos Athas.'' He settled more comfortably in his chair. ''I believe that a Greek man may be enticed by false glitter, but in the end, he adores the women in his family and will instinctively choose a wife who embodies some of their qualities. My observations suggest Nikos is this type of man.

''His mother had a full-bodied figure, which Stella inherited. Both women made the most of the dark hair color God gave them. Their strong bone structure adds character to their faces.

''You have lovely bone structure. Shedding twenty, twenty-five pounds at the most, will enhance your facial features and your figure. We won't touch the color of your hair. Keep in mind you don't want to look like all the other painted, shallow, emaciated creatures draped over his arm.

''His mother was apparently a warm, unpretentious woman, and by all accounts, Stella is the same. Those are qualities that I suspect are very natural to you—and not to his various blondes.

''When I'm through with you, and we've planned your entrée back into his life, I guarantee he'll fall madly in love with you.''

Dear God— This had to work! She had to make Nikos fall so hard there'd never be another woman for him.

''You're very convincing, Carl.'' After a slight pause, she said, ''When he's laid his heart at my feet, I have to admit I want the pleasure of watching his face when I tell him I'm the short, fat, funny-looking American Army brat he once told Stella to avoid at all costs.''

"Hell hath no fury like a woman scorned.'' But he said it with a frown. "The only problem I foresee is that you're not in love with him. A marriage without love on both sides is no union.''

"I didn't say I didn't love Nikos. I'm sorry if I gave you the wrong impression. I've *always* been in love with him,'' she replied honestly. "Besides, I've forgiven him.

"Oh, I won't pretend that I didn't entertain some drastic notions of revenge back then. Older boys are known to be pretty cruel before they grow up, and the truth of the matter is, I was an unattractive teenager.

"However, the time that's gone by has changed me a great deal, and I'm sure it's changed him, too. If the institute can do what its mission statement claims, within six months I'll be the woman Nikos wants to settle down with. I'm looking forward to that day.''

If that day didn't come, Rachel didn't know what she'd do or where she'd turn. More and more, Nikos had become the focus of her life.

"With determination like yours, I'm convinced you can realize your dream. I only hope—''

"I *have* to realize it, Carl.''

He studied her for a long moment before he said, "I know you graduated from college with a degree in communications. Let's discuss what you've been doing since graduation.''

"My father was eventually moved out of the space program and given the command over Red Crater Air Force Base near Las Vegas, Nevada. He died three months ago. March fourteenth.'' She swallowed hard.

"Until his death, I was living with him on the base and working for a radio station in Las Vegas."

"You've been in a depression since his death, correct?"

"Yes," she whispered. "I started losing sleep and realized I needed to see a doctor. But I didn't know any of the ones on base the way I knew Dr. Rich, so I called him. We talked and he prescribed some medicine to help me sleep."

"Are you still taking those pills?"

"Only once in a while, so I won't have bad dreams."

"Tell me about them."

"I dream about being left alone, then I wake up sobbing." She'd only had that dream once since the funeral. It was the other nightmares that caused her to thrash about in the middle of the night, screaming.

Much as she'd like to confide in Carl, who seemed kind enough and had gained her respect, she wasn't ready to divulge her innermost secrets quite yet.

"Since your father was often stationed in other parts of the world while you were growing up, you've been on your own a great deal, yet you've always known he was there for you. Now that he's gone, it's no wonder you're suffering this sense of loss.

"Continue to use the medicine if it helps. If you need something stronger, we have a physician on staff to deal with medical problems. But in time your mind will come to accept your loss, and you'll no longer be disturbed by your dreams. You're a strong person, or you wouldn't have acted on your doctor's suggestion to enroll here."

I'm a frightened person, Carl. Desperate enough to try anything.

"Do you speak any Greek?"

"No. Stella taught me a few phrases, but I've forgotten them."

"Then we'll send you to night school at the Greek Orthodox Church around the corner. If you're going to become the wife of Nikos Athas, you need to be able to communicate, at least on a basic level.

"As for your physical self, you'll spend a portion of every day getting in shape, learning about nutrition, taking lessons in how to do your hair and makeup, how to buy clothes that suit your height and figure, all of those things to make the outer covering as attractive as possible.

"The rest of your time will be spent with me while we work on the inner you and develop a strategy to bring about the reunion."

"I wouldn't know where to start trying to find him, how to connect with him."

He gave her a pleased smile. "That part's easy. You'll renew your friendship with Stella Athas—which will be a nice bonus for her *and* for you, Rachel. And once you do, Nikos will find you. Little does he know that in half a year's time, his life's going to change completely."

My future husband.

No male of her acquaintance at home or abroad could match Nikos's Adonislike face and physique. She already knew the truth about his womanizing, so she paid little heed to the gossip written about him in the tabloids.

Naturally, she hoped the past six years had added the needed maturity that would make him her companion and protector, as well as her lover and the father of her children. By Christmas, she would find out.

In the meantime, the Michelangelo Institute was the

only place where she could remain hidden and, please God, safe....

"AS THE SUN RISES ONCE AGAIN from the deep black void of space, sending its rays streaking across the Red Crater Desert of Nevada, this is Draco of the Constellation 1060 network signing off. Soon I'll succumb to the embrace of Morpheus."

In the middle of Manny Novak's closing monologue, a message from one of the daytime producers flashed across his call monitor.

"Hey, Manny— The same dude who's phoned a bunch of times wanting to know how to reach Rachel just came to the station. He drove a Jeep, looks like brass from the base. I spoke to him through the intercom, and told him the same thing I told him before. We don't have her phone number or forwarding address.

"He got mad as hell and walked around to the back door trying to get in. When he couldn't do that, he tried our car doors. Just thought you ought to know."

Manny cursed under his breath. Those bastards never knew when to quit. As far as he was concerned, they could rot in hell.

Over the past three years, Rachel's broadcasts had helped push the show's ratings through the roof. Before she left, her programs hinting at a cover-up behind the Mars probe findings had obviously alarmed some of the military brass. Talk about risky behavior. But Rachel had guts. Good for her. Damn if he didn't miss her.

He leaned forward; he still had to end the show. "To all my friends out there, don't forget to join me, Draco, every weeknight at midnight. Together we'll explore the cosmos where the impossible is truth, where the 'can't be' just is. Are you enlightened enough to deal with it?''

He pressed the button on the console that played his theme off the digital hard drive, then sat back in the chair and stretched.

At sixty-one years of age, with forty-five years in radio behind him, he'd supposedly reached the pinnacle of success: a nationally syndicated show that could be heard on fifty stations all around the country via satellite, a state-of-the-art broadcasting studio on the outskirts of Las Vegas. It was housed inside an adobe shell reminiscent of the architecture of Frank Lloyd Wright, so it blended with the desert and was protected by the latest electronic security surveillance system.

Great as everything was, however, there were times—like now—when he yearned for his early years in radio, the broken-down shack where he flew by the seat of his pants putting his reel-to-reel programming together.

Long gone were the days when he'd hunker down in front of his parents' old Philco and listen to Wolfman Jack out of Tijuana on 50,000 watts. That would be on a good night, when the ionosphere was high. Sometimes, back in his teens, he could even catch the sky waves of WLS out of Chicago and imagine himself doing an all-night show.

For Manny, the AM band was magical, a voice in the night that went out into space forever. Who knew where those signals had traveled by now? Beyond the solar system?

Hell, the earth was still receiving information through a mere .003 trillionth of a watt from the Voyager spacecraft launched in 1972. Fantastic.

Through the skylight, he could see the top of the red-

and-white tower rising 450 feet above the ground. Though silent now, the red beacon blinked at night to warn planes away. Too bad it didn't create an invisible shield to keep out the undesirables who controlled those planes.

There was always something top-secret going on at Red Crater Air Force Base. Manny had several reliable friends in high places who leaked enough information to put the powers-that-be in a continual uproar.

None of them had known as much as Rachel, one of his infallible sources for certain classified military information.

She'd quit her job with him three months ago and left the state. He still had no idea where she was.

Her night segments over the network had shown real brilliance. The listening audience loved their Cassiopeia and still asked about her. As for Manny, he missed her too much.

Unfortunately, her father's sudden death had devastated her to the point that she needed to get away. Manny hoped that when she had overcome the worst of her grief, she'd come back to work.

To his chagrin, she'd moved off the base and left no forwarding address or phone number. Because she loved the night show as much as he did, he figured that one day soon she'd miss it enough to phone him at the station. He had a tempting career offer waiting for her.

If he were thirty years younger, he'd ask her to marry him. She had no idea he felt that way about her; she thought he loved her in a brotherly way—as a friend and colleague. But his love for her ran a lot deeper than that. He hadn't realized it himself until after she'd tendered her resignation twelve weeks ago. They seemed like twelve months.

Maybe he was fooling himself. Maybe he'd given himself away and that was why she'd moved on without leaving him a number where he could contact her.

He got up from the console with a heavy heart. Before he did anything else, he needed to go home and sleep. Then he'd try to work out how he could get in touch with Rachel—and what he would say when he did.

CHAPTER TWO

SEPTEMBER FIRST.

Tonight marked the halfway point for Rachel.

Three months had gone by, and she was still safe! There was no doubt in her mind that coming to Michelangelo's had literally saved her life. Only three more months to go, and then she'd have to leave the institute. Three more months before that gnawing fear of being found would begin again.

She took a deep breath and continued to study the latest ski magazine containing photographs of Nikos Athas. The camera loved his dashing image. So did the starlets and models who grouped around him.

Thanks to Carl's investigative research, Rachel had been able to track his movements over the past six years. When Nikos wasn't skiing in races throughout Europe, or endorsing Brousillac skis and boots for the French-based manufacturer, he spent his time gambling in Montreux, Switzerland, where he kept an apartment.

The more Rachel learned about Stella's brother, the more she agreed with Carl. Though Nikos was a fabulous athlete, he was also a restless man who played at life without any sort of plan. She concluded that no matter how much money he made through endorsements, his earnings could never support his expensive lifestyle without considerable help from the Athas Shipping Lines fortune.

Long ago in Chamonix, she'd overheard him tell Stella that he rarely spent time in Greece because he didn't have an interest in the family business. He'd also said he hated feeling guilty about not measuring up to their father and autocratic brother's expectations.

Rachel could see how no man would want to be reminded that he couldn't stand on his own two feet financially. Nikos possessed more than his share of pride in that department. Coupled with his feelings of inadequacy—induced, no doubt, by the older Athas men—it explained why he avoided home. A home that also served as a painful reminder of his mother's death.

What he needed was someone who believed in him. Someone who could help him turn his natural talents into a lasting legacy for his own wife and family one day.

With Carl's assistance, plus the smattering of knowledge she possessed about the Athas family's inner workings, Rachel felt she'd put together a fairly accurate picture of Nikos's complicated psyche. She was convinced that she could assist him in finding the strength and integrity she knew he possessed.

The minute she met Nikos again, she would tap into that vulnerable part of him ignored by the shallow women in his life. This would give her the edge—and, she hoped, the prize....

Unless those men found her first. Unless they succeeded in hunting her down.

She shuddered in fright before she turned out the bedside lamp. For the first time in months, she wished there was someone to turn to. Tonight, while she'd been leafing through the ski industry magazine with Nikos's pictures, she'd come across an ad for an international skiwear convention in Las Vegas, Nevada.

The aerial shot of the city highlighting the Strip at night brought an attack of homesickness—for her father, most of all, and for her life at the radio station. She missed her long fascinating talks with Manny. His interest in the possibility of life existing in the unexplored universe rivaled her own. Dear Draco, her mentor, guru and friend all in one.

It had been weeks since she'd let any thoughts of the past interfere with her concentration. On Carl's advice she'd stopped watching TV or listening to the radio. That could come later, he said, when she'd reached her objective.

Rachel had abided by his rules, but a compulsion to hear Manny's voice for just a few minutes drove her to break them this once.

She turned on the radio, to 1060 AM. The second she heard Todd Elder hosting the nationally syndicated "Washington Lineup," she realized her mistake. The three-hour time difference between coasts meant Manny's nationally syndicated show wouldn't start until three in the morning her time.

She propped herself up on one elbow and set the clock radio to wake her at three. But try as she might, she couldn't fall asleep. Too tired to get up and study, she lay there and listened to the other program.

At five past three, after the news at the top of the hour, the sound of static with a high-frequency pulse blared in her ears, drowning out Manny's "Draco's World" opening monologue.

She shot straight up in the bed. It was the same sound she remembered hearing after the Air Force had blocked out one of her programs.

They didn't like the fact that she was broadcasting evidence. Some people within the government were involved in a cover-up of test pilots' UFO sightings. In retaliation, they'd broadcast a phantom signal on the same frequency of 1060 kHz to purposely interfere with the station's phasing.

The first time it drowned out her program, she was afraid Manny would fire her for going too far. Instead, he gave her a raise and told her to keep the truth coming. He said her show had picked up hundreds of new listeners.

During the time she'd been host of "The Cassiopeia Dimension," there'd been two other ugly accidents, as well. One involved a light plane that toppled Manny's radio tower. The other involved a small plane that wreaked temporary damage to his satellite dish uplink.

No matter how much the Air Force denied it, Rachel knew the powers-that-be wanted Manny's show off the air. Her own deceased father had provided her with indisputable proof of their sabotaging activities.

Since his unexpected death, she feared for her courageous ex-boss. Manny continued to broadcast the truth to an ever-growing population of listeners who were sick to death of lies.

Before Rachel left Las Vegas, Manny had extracted the promise that she would stay in touch with him. But for his safety, as well as hers, she hadn't dared to make contact since coming to Michelangelo's.

At this point, she worried he might be under surveillance, his phone lines tapped or his mail tampered with long before it was delivered to the station. For those reasons, she hadn't written or phoned him. His radio show provided her only link to him. Now even that pleasure was denied her!

Rachel could feel her rage building, along with her

fear. How long did those evil men plan to put Manny's show out of commission this time?

The question kept her awake the rest of the night. By midmorning of the next day, she couldn't stand it any longer and decided to phone the Dime Slot Café in Las Vegas. Manny always stopped there for breakfast after his show. Sometimes Rachel joined him. Everyone who worked there loved Draco's World, and Manny was a favorite celebrity.

Taking advantage of a break in her schedule, Rachel left the institute and walked several blocks to a pay phone. After obtaining the number from information, she punched the buttons and waited for someone to pick up on the other end.

"Dime Slot Café," a male voice answered.

"Hi. This is a friend of Manny Novak's calling. You don't happen to know if—"

"Just a minute, I'll get Betty," he interrupted before Rachel could finish her sentence.

Rachel hated bothering the manager, but she had to know that Manny was all right.

"Yeah? This is Betty." She sounded more brusque than usual, probably because they were often extra-crowded this time of day.

"Betty? This is Rachel Maynard." When there was no response, Rachel said, "Maybe you remember me better as Cassiopeia. Before I moved from Las Vegas, I sometimes came into the café with Manny Novak."

"Sure I remember you, especially your shows on the UFO stuff. They were great! Damn shame about Manny, though. He was a legend around here. We're all going to miss him."

Rachel's body went icy cold. "I've been out of touch for a long time. W-what happened to Manny?"

"You mean you don't know? He had a stroke and can't do the show anymore. The poor guy's gone to live with relatives in California."

Dear God.

"WHAT ARE YOUR PLANS for the Christmas holidays, Nikos?"

From Stasio's voice, Stella knew what was coming and wished herself miles away from Athens. Stasio had already excused the housekeeper so the family could talk in complete privacy.

Except that her brothers didn't talk to each other. Stasio asked the questions their father would have asked if he'd been present. Nikos gave short, clipped answers.

"Must we discuss that right now?"

"I think so. December isn't that far off. I'm clearing my calendar and hoped you would, too."

Nikos drained another cup of coffee. "I have races up until mid-December, then I'm doing some more photo shoots for Brousillac in Chamonix."

"But you'll be home Christmas Eve to go to Mass with the family."

"I'm not sure."

"It's important to keep the tradition our parents set."

"What if I can't make it?" he challenged.

Stella shivered, hating it when Nikos became difficult.

"Then I guess we'll have to get along without you."

Stasio never rose to the bait Nikos threw his way. Stella loved both her brothers, but she lived in awe of Stasio and never wanted to find out what it would be like to really cross him.

"Before you get up from the table, there's a matter I want to discuss with Stella. I'd like you to be a part of this, Nikos, since it will affect you, as well as our sister."

Intrigued, she turned to him. "Did you and Eleni set a wedding date?"

"I've asked her to marry me, but the exact date has yet to be determined."

His answer deflated her. "Why?"

"Because there's one important thing left to be resolved before we can make definite plans. Marriage is a binding commitment. I want mine to last."

"What's there not to be sure of? What haven't you got resolved?" Stella knew Eleni was highstrung and temperamental. But Stasio must have decided to overlook those flaws from the beginning, or he wouldn't have gone on seeing her for the last two years. At this point, the extended families on both sides were expecting an announcement.

He rubbed the stem of his wineglass several times. Stasio was hesitant. She'd never realized he had nerves like other people, that he sometimes felt uncertain.

"Something terrible's happened, hasn't it?" she cried out in alarm. "What's wrong?"

Nikos always acted bored around the family—Stella knew it was to cover his feelings of inferiority—but even he had lost some of his sangfroid waiting to hear the answer. Everyone knew Eleni had loved Stasio since he'd started seeing her two years ago. Stella couldn't understand how any woman could have been patient this long.

Ignoring her question, he said, "What I'm about to say is going to affect your life forever, Stella."

Her lower lip quivered. "You're not ill or something, are you?"

"Stop being cryptic and just tell us!" Nikos erupted.

Stasio sighed. "Don't worry. I'm in perfect health." He reached out and covered her hand with his own. Looking her straight in the eye, he said, "This is about the baby you gave up for adoption."

An eerie quiet filled the dining room.

Not a moment of Stella's life went by that she didn't regret her decision to allow the baby to be adopted. At the time, she and Stasio had agreed it would be best for the child to grow up in the U.S. For one thing, that would reduce the chances of any scandal being attached to her name or Theo's. All the counseling Stasio had arranged at the time had influenced her to give up the baby once it was born.

The chances of an eighteen-year-old unwed mother leading a normal, productive life with a full education and a chance for a good marriage diminished if she kept her baby.

The chances of the baby leading a normal life in a happy environment where all of his or her needs were met by loving parents diminished if that unwed mother insisted on raising the baby herself.

The statistics were irrefutable.

Yet when the moment came to sign the paperwork, Stasio had told her she could keep the baby if she felt she had to. He'd help her raise the child. If she felt any hesitation at all about her decision, then they would work things out.

Stella loved her brother for saying that, but she refused to add such a burden to his shoulders.

Their father, who'd held a high position in the government, had died of a heart attack just two months before Stella became pregnant. That meant Stasio had been forced to play a parental role to Stella, while at the same time running the Athas family business. Like her, he'd also been trying to cope with his grief at their father's unexpected death.

Too many responsibilities, including worry over the direction of Nikos's life, had prevented Stasio from leading a normal life of his own. Stella wouldn't allow her problems to stand in his way any longer.

Besides, it wouldn't be fair to her child, who deserved to have a mother *and* a father. In the end, she chose to give up her baby with the stipulation that a church-going married couple of her own nationality and religious background be selected as parents. Stasio had arranged everything through Costas, their family attorney. Stella knew it had been the right thing to do. Her child would find all the love and nurturing in a home where two doting parents were anxiously waiting to raise him or her.

Once the decision had been made, she'd been adamant about not seeing or holding the baby after delivery. Since that moment, she'd tried not to look back. She never talked about her child, except when Stasio brought it up. During the intervening years he'd broached the subject of her baby many times. Every so often he would remark that she was too quiet, too sad. Stella would immediately insist that she was fine with her initial decision—to let a good couple adopt her son. Over and over, she begged Stasio not to worry about her. But she knew he *did* worry; otherwise he wouldn't have continued to question her. Six years later, Stella still felt she had done the right thing for the baby.

But not for her. Not for her.

Every day she wondered if she'd given birth to a boy or a girl. He or she would be five years old by now. Did her child look like her? Or like Theo, the natural father, who'd done the cowardly thing and disappeared from Athens the second Stella told him the news?

There was a growing emptiness inside her that nothing seemed to fill. The normal daily pursuits and pleasures meant little anymore.

She knew everyone in her family, especially Stasio, was alarmed because she didn't want to meet any other men, didn't want to date or attend parties or have any kind of social life. She simply couldn't.

When Theo had abandoned her without as much as a phone call or letter of goodbye, she'd lost her faith in men. All she could think about was the fact that she'd given birth—that somewhere in the world, her child was being raised by other people.

"Why the hell are you bringing that up to her now?" Nikos's question rang with unconcealed anger.

"Because Ari was never adopted."

"Ari?" Stella's heart thudded. "I had a boy?"

A look of such sweetness, such tenderness, filled Stasio's eyes, she hardly recognized her brother. "Was he born with something wrong? Is that why nobody wanted him?" Her voice throbbed despite herself.

He squeezed her hand gently before letting it go. "Ari is perfect, Stella. He has Nikos's dazzling smile, your beautiful dark eyes and hair, our father's intelligence and our mother's charm."

She shoved herself away from the table and stood up, her heart racing. "And what part of him looks like *you?*"

"He's tall for his age."

"Where is he, Stasio? I have to see him!"

"If you'll sit down, I'll tell you everything."

"I can't sit!" She ran behind his chair and threw her arms around his neck. "You've seen him! Do you have a picture of him?"

"Yes."

He reached inside his suit pocket and pulled out a snapshot. With trembling hands she took the precious photograph and came face-to-face with her son. Ari.

"He's beautiful! Adorable! Oh—I can't believe it." She started to sob, hugging the picture to her chest.

By now Nikos had left his seat to come around and get a glimpse. She handed him the snapshot.

"What do you mean my smile? He's got Stella's smile and my good looks."

Hysterical with joy, Stella nudged Nikos, half laughing, half crying. He could be such a tease. She clutched Stasio's broad shoulders. "Where is he? When can I see him?"

"Maybe you shouldn't," Nikos warned.

Her head flew back. "How can you say that?"

He returned the picture to her. "Because if he doesn't know of your existence, it would come as too great a shock."

"But I want to tell him! I want to be his mother! Don't you understand? Ever since I gave him up, I've longed for him. And…and Stasio says he hasn't been adopted."

At this point Stasio rose from his chair and took her firmly by the shoulders.

"I knew in my gut that you regretted your decision. I've waited all these years for you to say something, but you never did. Not until tonight. Now I have the proof I've been waiting for.

"There are things you have to understand. He's still being raised by his foster parents, Anna and Giorgio Kiriakis, in New York. They love him and he loves them very much."

Of course he did. For five years he'd been raised by other people. Five years he'd bonded with them instead of her. The pain of that knowledge was almost unbearable.

"He's in New York?" One tear, then another, rolled down her hot cheeks. "Does he even know I'm alive?"

Stasio breathed in heavily. "He's been told that his mother loved him very much, but that she wasn't able to take care of him when he was born. So she made sure he went to live with some wonderful people who would love him. But if the day ever came when she could take care of him, she'd come for him."

"Good Lord!" Nikos muttered.

She swallowed hard. "Does he know what I look like?"

"Of course. I always take him a new picture of you. He has a scrapbook full of them."

His words filled her with inexplicable joy. "Stasio! Do you think he really wants me?"

"Every child wants his mother. Of course he wants you, even without having met you."

"I love him desperately. I want him. I've always wanted my child. Now that I have a secure job in our company office, I can support him. I'll do whatever it takes to get him back."

"I know that. Let's all sit down and talk this out."

Once more she took her place at the table, but Nikos remained standing a little distance off. Stella couldn't take her eyes off her son's photograph.

"Has Eleni ever seen him?"

"No."

"Have you seen him recently?"

After a long silence he said, "Whenever I'm in New York, I see him on a daily basis."

"All these years?" she blurted incredulously.

He nodded.

"You mean all the time I was in Switzerland at boarding school? All the time I lived with you while I went to university in New York?"

"That's right. As soon as Ari could understand, I explained that I was his godfather."

Nikos let out a whistle. "Does anyone else know?"

"Only Costas and I know the secret. Anna and Giorgio, who own a restaurant in New York, are distant relatives of his. Ari believes I'm a good friend of his mother's. I told him that I made her a promise to look after him."

Tears filled her eyes. The revelations were coming too fast for her to absorb. "You love him."

"Like my own son. I'll be adopting him right away."

Stella didn't think she'd understood him correctly. Apparently Nikos hadn't, either. "First you tell Stella about her son and show her his picture," he exploded. "Then you announce that *you* want to adopt him? And you've had the nerve to call *me* cruel!"

"Before you go off the deep end, Nikos, let me finish. Ari has been living with Anna and Giorgio all this time. When Stella gave him up, I followed her express wishes that only a married Greek couple active in their religious beliefs could adopt him.

"But Costas and I talked things over and decided Stella might change her mind one day. We were thinking of Theo, as well—that he too might decide to come back and try to make a home for Stella and the baby.

"So when Costas made private arrangements with Anna and Giorgio, he put in the proviso that for the first five years of Ari's life, he couldn't be adopted. If during that time no marriage took place between Stella and Theo, or Stella and any other man who'd want to adopt Ari, then after January first, Ari would be put up for adoption.

"January first isn't very far away, and time has finally run out. Ari can be adopted by any qualified couple, and there won't be anything we can do about it. Anna and Giorgio have already expressed their interest."

There was one other avenue—to simply have Ari turned over to Stella. But Stasio didn't feel this was the right time to discuss it. Costas was concerned that the judge might raise some tough questions on that score. To reduce the risk of a decision that could go against her, it would probably be better for Stasio to marry Eleni and adopt Ari outright.

His revelations continued to astound Stella. "You mean all this time you've been keeping him safe for me in case I wanted him back?" She couldn't comprehend his sacrifice.

"Of course. No matter how good the counseling, I wasn't sure any person who'd barely turned eighteen could fully understand what that kind of decision really meant. But our hands will be tied after the new year."

She stared hard at Stasio. "Every day since I gave him up, I've wanted to tell you I made a mistake."

"Somehow I knew it," he muttered, almost as if to himself.

"But I never said anything because I felt I couldn't give the baby everything he needed."

"You have the one thing no one else can give Ari," he said forcefully. "A mother's love. Six years of pain have forced you to grow up in ways that others who haven't suffered like this don't realize. I'm sure I speak for Nikos when I say we want Ari to know your love. You'll have the financial and emotional backing of everyone in this family. Isn't that right, Nikos?"

"Naturally. I had no idea you were still grieving for him, Stella."

"I've never stopped." Her voice quavered as she spoke.

"Good. Then it's settled," Stasio said. "I'll be leaving for New York next week. When I come back on the first of December, I'll bring Ari with me. We'll go straight through to Andros."

I'll see my son on the first of December? That was only a few weeks away! "This is like a dream. I'm afraid I'm going to wake up."

Stasio smiled. "Months ago I asked him if he wanted to spend the holidays with me in Greece. He was overjoyed because he knows it's the country where his mother was born, where his mother lives. He's always asking me about you, Stella—always wanting to know as much as I can tell him about his mother. When we get here, he's all yours."

"I can't wait!" she cried through her tears.

"It will be up to you to find the right time to tell him you're ready to take care of him and be his mother on a permanent basis. I'm sure you'll know when that moment comes. Be prepared for a barrage of questions. For one thing, he'll immediately find out that I'm his uncle, not his godfather. But there's something else you must understand. He loves his foster parents and will always want them in his life.''

''Of course. I'm so grateful to them for loving him all these years,'' she whispered, still in shock. ''It's more than possible that even after meeting me, he still won't want to leave them.''

''No.'' Stasio shook his head. ''You'll win Ari over with your sweetness. When he feels your love, when you can tell him in your own words how much you've always wanted him, he'll never want to leave your sight.''

''I pray you're right, Stasio.''

''I know I am.''

Moved beyond words, she practically fell out of the chair getting to her brother. Her emotions were too overpowering to tell him everything in her heart. All she could do was throw herself against him and cling.

''If the problem I referred to earlier is resolved, Eleni and I will have a quiet church wedding on Andros between Christmas and New Year's. No guests, just our families. That's why I was curious to know your plans for the holidays, Nikos. Naturally I'd want you as my best man.''

Nikos gave a noncommittal reply, and Stasio went on. ''What's important is that papers have already been drawn up for the adoption. After the wedding, Ari will be legally ours. Then we'll start proceedings for you to formally adopt your son.''

Nikos eyed his brother with a stunned expression. ''What you've done is incredible, Stasio. Why didn't you ever tell me?''

''Because I felt our sister should have the opportunity to start a new life with Theo, or a new man, if that was what she wanted. I was afraid that if you knew what I'd done, the secret would be too hard for the two of us to keep. We'd talk about it. I worried that one of us—if not both—would eventually break down and tell her the truth. Once she knew that Ari hadn't been adopted yet, it could jeopardize her newly found happiness.

"But..." His eyes searched hers. "Theo never came back, and you never looked at another man again. In fact, you've been in a state of depression that's only deepened over the last six years. You've seen doctors and therapists, but they couldn't provide what you needed. There's been no happiness, has there, Stella?"

"No. Since I was wheeled out of the delivery room without my baby, there hasn't been a minute of my life I haven't longed for him and regretted my decision."

Nikos took a step closer to his brother. "If this has all been a secret until now, have you told Eleni about Ari yet?"

"No. I had to have this conversation with Stella first."

Nikos made a sound in his throat. "When—if—she gets over the shock, I don't think she'll agree to get married on Andros. You know Eleni's never liked it there."

"Nikos is right, Stasio. Besides, it's the bride's prerogative to plan the wedding. Eleni's world is here in Athens. Her family would never agree to a private ceremony on Andros. It would be horrible to alienate my future sister-in-law because of my problems."

Stasio remained implacable. "Costas went to great lengths to keep things quiet. We can't afford the publicity. Securing your legal rights to Ari is more important than any lavish wedding I never wanted in the first place."

Stella wanted to hear confirmation that it was all right with Eleni. But when she tried to read the truth in his eyes, it was impossible to decipher their expression. She grasped his arms. "A woman only has one wedding day, Stasio. It should be perfect for her in every way. Are you *sure* Eleni won't mind? Can you say that in front of God and mean it?"

His mouth twitched. "I've already talked to God about your sadness, little sister. Believe me, I've never been so sure of anything in my life!"

CHAPTER THREE

"CARL?"

"Rachel! I've been waiting for you."

"I'm ready to leave for New York. I just wanted to say goodbye."

"I should hope so. Come all the way in and sit down."

Rachel did his bidding. It reminded her of that first day—with an important difference. When it came to her own attractiveness, she now had an inner certainty, reflected in her appearance. She was thirty pounds thinner, her hair was elegantly styled, and she wore a sage-green suit that was both simple and striking. "If Nikos Athas could see me now, eh?" she said with a smile.

Carl returned it. "He's going to eat the proverbial crow by the shovelful." There was a pause. "I can tell you're nervous."

"Yes."

Here at the institute, she'd been protected. But three months ago, when she'd heard about Manny's stroke, she was convinced that once she set foot outside Michelangelo's, she would never be safe, let alone know a good night's sleep again.

"That's not such a bad thing, feeling a bit nervous. Sometimes too much confidence is worse than too little. I'm going to tell you something. You're a beautiful woman. You were when you came here, but the weight loss has defined your face and figure. A golden redhead is rare. With your hair layered and styled, you're a real knockout.''

She shook her head. "I'm not tall enough."

"For what?"

"I don't know. I'd just like to be five foot nine instead of five-four."

"I'd like to be six feet, but that didn't happen to me, either," he confessed. They both chuckled. "But we shorter people are compensated in other ways."

"In your case that's true," she whispered. "You're a brilliant man and you've been wonderful to me—*for* me."

"Unfortunately not as wonderful as I would've liked. You're still keeping something from me, and I don't think it's because you're worried Nikos won't find you attractive. I had hoped you'd confide in me, but I can't force you to talk about it if you're not ready."

That was what she liked so much about Carl. He was intuitive, compassionate—a man she could trust. "I— I think someone could be looking for me." *I'm terrified.*

"And you don't want to be found?"

"No!"

"Well, that sounded emphatic enough. An old boyfriend you haven't told me about?"

"No."

"A distant relative who drives you crazy?"

"No."

"A former boss who wants you back?"

If only that were true. Poor, dear Manny.

"None of the above," she insisted.

"All right. I give up. Does anyone else know your secret?"

"No." Maybe Manny, if he still had any cognitive skills left.

"Then promise me one thing. Don't keep this to yourself much longer, or you'll make yourself sick. Find someone you trust, maybe a clergyman. Often in the confiding, tension is released from our minds and bodies. Be good to yourself, Rachel. You only have one mind, one body. They have to last you forever."

She shivered. "I know."

The only problem with Carl's advice was that a clergyman couldn't possibly protect her. And although she trusted Carl implicitly, she couldn't risk his safety by telling him the truth.

"I'm being serious now. I'd hate to see you lose sleep again and have to start taking medicine. That's no way to live."

"I don't want that, either."

"All right. So you're flying to New York this afternoon."

"Yes. Everything's been arranged, even my hotel accommodations."

He sat back with a smile. "Tomorrow your new life begins. You remember the steps we planned?"

"Yes."

"You'll keep me informed?"

"Of course."

"I'm not speaking as your counselor now. I hope you know I'm your friend."

"I do know that. I'm not sure what would've happened to me if I hadn't met you."

"If that's the way you feel, then call me soon. I'm going to miss you, you know."

Carl had been like a father to her and she would never forget him. "I promise to keep in touch."

"You do that. Good luck, my dear. I hope Nikos Athas has grown up enough to deserve you. One more thing. I insist on an invitation to the wedding."

"You'll be the first person on my list!" If I'm still alive…

She walked around his desk, kissed his cheek, then hurried out of the room. By now the taxi was probably out in front, waiting.

"HERE WE GO, ARI. All the way to the top of the building."

The second the private elevator started to ascend, Ari grasped Stasio's hand and clung to it.

"Stasi?"

"Yes, Ari?"

"My tummy feels funny."

"The first time I rode on this, mine did, too. Now I don't think about it."

"How long are we going to be at your work?"

"Not very long. My secretary, Mrs. Kostinc, will keep you company while I finish up some business. Then we'll leave on our trip."

"Anna says we're going on a fabulous voyage," he said importantly.

Stasio chuckled. "She's right."

"What's a voyage?"

"A long trip across the water."

"Goody." He jumped up and down. "Stasi? Is Mrs. Kostine nice?"

"Very nice."

"Is she old?"

"She's about the same age as Anna and Giorgio."

"How old is that?"

"Forty-five."

"Stasi? How old are you?"

"Thirty-five."

"I'm five."

"I know. In another few months you're going to turn six."

"Anna says I'm going to get a big surprise for my birthday. Do you know what it is?"

Ari, Ari. You're so much like your mother, I can't wait to see the two of you together. "If I told you, then it wouldn't be a surprise, would it?"

"Will I like it a lot?"

"I think you'll like it better than any present in the whole world."

"Better than my ship?"

Stasio chuckled. The toy facsimile of one of the Athas ocean liners he'd given Ari on his last birthday had been a tremendous hit.

"Much better than that. All right. Here we are."

The doors opened into a back hallway that led to his penthouse suite atop the Athas Building. With Ari still clutching one hand, he opened the private entrance to his office with the other. His secretary was waiting for them.

"Mr. Athas. I thought I heard the elevator."

"Mrs. Kostine? This is my godson, Ari."

"Hello, Mrs. Kostine. It's nice to meet you." He put out a hand to shake hers.

"It's nice to meet you, too," his secretary answered, visibly charmed by Ari's manners.

"I've heard a lot about you."

"You have?"

"Yes. Your godfather says you're a wonderful boy. I agree."

"Thank you. Stasi says you're very nice."

The two of them shared a smile over Ari's dark head.

"Come look out the windows of my office, Ari. You can see all of New York City."

Ari cast Stasio a wistful glance. This was a new experience for the boy. He'd never been separated from Stasio on an outing. Until now, Stasio had kept a low profile when he was with his nephew to avoid any hint of speculation or gossip.

If they went for walks, it was to the zoo or the park, someplace close to Anna and Giorgio's house, where Stasio could remain anonymous. In the unfamiliar surroundings of his office building, the boy was looking for reassurance.

"I'll be right here in case you have a question, Ari." The tension left his face. Stella's face.

Without saying a word, Ari put a trusting hand in Mrs. Kostine's and they left his office. She shut the door behind them, darting Stasio another private smile before it closed.

Ari delighted everyone who met him. Stella's heart would melt the very second she saw her boy. That day couldn't come soon enough. Before any more time went by, mother and son needed to be together.

Under ordinary circumstances he would have taken Ari to Greece with him in the company jet. But nothing about this situation was ordinary.

Before he'd left for New York, he'd finally told Eleni about Ari. He'd known she'd be surprised by the news, but he hadn't expected her explosive reaction. Among other things, she'd accused him of not loving her.

He'd tried to make her understand that this was about Stella and Ari, without success. She insisted on seeing herself as the injured party.

That was why he'd planned this trip back to Greece

by ship, and had asked Eleni to join them. The crossing would give her enough time to get well acquainted with him.

She couldn't help but adore the child who would be her nephew after their marriage. Toward the end of their journey, he would explain that a large wedding in Athens with all the attendant publicity and paparazzi could jeopardize the adoption proceedings. Therefore, their marriage would have to take place in total privacy on Andros, which was what he'd always wanted, anyway. He would drive this home to Eleni before they reached Piraeus.

As for Ari, he already knew about Eleni and didn't seem to mind that he'd have to share Stasio with her. He was a loving child, just like his mother. And soon he would be a member of the family.

Aboard ship Stasio would have the luxury of uninterrupted time to make Eleni understand that he could never be happy in his own marriage until he knew Stella had been legally united with her son. He needed Eleni's help in this. All it would take was for her to meet Ari....

Eleni had four brothers and sisters, whom she loved very much. Three of them were married with children. If she had trouble giving up her dream of a big wedding in Athens, Stasio would remind her that he knew she would make the sacrifice if this were happening to her own family. But using persuasion tactics would be a last resort. He had confidence that Ari himself would soften her heart.

On that hopeful note he forced himself to get down to business. A half hour later, he heard his secretary's voice over the intercom.

"Yes, Mrs. Kostine? Is Ari all right?"

"He's fine. Forgive me for disturbing you, but there's a Ms. Maynard in reception who'd like to talk to you before you leave this afternoon."

"I'm not taking appointments."

"I realize that. Actually, she's trying to get in touch with your sister. Apparently the two of them were friends at boarding school in Switzerland, but they lost contact."

Switzerland?

"Shall I give her Stella's phone number and address?"

Stasio frowned as he remembered back to that horrific period after Stella had given up her baby. Not only had those been lost, black months for everyone, poor Stella hadn't made any friends at school.

Except for one... Rosemary something. Or was it Ruthanne? An American name.

But she'd turned out to be a girl who only used his sister to supply her with a free vacation in Chamonix. As soon as they got back to the school, she'd dropped Stella without explanation. Her defection caused another wound to his sister that had never fully healed.

Stasio deeply regretted the incident. Between that experience and Theo's betrayal, Stella had no close friends except for family. She wouldn't allow anyone to get close enough to hurt her again. More than ever, he realized how desperately Stella needed her son.

"Will you come into my office for a minute?"

"Of course. Shall I bring Ari?"

"Is he asking for me?"

"No. He's lying on the floor looking at pictures in the latest *National Geographic*."

"Good. He probably won't notice if you step away

from your desk for a moment.''

"I'll be right there.''

ACCORDING TO CARL, Stasio Athas, the head of Athas Shipping Lines, spent the first part of each month in Athens and the latter half in New York. Her arrival at his office on November twenty-third was no accident.

She watched as the secretary disappeared into his private office. Naturally, the request for Stella's address and phone number had resulted in a small conference. People with as much wealth and notoriety as the Athas family had to protect their own.

She'd never met Stella's older brother, but Carl had produced recent photographs of all three members of the attractive Athas clan. Of the two dark-haired brothers, Stasio was the taller and more powerfully built.

Unlike the smiling Nikos, who wore his hair a bit longer and projected a dashing image, the older brother's harder, uncompromising features made him appear more striking yet less approachable.

From what she could tell, Stasio resembled their well-known father, Paul Athas, a highly placed official in the Greek government, now deceased. Nikos and Stella, on the other hand, bore a strong likeness to their mother, who had died years earlier.

While she waited to see what would happen next, the little boy, presumably the secretary's son, lifted his head from the magazine.

He had beautiful olive skin and dark, serious eyes that looked at her soulfully. Stella's eyes used to look at Rachel like that. Certain mannerisms of the five- or was it six-year-old, reminded her of Stella and Nikos.

"Hello." She couldn't resist talking to him, wondering if the boy could be an Athas. If so, Carl hadn't produced any information on him. "My name's Rachel. What's yours?"

"Ari." He got to his feet. He appeared to be tall for his age, remarkably lean and handsome. Her wore a dark navy pullover, matching pants and sneakers.

"I like your name. It sounds Greek. Can you speak that language?" she asked in Greek, anxious to practice with someone other than the intimidating priest.

The boy responded in fluent Greek, impressing her with his bilingual abilities. They both smiled at the same time. Again she had the strong feeling that he had Athas blood in him.

"I've been trying to learn Greek." She reverted to English once more. "But I know I make a lot of mistakes."

"You talk better than Barbara."

"Who's Barbara?"

"She cleans the house."

"Oh."

"Do you have any children?"

She shook her head. "No. But if I did, I'd want to have a boy just like you."

His eyes lit up. "You would?"

Rachel nodded. He had an endearing manner about him.

"I have a mommy, but she can't take care of me so I live with Anna and Giorgio."

Was Anna the secretary? More intrigued than ever, she said, "You're lucky. I live alone."

"All by yourself?"

"Yes."

"Don't you get scared?"

Yes. Terrified. "When that happens, I remember what my daddy told me to do."

"What's that?"

"Say a prayer so I'll feel better."

"I don't know if that will help."

"How come?"

"Because I heard Anna say something really scary to Giorgio."

"What did she say?"

"That pretty soon I wouldn't be living with them anymore."

His words had a disturbing effect on her. "Did they know you were listening?"

"No."

"Then maybe you misunderstood what she said."

He shook his head. "Anna cried."

"She sounds like a kind person. Why don't you talk to her and tell her what you heard. That way she can explain what she meant. It'll probably make you feel a lot better."

"Ms. Maynard? Please step inside my office."

Rachel hadn't realized they'd attracted an audience. She turned in the direction of the curt-sounding male voice. Her gaze collided with a pair of unfriendly black eyes made unfriendlier by the dark eyebrows above them.

Stella's oldest brother looked even stronger and more forbidding in the flesh. But like all the Athas family, he had inherited traits that made him a compelling figure. Maybe even more so because, unlike Nikos, he obviously didn't care what anyone thought of him.

"Stasi? Gues—"

"In a minute, Ari," he said not unkindly. "Mrs. Kostine, why don't you take Ari down the hall for a soda."

"I was just going to suggest it. Shall we go?"

The obedient boy waved a tiny goodbye to Rachel before following the secretary out the door. The gesture tugged at her heart.

"Come with me, Ms. Maynard."

Once they reached his ultramodern office, with various interesting graphics adorning the only wall not made of glass, he indicated a chair opposite his desk.

As soon as she sat down, she said, "I'm sorry to have bothered you when I didn't have an appointment, but I had no idea how else to reach Stella. I'm afraid we lost track of each other a long time ago."

By now he was seated in the leather swivel chair behind his desk. He made no apology for studying her at length. It surprised her to find disapproval rather than admiration in his unwavering regard.

Since leaving Michelangelo's yesterday, she'd been combating the stares of appreciation coming from just about every man who crossed her path. Unused to such blatant attention from the opposite sex, she was still trying to deal with the heady sensation of knowing most men found her attractive.

Carl had already discussed this aspect of her transformation, reminding her that for the first little while she'd be vulnerable to such flattering attention. He'd warned her to take it in her stride and remember that Nikos Athas was the man she loved and wanted to attract. What an irony to find herself the target of his older brother's patent disregard. At least, that was what it felt like.

She remembered another of Carl's many warnings. "A man like Stasio Athas isn't going to buy your story right away. He'll think you're coming on to him, either to procure a high-paying job or because you're interested in becoming his pillow friend.

"Either possibility will be repugnant to him, since his reputation appears to be the opposite of his younger brother's, at least in the public aspects of their lives. You'll need to appear at his office with indisputable proof of your former relationship with Stella."

Opening her handbag, she started to reach for her wallet when he said, "My secretary didn't hear your first name clearly."

She paused in the act of pulling out some pictures. "It's Rachel."

A disquieting silence filled his office.

"Rachel," he muttered, as if he'd just solved a complex riddle. The distaste in his tone was tangible now. "You can keep your photographs. I know who you are."

She froze in place.

Had someone been watching her during the time she'd been at the institute and followed her here? Did it mean there was no safe hiding place? Not even among the powerful Athas family? Had the past six months of planning been for nothing?

"You've gone pale, Ms. Maynard."

All the yelling in the world couldn't compare to the quiet rage in his voice.

"Dare I believe there's a smattering of conscience inside you that admits your extreme cruelty to Stella at the lowest point of her life?"

What?

"Or is this the look of genuine disappointment because your scheme to inveigle your way back into Stella's life—so you can use her again—has been thwarted at the outset?

"Or—" He paused. His mouth twisted unpleasantly. "Could it be that it's not Stella, but someone close to her you hope to befriend? Maybe because you've drained your latest lover of his last drachma and are now in the market for a new victim?"

His suppositions filled her with unmitigated relief. If she could have done it, she would have cried out for joy. She was still safe!

It didn't matter that Stasio Athas had hit upon the truth, even though it was flawed. She'd always loved Stella and Nikos. She always would.

"You have every right to despise me," she murmured.

"Because I was right on all three counts."

She braved his glacial scrutiny. "Because Stella deserves to know why I stopped being her friend. At the time, I thought it best to keep the reason a secret out of fear of hurting her. A couple of months later, while I was attending university in Pennsylvania, Madame sent me a letter from Stella.

"I couldn't bring myself to open it because I knew if I did, I'd want to see Stella again, and I still believed it wouldn't be a good idea. But I've lived to regret that decision because I lost the best friend I ever had, too."

He tapped the top of the desk with his immaculate, square-tipped fingers. "Even if you're telling me the truth, why try to reach her now?"

"My father died nine months ago. It was hard losing him. My doctor advised me to get away on a long vacation. I finally took his advice and quit my job. Right now I'm on my way back to Switzerland, which I consider my second home. I want to visit some of the old haunts.

"I thought if I could contact Stella and explain what

happened all those years ago, maybe she'd forgive me and we could renew our friendship, even travel together for a week or two. That is, if she's free. For all I know, she's married with a couple of children by now.''

He lounged back in the chair, eyeing her intently. ''My sister and I have no secrets from each other. Suppose you tell me the truth about your defection. I'll decide if Stella is capable of forgiving you.''

His honesty was even more brutally frank than Carl's. But it was a trait she prized as much as goodness and virtue.

''I have to admit I'd rather tell Stella than you.''

''How so? I'm a total stranger. What difference does it make?''

''It makes all the difference in the world, since you and Nikos had everything to do with my reason for letting Stella go.''

More than anything, his stillness told her she'd surprised him. Rachel had the impression that Stasio Athas was rarely surprised.

''Go on.''

As before with Carl, Rachel found herself relating the details of that night in Chamonix when Nikos had plunged the proverbial dagger in her heart, instantly humiliating Rachel and destroying her relationship with Stella.

The whole time she relived the painful experience, Stasio didn't move or make a sound. But when she looked in his eyes, she saw a bleakness alongside the anger. A bleakness that hadn't been there before.

''...and my problem was, Nikos only made veiled threats where you were concerned. Whatever Stella had done that put her under your thumb, I had no desire to make things worse.

"I was afraid you must be some kind of tyrant, especially if you viewed an American whose father was in the military with such contempt. If I was truly someone too undesirable for your sister to associate with, then I believed the only thing to do was take Nikos's comments to heart and bow out of her life.

"The last thing I wanted was to get Stella in more trouble with you, particularly when I knew she was deeply unhappy over something she couldn't talk about. Not even to me.

"Because of Nikos's comments, I assumed you'd forced her to walk a narrow line. In the end, I decided the only thing to do was end the friendship."

"Because you knew she wouldn't." He stated the obvious. The silence deepened. "I love my sister, Ms. Maynard, and I don't want to see any more hurt come to her. Since I have only your word for what happened, I feel it necessary to corroborate your story with the headmistress in Switzerland before I give you Stella's whereabouts."

Carl had warned her that Stasio Athas would want proof. "You're welcome to phone her, Mr. Athas."

He studied her for a moment. Obviously he hadn't expected her response. "Then I'll do so now. It's not too late for me to call Montreux for verification."

Confident that Madame would corroborate her story, Rachel sat back in the chair and waited while he looked up the number and made the phone call.

She shouldn't have been surprised he spoke French to Madame. A lengthy conversation ensued, one Rachel followed without difficulty. By the time he'd said *au revoir,* and had replaced the receiver, she could see from his frown that he not only believed her story, he was troubled by it.

"My apologies for having doubted you, Ms. Maynard. I had no idea Nikos was the person responsible
for your breakup with Stella."

Afraid she'd gone too far—that Stasio might seek a
confrontation with his brother—Rachel hastened to repair the damage by pulling out a couple of snapshots
taken at the Athas chalet in Chamonix. She put them
on his desk.

"In all fairness to your brother, that happened ages
ago, and I was a dumpy-looking teenager with a mop
of wild red hair. I'm sure every man who ever knew
me back then thought the same thing. Let's be honest
here. Stella was always lovely and never went through
the awkward stage. Nikos had every right to be proud
of her. I would imagine she's a raving beauty today...like your mother."

She watched him pick up the photographs and study
them for a long moment. It startled her when he admitted, "At that age I was too tall. I resembled one of
your American telephone poles."

Rachel couldn't help smiling at the picture Stasio
painted of himself. For a moment, he smiled back. She
enjoyed the feeling of camaraderie until his expression
unexpectedly sobered.

"But it would have been a fatal blow to my pride
had I heard a beautiful woman repeat my flaws aloud,
within my hearing."

"I understand a man's pride suffers more than a
woman's. I got over it and forgave Nikos a long time
ago."

A grimace stole over his hard-boned features. "I'm
afraid I'm the one who's going to have the more difficult time forgiving him. In a careless moment he hurt
you deeply. Ultimately that hurt translated to Stella,

who suffered unnecessarily when you turned away from her.''

Rachel sucked in her breath. ''We both suffered, but that's all in the past. We're adults now. I particularly don't want you to say anything to your brother or harbor any ill will toward him.

''Nikos is younger than you, not only in years. He couldn't help that his success in the Olympics went to his head. He's a fabulous skier. But he's obviously not as secure as you. I get the feeling he finds your presence rather daunting, even if you are brothers.''

He gave her a searching glance. ''Your generosity does you justice. But whatever my brother's virtues or failings, he committed an unconscionable act when he purposely drove you away from Stella. You both needed each other.''

''She felt like my sister.''

''Stella told me the same thing about you.''

The words were gratifying to hear. ''Do you think she'll forgive me?''

''If you tell her exactly what you told me, I have no doubt of it.''

Stasio was not the ogre Nikos had made his older brother out to be. In fact, he was so different from the autocratic despot she'd conjured in her mind, she could scarcely contain her shock.

''Then you'll give me her phone number?''

He seemed to be mulling something over in his mind. ''When were you going to leave for Switzerland?''

He'd answered her question with another question. Had she misread him, after all?

''Tomorrow night.''

''Have you ever traveled by ship?''

What? ''Many times.''

"Have you ever suffered from seasickness?"

"No. Why do you ask?"

"My fiancée and I are sailing for Greece this evening on one of our passenger liners, the *Neptune*. I'm inviting you to sail with us."

Fiancée?

Carl's research hadn't uncovered that particular piece of news, either. For some ridiculous reason, the revelation upset her.

The only person she should be worrying about was Nikos. As long as *he* didn't have a fiancée, her plan to become his wife was still a viable possibility.

"I couldn't impose like that. I've already purchased my airline tickets."

"I'll make sure the airline reimburses you."

A whole week on a ship with Stasio Athas, where no one could find her or track her movements?

"Only if you keep the money."

"A guest doesn't pay, Ms. Maynard. When we reach Piraeus, I'll send you on to Andros for a reunion with Stella. I'll be staying overnight in Athens, then I'll join you the next day.

"That will give you time to tell Stella what you heard Nikos say—and why you broke the friendship. She'll forgive you and insist you stay on."

Maybe. "I-it's all like a dream. Thank you," she said softly.

"It's the least I can do to rectify the damage Nikos inflicted."

"Please forget the past. If you asked Nikos today, he probably wouldn't even remember it."

"That's what worries me," he muttered.

"Please, Mr. Athas—Stasio. Let it go. I'll beg Stella to do the same thing. Nikos made a mistake, but he has many wonderful qualities. You don't want this to cause a breach in your family.''

His black eyes studied her while he appeared to weigh her words. ''You're right. Thank you for reminding me that we all need to pull together, not apart.''

Some of the tension left her body.

In the next breath, he said, ''When you go downstairs, there'll be a car outside to take you to your hotel. The driver will wait while you pack your things, then he'll drive you to the dock where you'll be taken aboard ship to your cabin. I'll ring your stateroom and we'll have dinner together.''

''Thank you again. Everything sounds wonderful.''

They shook hands. She felt the warmth and strength of his fingers long after the Athas company limousine had moved her through the heavy afternoon traffic.

Carl had been so right when he'd told her to confront Stella's oldest brother head-on. He was the force majeure in that household. Because of him, she'd be reunited with Stella. At some point Nikos would make an appearance. The rest would be up to Rachel and her ability to make him forget the other women in his life.

In the meantime, she would enjoy seven glorious, fear-free days on the ocean in the company of Stasio Athas.

Don't forget his fiancée, a tiny voice nagged.

CHAPTER FOUR

"Dr. Rich? I'm Colonel Sean Dodd."

"You're Air Force."

"Yes, sir. Thanks for fitting me in today."

"You're entirely welcome. When my nurse told me you'd flown all the way from Las Vegas to Philadelphia to see me, I asked her to rearrange a couple of appointments. What can I do for you?"

"I'm here on personal business, Doctor. Actually, I'm trying to carry out the wishes of a dear friend."

"The wishes?"

"Yes. One of my closest buddies, Colonel Charles Maynard, died about nine months ago. He had an only child, Rachel."

Hal Rich nodded. "I know her well."

"That's what I thought. She talked a lot about you after she moved back on base with her dad. Apparently you were her doctor while she was in college."

"That's right."

"Well, when Chuck got so sick and knew he wasn't going to make it, he begged me and Ruth to look after her. You know what I mean?"

"Of course."

"My wife and I used to have the two of them over for dinner all the time. After he died, we kept up the same tradition when we could. But a few months after the funeral, damned if she wasn't so depressed she moved from the base and disappeared!

"Everyone who knows her has been looking for her. She was in a bad way. It's no wonder. Chuck was a hero. Best of the best. Now we all feel like we're letting him down. Ruth's half out of her mind with worry.

"I finally told her I'd get on a plane and come talk to you. To be honest, you're the last lead we've got. Doctor? Would you have any idea, any idea at all, where she might be? I know it's a long shot, but Ruth and I aren't about to give up."

"Actually I do know where she used to be. I don't know if she's there now."

"I just knew this trip would pay off. Wait till I tell Ruth. She'll be thrilled! We've missed Chuck and Rachel. His death hit everyone hard."

Hal searched for the number on his Rolodex, then wrote it down on a piece of paper and handed it to the colonel. "I hope she's come to terms with her loss and is happier these days. There you go. Maybe you can still reach her there."

"You don't know how much I appreciate this. Is she staying with friends?"

"She was the last time I heard from her."

"That's the kind of news I like to hear."

The two men stood up. Hal walked the colonel to the door of his office. "When you catch up with Rachel, tell her to give me a call. I'd like to know how she's doing."

"You bet I will. Thanks again, Doctor."

They shook hands and the colonel strode into the waiting room. As soon as he'd disappeared out the front door, Hal returned to his office and buzzed his nurse.

"You can bring my next patient back here in five

minutes,'' he said as he punched in the phone number he'd given the colonel. Next he punched in Carl Gordon's extension and waited.

"Yes?"

"Carl? This is Hal Rich."

"Oh yes, Hal. If you're calling to speak to Rachel, she just left us yesterday. I'm sending you a copy of my report on her."

"What's your verdict?"

"She's going to make it in this life. She left here confident, beautiful."

"How about her depression?"

"It's no longer a problem."

"That's what I wanted to hear. It's one of the reasons I phoned."

"And the other?"

"A Colonel Dodd from Las Vegas, who was close friends with Rachel's family, was just in my office asking about her. It seems she didn't tell anyone where she was going when she entered the institute.

"Apparently he and his wife promised her father they'd look after her. They've been anxious to find her and make sure she's all right. I gave him the institute number, but I told him she might not be there. You should be getting a call from him any time now. Just thought I'd alert you."

"I appreciate that. Rachel plans to stay in touch with me. If she wants to talk to the colonel, I'll give her his number. If not...I won't."

"Sounds good to me."

"Talk to you soon, Hal."

Hal Rich hung up the receiver in time to greet his next patient.

"STASIO?"

His hand tightened on the phone receiver. "Eleni? The ship's ready to sail. Where are you?"

"I'm still at the hotel. After thinking it over, I've decided to fly back to Athens."

He frowned. "What's going on?"

"I—I just think it would be better this way." There was a curious nervousness in her voice.

Stasio didn't say anything for a moment. The night before last, she'd flown into New York to do some shopping as planned. It was decided that she'd meet Ari for the first time when she joined them aboard ship. But something had happened to make her change her mind. Or maybe someone...

Only Nikos and Stella knew about Stasio's plan to be married on Andros. Since his sister would never have divulged those details to Eleni, that left Nikos.

"Darling? You're not saying anything. Please don't be upset with me. I have a confession to make. I should have told you when you first brought up the idea of an ocean voyage."

"Go on." He wondered what kind of excuse she'd come up with.

"I'm not a good sailor. Being on a sailboat or ferry for a few hours in good weather, I can handle. But not seven days on an ocean in winter. Did you know they're forecasting a hurricane?"

He was sure of it; Nikos had gotten to her.

For all her attributes, there was just enough of a selfish streak in Eleni to be vulnerable to his brother's arguments.

Stasio hadn't been fooled by Nikos's agreement to support him in this plan to bring Ari into the fold. For reasons still to come to light, Nikos wasn't happy about the new turn of events in the Athas household. Stirring up trouble with Eleni fit right into his agenda.

"Don't worry about it," he said quietly. "I wouldn't want you to be seasick."

"If you'd take the plane, we could be together before morning."

She was so transparent that his irritation with her bordered on the same kind of anger he'd been harboring against Nikos ever since Rachel had supplied him with certain revelations earlier today.

Ari's and Stella's lives were at stake here! Everything else took a backseat.

"My nephew has never been on a real vacation. He's always wanted to go on a ship. I can't disappoint him now."

"Sometimes I think you'd rather play uncle to him than fiancé to me. Stasio—I won't be waiting at the dock. If you want to see me, you'll have to come to me."

"Eleni…whatever is wrong, we'll work it out. Don't draw lines."

"They were drawn before we ever met." The phone went dead.

Since he couldn't tell her that he'd fly to Athens tonight, he hung up without calling her back. He would have to wait until they reached Greece before he could reason with her. For Ari's sake, he had to.

"STASI?" HE HEARD a gentle knock at the adjoining stateroom door. "Are you off the phone yet?"

"I am. Come on in. How was your shower?"

"Fine. They have a whole bunch of soaps. Can I keep them?"

"Of course. But why would you do that?"

''Because the papers have ships on them. I'm going to make a c-collection.''

''That sounds like a very worthy project.''

''What's worthy?''

He tousled Ari's dark locks, still moist from the water. ''It means your project is worth going to all the trouble to do. Now, before we go to dinner, how would you like to talk to Anna and Giorgio?''

''They already called me in my room.''

Stasio shouldn't have been surprised. Another reason for this trip was to help Ari's foster parents deal with future separations from him. But the bond among all three ran deep. None of this was going to be easy.

''Are they fine?''

''Yes. They said they miss me.''

''I'm sure they do. How about you? Do you miss them too much to take this trip?''

''Of course not.''

On a rush of emotion Stasio picked him up and gave him a hug. ''Guess what? Someone special is going to have dinner with us tonight.''

''I know that.''

''You do?''

''Of course. It's Eleni. You're silly, Stasi.''

''Ari? That was Eleni on the phone. Something came up and she won't be coming on our trip after all.''

Always sensitive, he patted Stasio's face. ''Are you sad?''

The simple question was an illuminating one. He answered it truthfully. ''No. Now we can do all the things men like to do.''

''What things?''

"Well, after dinner we can visit the bridge and you can see where they drive the ship."

"Goody!"

"First though, we have to call our guest in her stateroom and invite her to dinner."

"Who is it?"

"Her name is Rachel. She's the woman you were talking to in my office."

"She was nice. Did you know she can speak Greek and her daddy told her to say her prayers when she gets scared?"

Stasio couldn't help smiling. "No. I didn't know that."

"She's pretty, huh?"

"Yes."

"'Specially her hair."

Gorgeous.

"She's lives all alone."

"Well, she won't be alone while she's on this ship."

"Where's her stateroom?"

"Right next to yours."

He seemed pleased by the prospect. "Do we have to call her? Why can't we just go get her?"

"I guess we can do that."

"Can I invite her?"

"If you'd like. I'll tell you a secret about her," he said as they left his stateroom and worked their way down the hall to hers. Already the ship had moved past the Statue of Liberty and was headed into open sea.

This close to Christmas the crossing would be rough, with gale-force winds predicted. Ari had already been told about the bad weather. It'd only made him more excited.

"What secret?" His eyes were shining.

"She's a friend of your mother's."

"My mother's?" Clearly this put Rachel Maynard in a category right on top.

"Go ahead," he whispered. "Knock."

"Who is it?" she called.

"It's Ari."

"Ari?"

The door opened and Rachel Maynard appeared in a simple black dress that was so stunning on her figure, Stasio couldn't say anything for a minute. Thank heaven for Ari, who had no problem communicating whatsoever.

"Hello, Rachel."

She looked totally bewildered as her shocked gaze passed from Stasio to Ari. "I didn't know you'd be on this ship!"

Ari laughed at her surprise. "Stasi's my godfather. He says you know my mommy."

The relationships were getting complicated. She lifted questioning eyes to Stasio's. This close, he could see tiny specks of silver in those china-blue depths. Her coloring was right out of a Raphael painting.

"I do?"

"Show her a picture of your mommy, Ari."

The boy pulled out a packet of pictures from his suit pocket. He never went anywhere without them. "See? That's her."

She took the packet from his fingers and looked. Stasio heard the slight gasp before she lifted her head. A stream of unspoken words passed between them.

"Stella was always beautiful, Ari. I—I have some pictures of her, too. Just a minute and I'll get them." After handing him back his pictures, she reached for her purse and opened it to find her wallet.

"These were taken when your mommy and I went to school together in Switzerland. We were a lot younger then. I look kind of funny, but your mommy was as beautiful then as she is now."

Stasio watched his nephew study the photographs intently. Finally he lifted his head. "Did she tell you about her little boy named Ari?"

"No," Rachel said before Stasio could intervene. "Because you weren't born yet. But we used to talk about the names we'd give our children one day. Ari was one of her favorites."

"It was?"

She'd handled the shaky moment beautifully. Ari was enchanted. So was Stasio, whose instincts told him she was perfectly capable of counting and had already guessed the reasons for Stella's great sadness. The details would come later.

"Yes."

"What was your favorite name?"

"Charles."

"You mean like in Charlie Brown?"

"Exactly like that." She leaned across and hugged him before Stasio set him down once more. "My daddy's name was Charles. But all his friends called him Chuck. Someday I want a little Charles who'll fly around the house like an airplane."

"I can't fly."

"That was a figure of speech," Stasio explained while he tried in vain to stifle his own laughter.

"What's a figure of speech?"

"Why don't we all go to dinner and I'll explain it to you."

The three of them started down the hall. To his consternation, Stasio found himself vitally aware of the

American woman at his side. Once or twice, their thighs brushed against each other. He felt a sudden rush of desire, something that hadn't happened for such a long time, he was at a loss to explain it.

"Are we meeting your fiancée there?" She had an appealing voice, low and well-modulated. He wondered if she might be a singer.

"Eleni changed her mind. She's not coming on the trip," Ari announced for him.

"Oh."

RACHEL GAVE A START when she heard a soft rap on the door to Ari's room. She'd put him to bed, at his own sweetly worded request.

Though she felt that the people who were looking for her hadn't caught up with her yet, she couldn't quite shake the premonition that one day her greatest fear would be realized.

"Yes?"

"It's Stasio."

"Come in," she murmured as he entered the room still dressed in the blue silk shirt and charcoal pants he'd worn to dinner earlier in the evening.

In the semidarkness he looked big and powerful, yet he moved around the room with surprising stealth as he picked up Ari's clothes and hung them in the closet. She shouldn't have derived so much pleasure from just watching him; there'd been enough of that at dinner, where they'd been given a private table and fed course after course of sumptuous food.

Ari had supplied ninety percent of the conversation. Rachel had only been required to answer the odd question when Stasio was otherwise occupied enjoying his meal. She loved watching him eat.

The truth was, she loved watching him do *anything*.

Everyone on the *Neptune,* from the staff to the passengers, knew the head of Athas Shipping Lines was on board. To their credit, they left Stasio alone, even when the three of them took a walk on deck in the freezing sea air. It was the kindest thing people could have done.

Rachel couldn't remember when she'd spent a more wonderful evening in her life. She would treasure this night forever. She could almost fantasize that she was on a cruise with her husband and son....

But she had to remember that Ari was Stella's son, and Stasio belonged to Eleni. She'd only been allowed to borrow them for a little while.

"He's asleep now. Come to my room. We need to talk," Stasio whispered close to her ear. His warm breath against her cheek sent delicious chills through her body.

Like a sleepwalker, she moved off Ari's bed with as much care as possible and tiptoed through the adjoining door into Stasio's suite. It looked like a nineteenth-century French drawing room.

He'd left only one light on next to his bed. There was something very intimate about being enclosed in such a room at this time of night with an exciting man like Stasio. She knew she shouldn't be alone with him at *any* time, but especially not tonight. For some reason, she had difficulty even recalling Nikos's image.

Carl had warned her there would be occasions like this, when she felt beautiful and desirable with a man other than Nikos. Whenever Stasio looked at her, he made her feel that way. But he was engaged to Eleni, so nothing personal was implied or intended. Any woman who'd been attractive to men all her life would understand that. She wouldn't let it go to her head.

But Rachel wasn't any woman. This was a new experience for her. Without Ari to act as a buffer, she felt out of control.

"You'd better sit down before you fall down, Rachel."

His warning came just in time. As a swell lifted the ship before dropping it again, she fell into the nearest chair. He, on the other hand, sat with enviable calm in the chair next to hers. Both chairs were anchored to the floor.

"I want to thank you for staying with Ari until he dozed off. I know he misses the feminine touch without Anna to tuck him in."

"It was a privilege. He's so precious, and he looks so much like Stella. When I first met him in your office, he reminded me of her and Nikos."

"Genes don't lie, do they?" He paused. "You were presented with several shocks today."

"So were you," she countered.

The corner of his mouth lifted—and her pulse rate suddenly accelerated. "My compliments for the discreet way you handled Ari's questions," he said quietly.

She swallowed hard. "Stasio—"

"I know what you're going to ask. Since you were completely honest with me earlier today, I plan to return the favor. I suppose I should start by telling you about Theo, the young man who slept with my sister, then ran away from responsibility when he learned she was pregnant with his child."

"Is he from a good family?"

"Yes. They live in Salamis. Theo came to work for

his uncle in Athens. His uncle's family attends the same church as ours. That's how Stella met him. He's her age."

"Then he's still young."

"That's right."

"Does Stella love him?"

"Obviously, she thought she did, but she hasn't seen him for six years. Still, they've had a child together, which should mean something."

"But not always. Not if he hasn't made one inquiry about Ari."

"No. He hasn't."

"Does anyone outside the two families know Stella was pregnant?"

"I don't think Theo even told his family about it."

Her eyes closed tightly. Poor Stella.

"But to answer your question more completely, I found a clinic in New York close to me where my sister could be with other unwed mothers until the baby was born."

Rachel took a fortifying breath. "When I first met Stella, I felt this great sadness coming from her. I think I told you that."

"Now you know it's because she gave up her baby for adoption."

For the next twenty minutes Rachel sat spellbound as Stasio explained about his sister's painful decision and the years of regret and depression that followed.

When he told her his reasons for not allowing Ari to be adopted by strangers—in case Stella changed her mind—Rachel had trouble holding back the tears.

"I know my sister wants to be a full-time mother to him, and I honestly believe that Ari won't ever want to leave her once they meet."

"He won't!" Rachel assured him. "Stella is the sweetest, kindest girl I've ever known. Ari will adore her on sight."

Their eyes met in mutual understanding before he said, "But Ari also loves Giorgio and Anna."

"Of course. They were there from the moment he was born. Stasio—there's something you should know." In the next breath she told him what Ari had overheard at his foster parents' home—that he'd be going away. She told Stasio he'd heard Anna cry and it had frightened him.

Stasio grimaced. "I was afraid of that. Intellectually, they've known the day could come when Stella might want to claim her son. But on an emotional level, they've never wanted to deal with the possibility."

"I can understand that. Couldn't they move to Greece to be near Ari?"

"I've already discussed it with them. But it means uprooting their lives, leaving their friends. They also know that Stella will need time alone to bond with Ari. That's why it's so hard on them right now."

"What does Stella say?"

"She's trying to come to grips with the realization that Ari will instinctively turn to Anna and Giorgio for emotional support. Stella hasn't said it in so many words, but I know she's afraid Ari won't be able to handle a separation from them."

Rachel sighed. "It's complicated, but not impossible to work out when there's so much love. Right now he's perfectly happy to be with you."

His eyes grew tender. "I love him."

Anyone could see that.

"If Anna and Giorgio can eventually move to Greece to be near Ari, then every desire of his heart will be fulfilled—because you'll be there, too. Surely you know you're his hero.''

''He's a wonderful boy.''

You're a wonderful man. So wonderful, in fact, it would be unfair to compare you to other men.

Rachel might have been an only child, but even she could imagine that if she'd been blessed with a brother and found herself in Stella's circumstances, that brother would never have sacrificed for her the way Stasio had sacrificed for his sister.

Such selfless love went beyond the norm. No wonder Stella had loved him with a love that bordered on worship. Ari was no different. One day soon, when he learned that Stasio was his uncle by blood, it would only cement the love they already shared.

Meeting Stasio explained Nikos in a way that nothing else could have. What Rachel had learned tonight made her realize that Stasio and his younger brother were leagues apart, unless Nikos had changed a great deal.

The Nikos of six years ago hadn't been made of the same stuff as his brother, or he would never have tampered with her and Stella's friendship when his sister was so fragile.

But that was the whole point, wasn't it? It took a man of great integrity and intelligence like Stasio to recognize Stella's fragility and understand her deepest needs.

Rachel had never envied another person before. But she envied his fiancée.

So far he hadn't talked about Eleni. Maybe it was time to bring her name into the conversation. That way, Rachel wouldn't be tempted to forget the other woman existed.

"Did your fiancée become ill at the last minute? Is that why she couldn't join you?"

The answer seemed a long time in coming. "This is Ari's first trip anywhere with me. At the last minute, Eleni decided he and I should have this time to ourselves."

She lowered her head. "Knowing how crazy Ari is about you, I don't suppose he's aware of her sacrifice. Does your fiancée love him as much as you do?"

There was another significant pause in the conversation before she heard him say, "Eleni has never met my nephew."

"Never?" she cried before she realized her mistake. "I'm sorry. It's none of my business."

"Don't apologize. I made it your business when I invited you to sail with us. You couldn't have known it was only recently that I told Eleni about Ari. It's taking her a little time to deal with the fact that he is and always will be an integral part of my life."

Obviously, something was going on here that Rachel didn't understand. She wanted to ask him what, exactly, there was for Eleni to deal with, but she didn't dare. Instead, she asked, "Aren't Stella and your fiancée close?"

"They're friends, but Eleni is six years older and they don't share a bond like you and Stella did. I'm afraid my sister has kept to herself too much over the past few years. It will be a double blessing to have you back in her life and know that Ari already likes you. You couldn't have shown up at my office at a more propitious moment."

His last sentence sounded cryptic. She sensed there were things he hadn't told her. Private things. She discovered she wanted to know everything about him and realized she was getting far too involved.

Her hands clung to the arms of the chair. "Stasio? I—I don't know how long I'll be able to stay in Greece." *I don't know how long I can be around you and pretend your nearness doesn't affect me.*

A new tension crackled between them. "I thought you wanted to vacation with Stella."

I did. I do. I planned everything so I could be with my best friend and get Nikos to fall in love and marry me. What I hadn't counted on was meeting you.

"If you recall, I meant for Stella and me to travel to Switzerland. But that was before I knew about Ari. Everything's changed. Once she's with her son, she'll need time alone and she won't want to go anywhere else."

"Andros has its own charms. I promise you won't feel deprived."

That's what I'm afraid of, especially if you're there. "I'm sure I won't. Now if you'll excuse me, I'd better get to bed."

"Let me walk you back to your stateroom."

"No!" She jumped to her feet. "Thank you." With some difficulty she made her way to the door, which opened into the hallway. An angry ocean boiled outside. "I'll be fine by myself." *As long as you don't touch me.*

CHAPTER FIVE

"YES?"

"Good afternoon, ma'am. My name is Colonel Dodd. I've flown all the way from Nevada. Dr. Hal Rich gave me your phone number, but I could never reach a live operator so I decided to drive over here. It's a beautiful old place."

"What is it you want?"

"Well, ma'am, I'm trying to touch base with the daughter of my best friend, Colonel Maynard. Her name is Rachel Maynard. Dr. Rich from the Whitestone Clinic said she lives here."

The woman shook her head. "There's no one here by that name."

"She's on the shortish side, a bit heavy, with fairly long red hair she wears in a ponytail. Does any of that ring a bell?"

"No." She started to shut the door.

He reached for his wallet and extended a hundred-dollar bill. "Will this help your memory?"

"Keep your money."

"Now see here, ma'am. All I'm try—"

"I know exactly what you're trying to do. I can't help you."

She shut the heavy paneled door in his face.

He walked to the corner before making a call on his cell phone. When T.J. answered, he said, "Bring the van around. It looks like we're going to be camping out for a while.

"Make sure you've got the night vision goggles. While you're at it, pick up some Chinese food with a double order of Char-Shu. Oh yeah, and a couple of six-packs."

STELLA WALKED INTO THE living room and gave Eleni a kiss on both cheeks. "I was surprised when Maria told me you were waiting down here. You look like you've been crying. Something's wrong."

"Your brother and I had a fight."

Stella could see that at a glance. Normally Eleni's makeup would be immaculate. Today her eyes were puffy and red. The way she'd pulled her long black hair into a chignon, she looked every one of her thirty years.

But even in this state, her brother's fiancée was a striking woman with her long legs and slim model's figure. She could wear any outfit and look terrific.

"When did this happen? He's on the ship with Ari right now."

"I know. We talked before they set sail two days ago. One thing led to another. He wouldn't back down. Neither would I. He said some disturbing things to me."

"Stasio?"

Eleni's features tautened. "You can't imagine that, can you?"

"Yes and no. The thing is, I'm not in love with him. You are. Sometimes love makes people say and do things they don't mean. When Theo didn't want anything to do with the baby, I lashed out at him. I've never done anything like that before in my life."

The other woman's brown eyes remained fixed on Stella. "Tell me something. After you fought and he ran away, why didn't you let Stasio talk to Theo's parents? He could have influenced them to bring their son back and make him face his responsibilities."

"That's true. But let me ask you a question, Eleni. You say you've had a fight with Stasio. Would you want him if the only way he would come back was because someone made him?"

Eleni's eyes glittered. "We're not talking about Stasio."

"You mean it would've been all right for *me* to marry someone who didn't love me," Stella clarified.

"If I'd found myself pregnant, I would have done what had to be done to make sure I didn't burden anyone else."

With that remark, Eleni had revealed her true self. Stella had always felt Eleni's resentment, but she'd thought it stemmed from the fact that as brother and sister, she and Stasio were close. Eleni didn't like sharing Stasio with his own family. A lot of selfish women were like that.

"I *did* do what had to be done. I gave my baby up for adoption."

"But you made sure Stasio would always feel your suffering."

"Not deliberately!" Stella defended herself.

"Maybe not. But since the issue's been raised, there's something I want to say to you. It will probably hurt, but you have to believe me when I tell you that's the last thing I want."

Stella sensed that Eleni had been building up to this for a long time. With Stasio gone, she could speak her mind without fear that he might walk in and want to know what was going on.

"What is it?"

"By now you must be aware that Stasio loves Ari like his own son."

"Yes." *And I love him for it.*

The tension thickened. "I don't think you fully comprehend what that means."

"Oh, but I do, Eleni. Stasio has a great capacity to love. He was born to be a family man. It's in his nature."

"Are you equally prepared for Ari to love him the way a son loves his own flesh-and-blood father?" Stella could hear Eleni's voice shaking. "Stasio has had an ongoing relationship with your son since his birth. Doesn't it trouble you the least little bit that the boy has bonded with your brother instead of you?"

With that question, Stella realized Eleni's paranoia went much deeper than she'd first suspected. Eleni was jealous of Ari's place in Stasio's heart!

The knowledge didn't hurt Stella, but it saddened her because she could see that the mere existence of her innocent little boy had become a wedge driving her brother and future sister-in-law apart.

Because of Ari, Stasio hadn't been in any hurry to get married. That had been a wound to Eleni's pride. Maybe he'd already told her they'd have to marry in secret on Andros, thereby denying her the chance to let the world know she was now Mrs. Stasio Athas, a title many women had coveted over the years.

Stella sank down on the sofa beside her. "Look—I understand your pain, Eleni. I've been wrestling with my own demons. As Stasio has reminded me, the man and woman who've been raising Ari might be called foster parents, but in reality, they're his parents. Ari loves them. I'm trying to come to terms with the fact that I'll have to share Ari with them.''

Eleni's knuckles were white as she pressed her fist against the pillow. ''I don't think you've really thought about what you're doing, Stella.''

Her remark cut to the quick.

''You mean you don't think I've considered the possibility that Ari won't love me, won't want to live with me?'' she cried. ''Oh yes, I have. It's my greatest fear.''

''As it should be,'' Eleni shot back. ''It seems to me that in all of this, neither you nor Stasio has thought about Ari's feelings. The boy's going to be torn apart by conflicting loyalties. You don't uproot a child just because you decide you want him.''

Stella felt like she'd been slapped in the face. ''I always wanted him and Stasio knew it.''

''I know you think it's a wonderful thing Stasio did when he prevented anyone from adopting him. But are you sure it was such a wonderful thing for Ari, who's perfectly happy living in New York with the parents who raised him?''

''I've been asking myself those same questions.'' A familiar male voice broke in on their conversation.

Nikos!

Stella's head whipped around in surprise. She was still reeling from her agonizing conversation with Eleni.

''Hello, Stella. Eleni. I'm only in town for a few hours.'' He crossed the room and kissed them both on the cheek. ''I didn't mean to eavesdrop, but since I couldn't help overhearing what you were saying, I have to admit Eleni's got a point. Stasio enjoys playing God with people's lives. But he may have gone too far where Ari is concerned.''

Nikos could be cruel, but this time he'd crossed the line. "Why are you attacking him like this?" By now Stella was on her feet, her body trembling.

"Why?" Nikos demanded. "Because you've got a blind spot when it comes to Stasio. He's not infallible you know. He was born of an earthly mother and father, like the rest of us. I admit he rarely makes a mistake— but he's made one this time. Fortunately, I'm not blinded by hero worship, and neither is Eleni."

"Listen to your brother, Stella," Eleni begged, getting to her feet. "No harm will be done if you never meet your son face-to-face. Stasio can always supply you with pictures and keep you advised of his progress. You can continue to love him in your heart."

Nikos slid an arm around Stella's shoulders. Not wanting it there, she moved away from him. His eyes narrowed. "Do you hear what Eleni's saying? It's not too late to keep everything the way it is. Stasio hasn't told Ari he's coming to Greece to meet his mother. Not yet. Ari thinks he's on a pleasure trip with his godfather. Nothing has to change."

"One day you're going to meet a man who'll love you and want children with you. You'll be the parents of that child from the day it's born," Eleni reasoned. "There'll be no conflict for anyone. You want that for Ari, don't you? You want him to grow to adulthood without trauma or confusion. His foster parents love him. Why don't you leave it alone?"

Stella felt as if she'd been thrown in a pit to be tortured. She suspected that Eleni, out of sheer desperation, had asked Nikos to join forces with her.

"There's one thing you've both forgotten," Stella

began in a barely controlled voice. "Ari knows about me. He knows I would've kept him if I could. He's been told I'll come for him when I can. A child longs for his birth parents. Stasio says Ari's been waiting and waiting for the day I could take care of him."

Nikos shook his head. "It always comes back to Stasio, doesn't it? You still don't get it. The only reason Stasio wants Ari here with you is so he can have a permanent hold on the boy."

"What?" Even for Nikos, this accusation sounded ludicrous.

"Come on, Stella! You don't honestly think he'll let another man be a father to Ari, even if you were to marry again. The way he feels about your son, you'll be lucky if any man *wants* to marry you, knowing he'll have to take on Stasio.

"As for Stasio and Eleni's marriage, I don't give it a chance in hell if Ari lives in Greece. Can't you see that what you're about to do will undermine their whole relationship?"

In shock, Stella switched her gaze to Eleni's. "Is that what you think, too?"

"A lot of damage has already been done." Eleni underlined Nikos's words. "What I think is that Stasio's so preoccupied with your son and your happiness, he doesn't realize he's put both of you before everything else in his life."

You mean he's put Ari's and my happiness before you, Eleni.

Stella had always known that Nikos was jealous of Stasio. What she hadn't realized was that Eleni's jealousy was every bit as destructive. Eleni felt she needed to be the only one in Stasio's affections.

Eleni and Nikos were like two dogs who had joined

forces to fight for a bone already in their possession. Stasio had plenty of love to go around, but apparently that wasn't enough for them. They wanted more. A psychiatrist would have a name for it.

"I think we've all said enough for one day," Stella whispered brokenly. "Nothing's been discussed in this room that I haven't been struggling with myself."

"As long as you haven't made a definite decision, we can't ask for more than that, can we, Eleni?" Now that he'd done his worst, Nikos could speak in a conciliatory tone and pretend nothing was wrong.

"No. We're only trying to make you see reason. But Stella, I meant what I said earlier. None of this was said to deliberately hurt you."

Crazed with pain, Stella turned on her heel and started for the hall. When she reached the doorway, she paused to stare at them. "In case I haven't said it yet, I want to thank you both for all your love and support at this crucial time. Your confidence in me and my ability to do the right thing is overwhelming."

"Stella?" Shades of panic and pleading laced Eleni's voice while Nikos stood there with a stunned expression on his face.

"Don't worry," Stella said sarcastically. "I won't say a word about this conversation to Stasio." Some things were better left unsaid. If he knew what had gone on here today, the love he felt for Eleni would crumble to dust.

"Thank you."

"You needed to hear this for your own good." Nikos threw in another brotherly salvo.

What I need is someone to talk to.

I know Stasio did everything he's done out of a selfless love. Father would have approved of what Stasio did. He would have told me to follow my heart, not my head.

My heart wants Ari, but I have to be sure that what I want is the right thing for my son.

I wish I could talk to Mother. She always knew what to do. I wish she were still alive.

I wish I had a friend.

"STASI? I CAN SEE LAND!"

"Let me look."

Ari handed Stasio the binoculars. "You're right. You've got a great eye there. Do you know what this means?"

"What?"

"We're passing through the Strait of Gibraltar and getting closer to Greece. From now on, we'll be sailing in the calm waters of the Mediterranean like the Phoenicians of old. Nobody will be sick anymore."

"We didn't get sick, and Rachel didn't get sick."

"That's because we're born sailors."

"How come Rachel didn't come up on deck with us?"

I miss her too. Only five days at sea and already I can't imagine my life without her.

Following that thought came another one even more troubling. She'd been avoiding him for the greater part of each day throughout the crossing.

"I believe she's reading to Mrs. DeMaio, the woman who broke her leg during the storm the other night."

"She's the one who fell down the stairs, huh?"

"That's right. The steward told her to stay in her cabin, but she insisted on leaving it."

"I love it when the waves make me fall."

"You won't feel that way when you're seventy-five years old."

"That's really old, huh?"

"Pretty old. Of course you can get even older than that."

Ari turned his head and looked up at Stasio. The wind blew several dark strands of hair across his forehead. "How much older?"

"You could be a hundred."

"A hundred—"

Stasio laughed out loud at the boy's shock.

"Stasi?"

"Yes?"

"Is Eleni as nice as Rachel?"

Lord. Where did that question come from?

"Yes. She's very nice."

"Does she like to tell stories?"

Stories? "I don't know."

"Rachel tells better stories than Giorgio."

"Is that right?"

"Yes. Last night I had a bad dream and knocked on your door but you were asleep, so I went to her room. She let me in."

He'd had no idea. "You should have wakened me anyway, instead of disturbing Rachel."

"She said I could come anytime if I couldn't sleep. Are you mad?"

"No. Of course not. I'm glad she made you feel better."

"She's fun! We ate some chocolate and she told me all this stuff about UFOs."

Stasio burst into laughter. Caffeine and little green men. Hardly the fare for a frightened five-year-old. "Did she tell you what a UFO is?"

"Yes. She even showed me a picture of one."

He blinked. "She showed you a picture?"

"Yes. She has a collection. When she used to do her radio show, she put them on the Internet," he said importantly. "Stasi? Do you think people live on Mars?"

That must have been quite a conversation they had last night. "I think anything is possible."

"So do I."

"You do, huh?"

"Yes. She says Draco and I would get along fine." Draco? "I don't think I've ever heard of him."

"Rachel loves him."

Stasio sucked in his breath. "Is that right?"

"Yes. They stay up all night looking for UFOs."

I'll just bet they do.

"Stasi? Can we do that sometime?"

"You mean look for UFOs? I don't see why not."

"Can Rachel come, too?"

"Of course. She's the expert."

"Goody. Do you like Rachel?"

"Why do you ask?"

He let out a little sigh. "I don't know."

Yes, you do, Ari. Because you've never met Eleni, and now you've taken to Rachel. So have I.

You should have come on this trip, Eleni. You should be the one occupying my thoughts. You should be here now where I can see you and hold you. We should be planning our wedding.

He looked down at Ari and tightened his grip on the boy. *If there isn't going to be a wedding, then I need to get hold of Costas and discuss the problems he thinks the judge would raise if we petitioned to have Ari returned to Stella outright. Somehow...*

"Come on, Ari. Let's go work out in the gym."

"I THINK IT'S TIME TO TURN OFF the light, Mrs. De-Maio. Your pain pill has started working. Just think, tomorrow morning your family will be waiting for you at the dock in Piraeus."

"I would never have made it this far without your help. You're an angel, Rachel."

"Nonsense. I had nothing else to do." *Thank heaven, you needed me.*

It had been a huge mistake to come by ship. There were only so many places a person could hide, even on the *Neptune.* Ari had found every one of them. Stasio was never far behind.

"Is there anything else you want before I say good-night?"

"Nothing. Thank you, my dear. Now it's late. You need your sleep, too."

There would be no sleep for Rachel. Tomorrow, not only would she be on dry land where the people hunting her could find her more easily, she would be separated from Stasio.

She glanced at the clock on the table. It said twelve-thirty. Their last night aboard ship. Rachel had purposely eaten dinner with Mrs. DeMaio, then read to her for the rest of the evening in order to avoid Stasio's company. The temptation to linger with him would have been too great.

"Good night, then. Pleasant dreams."

Rachel slipped out the door and hurried down the hall to her own stateroom. Luckily no one was about. When she paused by Ari's door and listened, all was quiet.

Soon he would be meeting his mother for the first

time. Rachel could only imagine what that would mean to a little boy who'd only had pictures of her before this. Pictures and dreams.

As for Stella, she would die of joy when she finally held Ari in her arms and discovered how wonderful he was. No mother could ask for a more perfect child.

Ari had a lot of his uncle in him.

No woman could ask for a more perfect man.

Eleni had to be the most fortunate woman alive.

When Rachel went to bed ten minutes later, she determined that the best cure for her heartache would be to watch Stasio greet his fiancée at the dock. Wasn't the refiner's fire meant to consume everything until one was past feeling?

A tap on the door pulled her back from sleep. She propped herself on one elbow and listened to make sure the noise wasn't a figment of her imagination.

"Ari?" she called out when she heard it again. "Just a minute."

No doubt thoughts of waking up in Greece tomorrow morning had kept him awake. She unfastened the lock and opened the door. "Couldn't you sleep?"

"No. I had a bad dream."

Stasio.

CHAPTER SIX

"CAN I COME IN AND HEAR A UFO story?"

Naturally Ari had told him. "I don't know. They're kind of scary in the middle of the night. Are you sure you're up to it?"

Rachel felt his gaze sweep from her bare toes to the top of her disheveled red hair. It missed nothing in between. Too late it dawned on her that the light from the hall revealed her state of undress. Her creamy nightgown was by no means immodest, but she felt suddenly vulnerable, exposed.

With a face to match her hair, she dived for the bed to cover herself. Stasio's low laughter followed as he came inside and shut the door.

"If the sky weren't overcast, I'd take you up on deck to look for extraterrestrials. But Ari tells me the desert is a much better place."

"It is," she muttered into the sheet covering her chin. "You need a telescope."

"Plus someone to watch with you?" He pulled a chair next to her bed and sat down.

"T-that, too."

"Who's Draco?"

Was there nothing Ari didn't tell him?

She answered quietly. "A friend."

"Is he anxiously awaiting your return from this vacation?"

"No."

"Why not?"

Rachel stared hard at him. "Why are you asking me all these questions?"

He stretched out his long powerful legs and folded his arms as if he had every intention of staying for a while. His nearness made it oddly difficult to breathe.

"Ari has the impression that you're in love with this man," he said bluntly. "I'm just trying to determine how long Stella can hope to enjoy your company before you go running back to his arms."

In a nervous gesture she brushed some wayward strands of hair out of her eyes. "I wish I *could* go running back to him, but he's had a stroke. I doubt he'd even recognize me if he were to see me again."

"I'm sorry." The teasing had left his voice. "Were you lovers?"

There were certain questions that shouldn't be asked. But something about Stasio's words and manner invited intimacy—or, perhaps, demanded it. This had to stop.

"Manny Novak is at least thirty years older than I am. He was my boss at the radio station."

"I thought his name was Draco."

"Draco was his radio name."

"What was yours?"

"Cassiopeia."

"One of our cruise ships has that name. But you didn't answer my question," he persisted.

Why? Why did he really care?

"I believe he was in love with me, but I didn't have those kinds of feelings for him. He was my idol, my mentor. We spoke the same language, dreamed a lot of the same dreams. I loved the questions he asked. They were the same questions *I've* always asked."

"Like what, for instance?"

"Like, are there really people living deep under the polar ice cap where you can see green vegetation? Or are the remains of earliest man really bones from a more ancient planet that was used to put this one together?"

Silence filled the stateroom.

"Aren't you sorry you asked?" she murmured.

"On the contrary. I've always wondered if there was life beyond our solar system."

"So you don't mind that I told Ari those stories?"

"Of course not."

"Some people aren't nearly as open-minded."

"When you see the beauty of the Cyclades for the first time, you'll know why I believe anything is possible."

"Andros is part of the Cyclades, isn't it?"

"Yes. Palaiopolis, my birthplace, was its ancient capital."

"Naturally you're not the least bit prejudiced."

He smiled, and the warmth of that smile reached out to her like a living thing. *Don't look at me like that, Stasio.*

She averted her eyes—which didn't help. His image remained in her mind. She was worried it would always be there to haunt her.

Tonight he had dressed in dark trousers and a wool turtleneck, much like Ari's outfits on board ship. There ought to be a law against any man being so attractive! His black hair looked disheveled, evidence that he'd been walking on deck in the wind.

"Ari missed you at dinner. You didn't even come to the movie afterward."

"Mrs. DeMaio has been in considerable pain since her fall. Reading to her seems to distract her a little."

"I'm sure she appreciated your help, but I needed a word with you before we went to bed."

"I'm sorry I wasn't available. I assumed we'd see each other in the dining room at breakfast."

"Not tomorrow."

"I don't understand."

"Tomorrow, or I should say today, the three of us will be eating a special breakfast in my stateroom at seven."

"So early?" The excitement of that prospect set her body trembling.

He nodded. "We dock around five in the morning. We'll leave the ship after breakfast and drive to the heliport. While Ari and I fly to my office in Athens, you'll be flown to Palaiopolis. There'll be a car there to drive you to the family villa—where you'll see Stella."

"What if she takes one look at me and slams the door in my face?"

He eyed her shrewdly. "You know my sister better than almost anyone else. Do you honestly believe her capable of that kind of behavior?"

"No. But you have to admit my presence is going to come as a huge shock."

"The best kind, Rachel. She needs a good friend more than you know, especially right now, while her nerves are so frazzled."

"I can't wait to see her." It was the truth. "Stasio, Ari doesn't know what's happening, does he?"

"If you mean, does he know he's going to see Stella the day after tomorrow, no. I'll give him that news tomorrow night. But he does know you're leaving us tomorrow to start your vacation. He already misses you and said he wishes the three of us could travel together.''

So do I.

''What did you say to that?''

''I promised him we'd meet you again very soon. It kept the tears from flowing, but he's not happy about it. You've made a friend for life.''

She half laughed, half cried, then used the sheet to brush at the moisture beading her eyelashes. ''He's so smart, so adorable. Stella's not going to believe it. I envy her a son, let alone one like Ari.''

''You took the words right out of my mouth.'' In a swift, graceful movement, he got to his feet and put the chair back in place. ''Good night, Rachel, for what's left of it. Before I go, where's my chocolate?''

She smiled in the darkness. ''I'm afraid Ari and I ate it all.''

''Next time remember to save me a piece.'' The door opened and closed.

Next time.

What I wouldn't give for a next time.

It'll never happen. Not with Eleni waiting for him. His fiancée, she reminded herself. *Remember Nikos,* she thought desperately. *The man you love, the man you want.*

No, it'll never happen. Not if the person who killed my father catches up with me first...

Letting out a groan, Rachel turned over on her stomach to stifle her tears with the pillow.

''WHAT'S ALL THIS?''

Stasio chuckled because the incredulity in Rachel's voice had heightened Ari's excitement.

''It's a surprise! I told Stasi what you liked for breakfast, and he told the cook!''

To his nephew's delight, her blue eyes widened and she made hungry noises as she walked around the table to examine everything.

Now that the ship had pulled dockside for disembarkation, there was no more motion. As Ari followed her, Stasio took in the slender yet voluptuous shape of her body. She wore a two-piece knit suit, and the effect of the pale blue against her glistening red-gold hair took his breath.

She looked both elegant and natural. Expensive. Healthy. *Beautiful.* Everything about her was in the best of taste. But it was more than that. There was a goodness about her, a genuineness and compassion that he'd rarely seen in others. He couldn't help wishing their ocean voyage had just begun.

If he didn't have the vital mission of delivering Ari to the mother he'd been waiting years to meet, Stasio would have been tempted to order the ship turned around to sail back to New York. Another week with Rachel…

''Let me see. Scrambled eggs done extra dry, sausage patties, peach nectar, popovers with sweet butter and satsuma plum jam.'' She suddenly wheeled around, raising her arms in an expansive gesture. ''You remembered *everything!*''

She lifted Ari off the ground and gave him a big hug.

He squealed with joy. The happy sound of their combined laughter resonated inside Stasio's body.

Rachel was good for everyone. He knew in his gut she'd be good for Stella who, in her pain, had unwittingly pushed too many people away. He'd held out the hope that over time, she and Eleni would draw closer despite their age difference. But that hadn't happened yet.

"This is the best surprise anyone ever gave me in my whole life!"

"Really?"

The expression in her eyes softened. "I'd never lie to you. You're a very special boy. In fact you're just like your mommy, who's sweet and kind. She's very special, too."

With a kiss to the top of his head, she put him down. "Shall we eat this feast? I don't know about you, but I'm starving."

"We're hungry, aren't we, Stasi?"

"Always."

While Ari took his seat, Stasio helped her to the table. Unable to resist, he brushed his hand against the ends of her hair where it curved into place near her neck.

Since the afternoon he'd asked her to step into his office, the urge to touch her, to explore her creamy skin, had flared into a need he could scarcely control.

As he sat down to eat, he reflected that a man had several appetites. He was about to satisfy one of them. As for the oth—

"Stasio?" There was a knocking at the door. Someone was trying to get inside his stateroom.

He frowned.

That was Eleni's voice on the other side of the door. "Let me in, darling."

Two pairs of questioning eyes swerved in his direction. In a flash, the joyous feeling of moments ago had vanished. Neither Ari or Rachel could be in any doubt as to their visitor's identity. They lowered their heads and continued to eat their breakfast in silence.

For the first time in his relationship with Eleni, she had done something totally unexpected. In reconsidering her threat to stay away from the ship, coming here to see him, she'd revealed an anxiety he hadn't observed before.

There was a frantic tone in her voice. She sounded anxious to mend their quarrel. Maybe she regretted her conversation with Nikos and was prepared to marry Stasio on Andros.

For Stella and Ari's sake, he ought to be feeling intense relief over that possibility. He *was* relieved.

But for the life of him, he couldn't summon even a particle of desire to see his fiancée. Except for resentment at the intrusion, he felt nothing—and the deadness of his emotions alarmed him.

If this was a permanent condition, he was in the deepest emotional peril. Because the woman outside his door was the woman he'd promised to marry.

"Excuse me." He put down his napkin and got up from the table. The second he opened the door, she flung her arms around his neck. He'd never realized before how tall she was. Since Rachel had come into his life, he'd started making comparisons—even trivial comparisons like this—and couldn't seem to stop.

"Darling! Forgive me for that awful phone call. I should have come on the trip. I've missed you."

To his chagrin, Stasio couldn't say those words back to her and mean them. The best he could do was move her out into the hall and kiss her, hoping to ignite some small spark that would assure him his lack of response was transitory.

Eleni eventually pulled away from him. Her hurt

brown eyes searched his. "I did more damage than I thought, didn't I?"

"We'll talk later, Eleni. In case you didn't notice, we're not alone."

She frowned. "I just spoke to the steward. He told me Ari's in the stateroom next to yours."

"He sleeps there, but right now he's having breakfast with me and a guest."

"What guest?"

He hesitated. "Come in and I'll introduce you."

Stasio dreaded the moment Eleni laid eyes on Rachel. Guilt was a new feeling for him, but there was no other name for it.

He was sure that during the crossing, Rachel had been unaware of his feelings. But he recognized the significance of his own reactions. Though he might not have acted on his feelings, he'd been unfaithful to Eleni in his thoughts.

Not at any time throughout their relationship had she ever given him reason to think he couldn't trust her. He'd always valued that. Trust was everything in an engagement, in a marriage. It was the rule he lived by. Or so he'd believed...

When confronted with his first real test of fidelity, how could he have deserted his principles so easily? How could he have spent a whole week aboard ship enjoying another woman's presence when he should have been missing Eleni? What kind of man was he?

He had no answer for that question. He might order his mind to stop thinking about Rachel, but he could do nothing about his heart, which raced whenever she walked into a room.

With reluctance he ushered Eleni in. When he felt her body tense, he knew she'd seen Rachel.

"Ari? I'd like you to meet my fiancée, Eleni Souvalis. Eleni, this is my wonderful godson."

Stasio watched with pride as his nephew displayed faultless manners and got up from the table to shake her hand. "Hello, Eleni. I'm happy to meet you."

"Hello, Ari."

When nothing else was forthcoming on her part, poor Ari didn't know how to respond. Even in his innocence, he sensed tension in the room. A slow-burning anger against his fiancée's deliberate refusal to make the moment comfortable for Ari began building inside Stasio.

"This is Rachel Maynard, Eleni."

Rachel rose smoothly to her feet and extended a warm hand of greeting. "How do you do, Ms. Souvalis. You're even lovelier in person than in the picture Mr. Athas gave his godson."

Somehow she always knew the right thing to say. It was a gift.

"I'm afraid I'm at a disadvantage, Ms. Maynard."

It was time for Stasio to step in. "She and Nikos are old acquaintances, Eleni." For now, it was the only part of the truth he intended his fiancée to know.

"Nikos?"

There was the slightest hesitation before he heard Rachel say, "Yes. I spent some time with him in Europe years ago, while he was training for the Olympics. Every teenage girl went crazy over him. I bought all his posters. They plastered my walls for a long time."

She sounded totally convincing. Stasio studied her animated features. The revelations about Nikos shouldn't have bothered him. But they did....

Were you in love with him six years ago, Rachel?

An unprecedented attack of jealousy jolted him. Until now, he hadn't thought he was vulnerable to that emotion, certainly not where his own brother was concerned.

But she didn't give anything away, standing there like a lick of flame in a colorless room. Aboard ship, she had dominated the attention generally accorded his striking fiancée. She had dominated *his* attention.

"How did you come to be on this ship with Stasio?" Eleni's voice was probably sharper than she'd intended.

"I'm on vacation from work. The first thing I did was stop by your fiancé's New York office to enlist his help in catching up with Nikos again. Since Greece was already on my itinerary, Mr. Athas made it possible for me to take the ship."

"I'm surprised Stasio didn't tell you that when Nikos isn't working, he spends most of his free time in Switzerland."

"He did tell me. Just as soon as I've seen the sights of your wonderful country, I plan to travel to Switzerland and—I hope—see Nikos again. Now if you'll excuse me, I'm anxious to be off on my holiday. It was lovely meeting you, Ms. Souvalis.

"Ari?" She turned to Stasio's nephew. "I have a little surprise for you. If you'll come to my stateroom, I'll give it to you."

Once again Rachel had handled a precarious situation with the kind of finesse he'd come to expect from her. She'd responded to his hint not to mention Stella, and she'd realized that getting Ari out of the room was paramount.

"Can I go with Rachel, Stasi?"

"Of course."

When they reached the doorway to the hall, Rachel turned. "I'm indebted to you for your help. The steward informed me you've sent a company car for me."

She lied with impunity to smooth the way for him. Another potential problem defused, at least for the moment. Later, if and when Eleni saw Rachel at Andros… He'd worry about that once it happened.

"You shouldn't have done it, Mr. Athas, but I admit I'm grateful that I don't have to try and find my own transportation from the port."

Stasio flashed her a brief smile. "Nikos would have my head if he knew you were looking for him and I hadn't done all I could to assist you."

Her lips curved upward. "Goodbye then. Thanks again."

"You're entirely welcome."

RACHEL GRABBED HOLD of Ari's hand. Deep in thought, she started down the corridor to her stateroom. Ari had clearly sensed something was wrong, because he didn't ask one question while he hurried beside her.

The second Rachel had heard Eleni's voice on the other side of the door, she'd seen a look of distress cross Stasio's face. All this time, Rachel had assumed his fiancée would be waiting at the port to welcome him home. But judging by his reaction, he hadn't been expecting her.

To add to the mystery, he'd preempted anything Rachel might have said by bringing Nikos's name into the conversation. That was a clear signal not to mention Stella's name in front of Ari or Eleni.

Whatever was going on in Stasio's mind, Rachel was convinced she only knew a portion of it. She understood even less about his relationship with Eleni Souvalis. All she knew was that there'd been enough tension in the room to set off an explosion.

Some part of these negative feelings emanated from

Rachel herself. For a week she'd been in denial. But no longer. His fiancée had arrived in the flesh. She wore his diamond.

Eleni Souvalis was everything Rachel could never be.

Through the crack in the door she'd watched them embrace. It felt as if the earth had somehow shifted, leaving her disoriented and confused. Leaving her with emotions she was terrified to examine too closely.

It was too late to go back to Michelangelo's and tell them she'd changed her mind. Too late to admit she was desperately in love with Stasio Athas and wanted to be *his* wife.

Not only could the institute not turn her into the kind of woman he'd want, Stasio was in love with Eleni. He planned to marry her.

Rachel's sweet plan of revenge had backfired. God had been right when He'd said, "Vengeance is mine." Even Carl had warned her, "You're not in love with Nikos."

Of course Rachel knew that. But the debilitating fear that had caused her to enroll at Michelangelo's in the first place had driven her to the point of irrationality.

It was irrational to have picked Nikos Athas, of all men, to be her savior. She'd willfully misunderstood her feelings for him—the long-ago attraction, the desire for revenge, the need to prove to herself as well as to him that she was a worthwhile person. Worse, it was morally wrong to have involved Stella in any of it. Even if Rachel had always loved her like a sister, she had no right to trade on their former friendship to get close to Nikos.

As for Stasio, the most honorable man she could

think of, Rachel felt a deep sense of shame for approaching him with her self-serving agenda.

Guilt came to her again and again when she realized how he'd gone out of his way to help effect a reconciliation with Stella. He'd confided private family business to Rachel. He'd trusted her with Ari. And look how she was repaying him.

The deception had to stop!

No matter how frightened she was, no matter how much she wanted to marry a man who would be able to protect her, no matter how much she wanted the emotional satisfaction of Nikos's approval, the fact remained that what she'd been doing since she'd gone to the institute was *wrong*.

Well, not all of it. She'd bought six months of safety, and naturally she was happy about the weight loss. It hadn't hurt to take classes that taught her how to buy the right clothes and do her hair. She wasn't sorry to have picked up some Greek. But she was mortified over everything else!

If she could, she'd leave the ship and head straight to the airport for a flight back to the States. But she now had a moral obligation to stay here and make amends.

She would start by visiting Stella. Rachel had always wanted a chance to explain the reasons she'd stopped being her friend. It was important to her that Stella realize how much Rachel, too, had suffered over that decision.

Evidently they'd both been crushed by the loss. What greater proof did Rachel have than Stasio's reaction when she first introduced herself to him? After six years he still remembered Rachel's name and the hurt she'd caused his sister.

Rachel sighed. That was all about to change. Once she'd made her peace with Stella, she'd catch the next flight to Los Angeles, where no one knew her. In a huge city like L.A., she would be difficult to trace. Manny's mother and sister lived there. Somehow, she'd find a way to contact him without being detected. If he was still alive...

Work in television or radio was out. Luckily she had enough money left from her father's investments to enroll in graduate school at U.C.L.A. Perhaps she'd study library science. Or take some kind of computer course. She could look into on-campus housing and try to fade into the horde of students.

"Rachel? Is your tummy sick?"

Ari.

You could never fool a child. His voice called her back from her tortured thoughts.

"No."

"Are you sad?"

When they'd entered her stateroom, she shut the door and knelt in front of him. "I always think it's a little sad when we have to say goodbye to people we love. But I'll be seeing you again very soon."

"Promise?"

"I promise. In the meantime, I'm going to give you these pictures." She pulled some of the snapshots from her wallet and handed them to him. "Every time you look at your mommy, you'll see my face right next to hers. That way you won't forget me."

"I'll give you one of my pictures."

"I was hoping you would."

He pulled out his packet. "Do you want this one? That's me, and that's Stasi."

"Yes. That's exactly the one I want." She grasped

it with a trembling hand and put it in her purse. Tonight on Andros, after she'd gone to bed, she would take it out and gaze at it to her heart's content. "Thank you, Ari."

She put her arms around him and hugged him tightly. "You're a dear boy. You're lucky, too, because today Stasio and Eleni are going to take you all over Athens."

When she let him go and stood up, he said, "I don't think Eleni likes me."

"I'm sure that's not true. Some people don't talk a lot at first. Give her an hour or two, and I know you'll become good friends."

After a silence, "I wish you could come with us."

"I do, too, but some other people are waiting for me to visit them." *Your mother, for instance. She'll take one look at you and you'll feel her love. Things will never be the same for either one of you.*

"My luggage has already been taken off the ship and put in the limousine, so I guess I'd better get going. Come on. Walk me down the hall to the elevator."

He slipped his hand in hers. Tomorrow he'd slip it in Stella's. That was something Rachel couldn't wait to see. And Stasio would be there....

THE KNOCK ON THE stateroom door brought Stasio's head around.

"Don't answer it, darling," Eleni whispered, seeking his mouth. "We haven't had a minute to ourselves since I came aboard."

"It's Ari. I have to let him in." *I want to let him in. Heaven help me, but I still don't feel like kissing you. I need a chance to try and understand what's going on inside of me.*

He released her shoulders with a mingled sense of

guilt and relief, then started across the room—but not before he glimpsed the brief flare of anger in her eyes.

"Mr. Athas? I'm glad you're still here!"

To Stasio's surprise, it wasn't Ari or one of the stewards. A man probably Stasio's age stood in the doorway.

"What can I do for you?"

"Forgive the disturbance. I'm Lorenzo DeMaio. The steward said you might know the whereabouts of Rachel, the American woman who spent time with my mother after she broke her leg. Mother would like her to come by her stateroom."

Stasio raked a hand through his hair.

"I'm afraid Ms. Maynard has already left the ship." Since she'd hurried out of the room with Ari, Stasio had been aware of a strange new emptiness inside him.

"Mother's not going to like that news. She wanted to exchange addresses and give her a gift for all her kindness."

That would please Rachel.

"I'll be seeing Ms. Maynard again. I'll give her your mother's present if you'd like."

"Excellent. Thank you. I'll be right back."

As the other man left, Stasio turned to Eleni. "I need to check on Ari." The fear that his nephew had been too intimidated by Eleni to join them had him worried.

"But, Stasio—"

He ignored her entreaty and opened the door between his room and Ari's. His heartbeat settled down to a more normal rate when he saw his nephew on the bed studying some pictures. He lay on his stomach, hands propping his face.

Stasio walked over and sat down beside him. "What have you got here?"

"Rachel gave me these. It's a present."

When Stasio looked, he could see they were the same pictures Rachel had shown him in his office.

"She knows how much you love your mother."

A little sigh escaped. He turned to Stasio with a sober expression. "I wish I could see my mommy."

Stasio's original plan had been to tell him the truth tonight, after he'd ironed out all the details of the wedding with Eleni.

But Eleni hadn't come on the trip, and it didn't look as if there was going to be a wedding. As far as Stasio was concerned, his nephew had just indicated that this was the moment.

Covering the little hand next to him, he said, "Ari? I have something very important to tell you. Tomor—"

"Stasio?" Eleni's voice broke in like a discordant note. "Mr. DeMaio wheeled his mother to your door. She insists on talking to you before she goes ashore."

Frustrated at every turn, he said, "Tell you what, Ari. We'll finish this conversation later. Let's go." He patted the boy's shoulder, then rose from the bed. They followed Eleni back into his stateroom.

"Mr. Athas!" the older woman called out from her wheelchair. "I couldn't leave until I thanked you for the flowers and fruit. It was my fault I fell. That's why I couldn't possibly accept the voucher you gave me for a free trip next year. I wouldn't feel right about it."

"Accidents happen, Mrs. DeMaio. When you're well again, I'd like you to take another trip on Athas Lines so you'll be left with a happier memory."

"You're very kind. Please accept this token gift from me. It's a CD. I have another one for Rachel. You see, my husband was a Brazilian who had the most beautiful singing voice. His band made recordings of many Portuguese love songs. I believe the two of you would enjoy the music.''

Mrs. DeMaio had no comprehension that her words might give Eleni a reason to wonder what exactly had gone on for the past seven days between him and one of Nikos's ''friends.''

''Thank you. I'm sure we will.''

''She was truly an angel, but you already know that. After I broke my leg, I couldn't have gotten along those first twenty-four hours without her help. Please see that she gets this. I've attached a note with my name and address. Tell her I'll never forget her.''

He took a deep breath. ''Rest assured I'll deliver your message and your gift. Try to enjoy the rest of your holiday. No more ocean voyages in midwinter.''

''No.'' Her warm laughter echoed all the way down the hall.

Ari's hand crept into his. ''Stasi? I feel funny.''

''That's because you've been on the ocean, and your head and tummy still feel like they're going up and down. Some people feel so funny after being on a ship, they fall over. But it soon passes.''

''Do you think I'll fall over?''

''Not if you hold on to me.''

''I'll hold on. When are we going to fly in the hel-icopter?''

''Right now.''

''Goody!''

''As soon as we reach my office, you can phone Anna and Giorgio. They'll want to know you arrived safely. Then our adventure can begin.''

Eleni made no move to leave. In a brittle voice she said, ''Stasio, we have to talk.''

You think I don't know that?

"We will," he told her in a quiet voice out of Ari's hearing. "But it's going to have to be after he goes to bed. For now, let's enjoy this day. I promise that by the end of it, you'll understand why Stella and Ari were always meant to be together."

And you'll understand why my feelings for you have changed.

CHAPTER SEVEN

IN THE MIDDLE OF THE STAFF meeting, General Berman's pager went off. Only one man knew his number.

"Gentlemen, we've been at this awhile. I think we ought to break for lunch and reconvene at 1400 hours."

Everyone agreed. There was the sound of shuffling feet as the men filed out. He waited till they'd gone, then shut the door and locked it.

"Sean?" he barked into his cell phone after he'd punched in the number. "How come I've had to wait so damn long to hear from you?" He pulled a toothpick out of the drawer and started chewing on it.

"Have you ever tried to find a missing person who didn't want to be found?"

"Are you telling me you think she suspects something?"

"Maybe."

"Damnation, Sean! I didn't make sure you were promoted to full colonel on maybes!"

"I got rid of her boss. That ought to earn me another rank, at least."

The general grunted.

"How the hell was I to know she'd vanish without a trace a few months after the funeral? But I've finally picked up her trail."

"Where is she?"

"Philadelphia. She's hiding out in some kind of

posh, live-in hotel for wealthy women, but there's no name on the building. The watchdog who opened the door wasn't about to let me in or answer any questions.

"I've spent the past week monitoring the place in the surveillance van, but I haven't seen her go in or out."

"Sounds like you've been wasting your time."

"Her doctor gave me her telephone number. My usual source linked it to that address. She's in there."

"Then flush her out!" The toothpick broke in two.

"All I need is your authorization and it's done."

"You've got it. And Sean?"

"Sir?"

"I don't care what you have to do."

"Understood, General."

AFTER THE DARK STORMY WATERS of the Atlantic, it was sheer joy for Rachel to look out over the brilliant aqua of the Aegean.

She had a hard time realizing that winter had come to the Cyclades; from the helicopter, she really couldn't tell. The sun was brilliant and the water peaceful, sparkling in the light. But the sixty-degree temperature in Piraeus had driven her to put on a jacket.

"We're approaching Andros, Ms. Maynard."

Stasio's island. Her heart picked up speed.

From the moment of liftoff, the pilot had given Rachel a colorful commentary on the history of each jewel-like island as it appeared on the horizon. She suspected that Stasio had instructed him to keep his passenger entertained.

"Straight ahead is Mount Kouvari, rising over three thousand feet. Because of its many streams, Andros was known as the Watery Isle of the Cyclades in ancient times.''

They flew breathtakingly close to the mountain. ''You see those square towers where the pigeonholes form geometric designs?''

''Yes,'' she said, trying to catch her breath. ''What are they?''

''Dovecotes introduced by the Venetians in the thirteenth century.''

Rachel marveled at the sight. But there was so much to see no matter which way she turned her head, she could scarcely absorb everything. Already, another fairy-tale village had come into view. The helicopter dipped, enabling her to pick out the network of stone walls separating the fields belonging to various owners. The town itself seemed to tumble down the mountain between lush valleys to the sea.

''How beautiful!'' She gasped the words as they passed right over an exquisite white villa built on the slope in the Cycladic tradition of a hundred years earlier. Rows of dark pines and sycamore trees surrounded the large estate, enclosing its tiled pool and terraced gardens.

The pilot grinned. ''All visitors react the same when they see the home of Kyrie Athas for the first time. Welcome to Palaiopolis, Ms. Maynard.''

So this was the village where Stasio grew up.

No wonder his eyes seemed to charge with light when he talked about his home. Seeing all this made her realize how hard it must have been for him to spend so much time in New York when his roots would always pull him back here.

More and more she was beginning to understand the depth of his love for Stella and Ari. Otherwise she imagined he'd spend every possible moment here, away from New York, away from the teeming metropolis of Athens.

She remembered snippets of past conversations with Stella. Her friend had loved Andros, too. She recalled how Stella had described taking hikes in lush mountain forests and walks along the white-sand beach.

Before they'd stopped being friends, Stella had begged Rachel to consider coming to stay with her on Andros. They would arrive in late spring after school was out, Stella had said, when the flowers were a riot of color on the hillsides, and the trees were heavy with lemons and limes.

If Nikos hadn't ruined everything, Rachel's father probably would've allowed her to come for a vacation. She would have met a younger Stasio. He would have been kind to her and she would have loved him with the intensity of girlhood.

Rachel had to pinch herself to believe any of this was real. Besides experiencing the indescribable beauty of the landscape for the first time, she'd never flown in a helicopter before.

It was a marvelous form of transportation. She knew Stasio used it without even thinking about it. Now she could see why. In no time at all, she'd been whisked from the bustling port where danger could conceivably lurk and been safely delivered to the town's heliport.

The pilot shut off the engine. "Kyrie Athas has sent a car for you. Yannis, the chauffeur, will drive you to the villa. Let me help you with your luggage."

"*Efcharisto.*"

Once they were on the ground and Yannis had transferred her bags to the trunk, she turned to the pilot.

"Thank you again for a thrilling ride. I'll tell Kyrie Athas I had an absolutely wonderful time."

"Do I dare tell you how urgently he warned me not to let anything happen to you?"

His words warmed her heart. "He worries about everyone."

"That is true," came the surprisingly serious reply. *"Kalimera, Despinis."*

When he had climbed aboard the helicopter, Rachel turned to Yannis, who she discovered spoke very little English. Now would be a good time to try out her Greek.

"Would you take me to a local hotel, please?"

The wiry older gentleman wearing a heavy sweater scratched his head. She knew he understood her, but undoubtedly he had orders to drive her directly to the house.

"I would like to freshen up in my own room before I meet with Despini Athas. You can wait for me in front. I won't be long."

"But...Kyrie Athas said nothing about a hotel."

"Because he didn't know my plans."

"Most of the hotels are closed from November till March."

"I'm sure you can find me a little inn. Please?"

He stood there pondering her request. Clearly he was not happy about the situation.

"It's all right, Yannis. I'll just take my bags with me and walk."

He waved his hands in panic. "No, no. No walking. I will drive you to a *taverna* in the upper part of town. It has a few rooms for guests. Kyrie Athas knows the owner and would approve of this place."

Pleased to have won the battle, she thanked him and

got in the backseat of the car. Once they were off, she could hear him mumbling under his breath. Obviously he didn't like the idea of going against his employer's wishes.

But if Stasio was wrong and the meeting with Stella didn't go well, Rachel didn't want to put her friend in the position of *having* to invite her to stay.

Of course, that wasn't her only concern.

Rachel already felt too beholden to Stasio to take any more advantage of his hospitality. She would pay her own way from here on out. Staying at a hotel was the best plan she could think of for a variety of reasons—chief among them, Eleni's presence at the villa.

Tomorrow everyone would arrive. Rachel didn't think she could bear to watch Stasio and his fiancée together for long periods of time. Better to have an excuse to leave. After the kiss Rachel had witnessed on the ship…she suppressed a shudder. She couldn't stand to see any more evidence of their closeness, their passion. It was too painful to watch. Because face it—she'd fallen in love with him.

"Come, *Despini*. We are here."

Rachel blinked in surprise. She'd been so deep in thought, she hadn't realized they'd wound up the hill to a small, charming *taverna* with balconied rooms facing the sea.

Yannis grabbed her bags and hurried up the narrow stone steps ahead of her. Rachel slid the camera case to her shoulder and followed him inside the attractive stucco-and-wood building.

The male proprietor working behind the bar recognized Yannis right away. The two of them held an animated conversation, most of which Rachel understood. The priest had taught her well.

At the mention of Kyrie Athas, the other man's face lit up. He took the bags from Yannis and motioned for Rachel to follow him out of the restaurant and up the stairs to the next floor.

After indicating the bathroom at the end of the hall, he opened one of the doors. The simple room with its twin bed, red-and-blue quilt and antique white washstand couldn't have been more perfect for her needs. Everything was neat as a pin—the wooden floor polished, white curtains pristine. She reached in her purse and pulled out enough drachmas for a tip.

He wouldn't accept it. She heard him say something about Kyrie Athas, then he deposited her bags, put the key on the bedside table and left. Rachel decided she'd add the amount to her bill when she checked out.

Not wanting to keep Yannis waiting, she made her preparations in less than ten minutes. After running a brush through her hair and refreshing her makeup, she felt a little more presentable—and almost ready to face Stella.

Just thinking about their reunion brought an adrenaline rush of excitement and anxiety. By the time she was back in the car and they were headed for the villa, she thought she might actually be running a temperature.

It occurred to her that if Yannis was part of the staff at the villa, Stella might already be aware that someone would be arriving shortly. Then again, maybe she knew nothing about Yannis's departure and took no notice of the noise made by the helicopter as it passed overhead.

All Rachel knew was that Stasio had made it clear he wanted this first meeting between Stella and Rachel to be a surprise. That was the way Rachel wanted it, too. She would be watching for her friend's first reaction. Stella was like her son Ari—her dark eyes told everything she was thinking and feeling. Rachel would know in an instant if that strong camaraderie of theirs was still alive. Or dead…

"AIYEE! YOU'RE STILL IN BED and you haven't touched your breakfast. I don't think you've eaten anything since you arrived on the island yesterday."

The elderly housekeeper, who'd come to the household a much younger woman, hired to wait on Stella's mother, put a weathered hand to Stella's forehead. "I think I should call Dr. Vassilus."

"I don't need a doctor, Melina. I'm simply not hungry."

"Then I will phone your brother and tell him to talk some sense into you."

"No! You mustn't disturb Stasio."

"In that case, drink your tea to give you some strength!"

Stella roused herself from the bed and reached for the cup of tea, which had gone cold. She couldn't afford to get into a battle with Melina.

None of the staff knew Stasio would be coming to the villa in the morning. No one had any idea he'd be bringing Ari with him, let alone that the boy was Stella's son.

She still wasn't positive it was the right thing to do for Ari. The ghastly confrontation with Nikos and Eleni a few days ago had increased her fears that no matter how noble Stasio's intentions might be, his plan could backfire with tragic consequences where her little boy's happiness was concerned.

But now that she knew he'd never been adopted, the maternal part of her refused to be quieted. Especially since Stasio had told her Ari knew she was alive and longed to know his mother.

Desperate to find some peace over her decision to meet him, she drank all her tea while Melina, hands on hips, stood watching. "I'm going to church as soon as I'm dressed," Stella murmured.

Melina nodded with satisfaction and picked up the tray. "That's what your mama used to do when something was bothering her. As soon as you return, I'll tell the cook to prepare *fourtalia.*"

Souli's potato omelet was her favorite meal, but food was the last thing on Stella's mind.

Yesterday in Athens, after Eleni had left the house and Nikos had stopped by her room to stay goodbye, he'd made it clear that if Stella insisted on claiming her son before the whole world, she should be ready to live with the consequences.

When Stella asked him if this was a threat, he said, "Take it any way you want, but this selfish desire of yours and Stasio's has already caused problems between him and Eleni. If their marriage turns out to be a disaster, we'll know who to blame—won't we, little sister?"

Her wants and her fears were at war, and she'd barely slept all night. The *Neptune* would have long since docked at Piraeus. By now Stasio would be showing Ari the sights of Athens.

She assumed Eleni had joined them. Despite that, Stella hoped her future sister-in-law had decided to let Ari spend this first special day in Greece alone with Stasio, the man he believed was his godfather.

Right now Eleni was upset with Stasio. Stella feared Ari might pick up on those feelings. From what she knew of children, they tended to blame themselves for the troubles between adults. Stella didn't want Ari thinking anything but happy thoughts.

That goes for me, too. I don't want to think anything but happy thoughts, she cried inwardly as she put on an apricot-colored wool sweater and matching skirt for church. After slipping her feet into low-heeled black pumps, she pulled her white lace mantilla from the drawer and thrust it in her purse.

A blessing from the priest. That's what I need.

Negotiating a series of corridors and steps, she finally reached the main foyer. "Melina? I'm leaving!"

"Ya sas!" The housekeeper shouted a goodbye from another part of the villa.

Stella had barely started down the outside steps when she saw the estate car approaching. Good. Yannis could drive her to the church, which was farther up the mountain, then she'd walk back. There was a slight chill today. It would do her good to fill her lungs with cool air. Maybe it would clear her head.

"Yannis? You're just in ti—"

But the rest of the words never made it past her lips. Someone was getting out of the backseat of the car.

Stella had known only one person with hair that looked like spun red-gold in the sunlight. But that person had been a teenager who'd worn it long and confined in braids when she couldn't stand its unruly behavior.

The stylish woman turned in her direction. Stella found herself staring into a pair of unforgettable chinablue eyes the exact color of her suit. They glistened with moisture and seemed to beseech Stella.

"Bonjour, chère amie," the well-remembered voice said in French. *"Est-ce que tu me souviens?"*

It *was* Rachel. What on earth?

"O-of course I remember you."

"But not with good memories," she said, reverting to English. "I hurt you horribly. In the hurting, I hurt myself even more."

Stella clutched her handbag tightly as memories of that dark painful time came flooding back.

For Rachel, of all people, to appear on her doorstep from out of nowhere and admit what she'd done to Stella—it was simply too much to comprehend.

She shook her head, hardly able to believe this was happening. "What are you doing here?"

"I could tell you I'm here on vacation, which I am. But it's you I came to see. I know it's six years too late, but I'd like to explain why I turned away from you and ended our friendship."

The sincerity this woman exuded sounded like the old Rachel, before their painful parting.

"If you can't find it in your heart to hear me out, I won't blame you. I'll just ask Yannis to drive me to the hotel."

She blinked in confusion. "How do you know Yannis?"

"It's a long story. Stella, if you want me to go away, I will. But before I leave, I want you to know that what I did six years ago was done out of love for you. No other reason. I've always loved you like a sister, and I always will."

She turned to get back into the car. The action jerked Stella from her stupor.

"Wait, Rachel! Don't go!"

Rachel hesitated, then turned around. "You mean that?" Her voice trembled, revealing a vulnerability Stella had no defense against.

"Yes. If you've come all this distance to see me,

then the least I can do is listen to what you have to say.''

"Thank God, you haven't changed, Stella!" she cried softly. "You're still the same wonderful person who became my best friend. But I hate imposing on you, especially when it's obvious you're on your way somewhere."

"I am. To the church up on the hill."

"Then maybe I could come back later, when it's more convenient."

"This is perfect. Why don't you walk up there with me? It'll be like the old days in Montreux when we used to go on those weekend excursions above the lake and spend all our time talking."

They both smiled in remembrance of those days before everything had gone so wrong.

Stella thanked Yannis for taking care of her friend, then gestured to Rachel. "Shall we go?"

They started down the tree-lined driveway to the winding street, which would lead them up the mountain.

After they'd been walking awhile in silence, Rachel blurted, "It feels so natural being with you again. It's as if we were never apart."

"I was thinking the same thing," Stella murmured. "Why don't you tell me what happened to ruin our friendship? I have to admit I've always wondered why you changed. I sent you a letter via Madame, apologizing for anything I might have said or done to hurt you. I guess you never received it."

"Yes, I did. I tore it up without reading it."

Stella couldn't prevent a gasp. Rachel stopped walking and looked directly into her eyes.

"Stella? I need your promise about something."

She took a deep breath. "That's hard to give."

"I know, but I'm asking you anyway."

"All right. What do I have to promise?"

Rachel moistened her lips nervously. "That you'll remember this all happened a long time ago, and that it won't affect your love or your relationship with Nikos."

Nikos?

Just the mention of her brother distressed her. But that distress had to do with what had occurred since he'd learned Stella's child had never been adopted and Stasio had kept it a secret from him.

Rachel was talking about something vastly different.

What had Nikos done to Rachel in Chamonix? Whatever it was, she couldn't talk about it at the time.

Had he slept with her, or worse, forced himself on her? Was it something like that?

"I promise," she lied. "Tell me what he did."

As they started walking again, Rachel reminded her of their last night in Chamonix, when Rachel had gone into the bathroom and heard Nikos talking to Stella.

Suddenly Stella heard again the deliberately cruel things Nikos had said—but she now realized that Rachel had heard them, too.

She groaned aloud in horror.

No teenage girl could have withstood such a brutal attack from a man like Nikos.

He knew Rachel had a crush on him, yet he'd mocked her, demeaned her physically and emotionally, disparaged her father's career, questioned her motives for hanging around Stella.

And he'd made Stasio out to be a monster. He'd frightened Rachel into defection through blackmail, crushing her under his heel.

No wonder Rachel had asked for a new roommate. No wonder she'd gone away to some lonely place to nurse her wounds. And in all that time, she never said one word against Nikos. Even now, she didn't want Stella to blame him.

Oh, Nikos. It was bad enough what you said and did to me the other day in Eleni's presence. But what you did to my best friend, I can never forgive.

Her grief and anger were too terrible to express. The only thing she could do was put her arms around her friend and cling.

For a long time they stood holding each other. The embrace was cathartic for both of them. Rachel, her face glistening with tears, pulled away first.

She grasped Stella's hands. "Staslo said that if I told you exactly what I told him, you'd forgive me."

Stella could hardly see through her own tears. "You've seen Stasio?" she cried out in an incredulous voice.

"Yes. I went to his office in New York to get your address and phone number. I hoped that if you could forgive me, we might travel to Switzerland together, even if it was only for a few days, so we could become close again. So we could relive the good times we had.

"He made me tell him about Nikos, then he called Madame to verify what I'd said. One thing led to another, and I ended up being his guest on the ship that brought us here."

Stella's mind reeled with too much information. "Then if you were on the ship, you met—"

"Ari?" she said before Stella could. A smile broke out on Rachel's face. "I spent seven fantastic days with him. He looks so much like you, it's uncanny.

"As soon as he found out you and I had been friends

in Switzerland, he couldn't stop asking questions about you. I gave him some pictures of you and me. He studied them for hours and he carries them in his pocket.''

By now Stella was sobbing brokenly.

More tears filled Rachel's eyes. ''Oh, Stella. You're such a lucky woman. He's so adorable, so precious, you're going to die when you see him tomorrow. If I ever have a son, I'd want one who looks and acts just like him! And I know Stasio feels exactly the same way.''

In seconds, Stella's pain had turned to joy, and all because of Rachel who had appeared at the villa like an answer to prayer.

She stared at her friend through new eyes. There was a radiance about her when she'd mentioned Stasio's name. Almost as if...

No.

It wasn't possible.

He and Eleni were going to be married.

But they'd had a fight.

Stella's thoughts flew faster and faster. For seven days and nights Rachel had been on that ship with Ari and Stasio.

Why hadn't he put her on a plane to Athens?

As she pondered that question, the answer came like pure revelation.

Because my brother wanted *her to sail with him.*

It was also a fact that what he'd done was entirely out of character for an honorable man contemplating marriage to another woman in the next three and a half weeks.

Dying of curiosity, she asked, ''Did you meet Stasio's fiancée at the dock in Piraeus?''

Rachel averted her eyes. "Actually she came aboard ship while the three of us were eating breakfast."

Stella would love to have been witness to that definitive moment.

"Ms. Souvalis is very lovely."

"She is." *But not as lovely as you, Rachel. Not inside or out.*

"After we leave the church, you're coming back to the villa with me. We have years of catching up to do. I'll send Yannis for your bags. We'd better do it before Stasio finds out you checked into a hotel. I know my brother. He wouldn't like it. I'm surprised Yannis complied."

Rachel blushed on cue. She'd been doing that ever since Stella had known her. The curse of a redhead.

"He didn't want to, but I left him no choice. Either he drove me to a hotel, or I took my bags and walked to one."

"Heaven forbid. Poor Yannis."

They both smiled, then Rachel's expression sobered.

"Stella—tomorrow's going to be the most exciting, and I daresay, the most emotional day of your life. You shouldn't have to worry about anything but getting acquainted with your son."

"That's exactly why I want you there, Rachel. He already knows you, and he's comfortable around you and Stasio. I think it'll make it easier for him to meet me if people he trusts and cares about are there, too. Especially if he takes one look at me and decides he'd rather hurry back to his parents in Ne—"

"Don't say it," Rachel cut her off. "Don't even think it. Tonight Stasio's going to tell him he'll be seeing you in the morning. I know it's something Ari's been waiting for ever since he was old enough to understand.''

''That may be true, but sometimes the reality doesn't live up to the dream.''

''Then just love him while he's here, and let him make the decision when he's ready. Maybe it'll take traveling back and forth to New York and Greece before he knows where he'll be the happiest.''

Rachel always did have a wise head on her shoulders. ''What you've said makes perfect sense. Do you have any idea how happy I am you're back in my life?''

''Why do you think I came? Nothing's been right since I left Switzerland with things unresolved between us.''

The tremor in her voice led Stella to believe her friend had suffered in other ways, too. Before long, Stella decided, she'd learn the truth. They'd shared almost everything with each other once, and now they had again. Stella marveled that the bond, which should have been broken years ago, seemed stronger than ever.

CHAPTER EIGHT

STASIO WAITED FOR ARI to put on his pajamas and climb into the big bed with the puffy white quilt. Once his nephew fell asleep, Stasio would join Eleni, who was downstairs in the salon counting the minutes until they could be alone.

At one time, he'd looked forward to spending intimate evenings with her. But there'd been a change in their relationship dating back to the moment he'd first told her about Stella's son. Today's outing seemed to have strained it even more.

He'd hoped Eleni would enjoy their walking tour through the Plaka and unbend enough with Ari to act more naturally around him. But she'd remained distant and uncharacteristically quiet. Ari, in turn, hadn't been his usual effervescent self.

But the news Stasio had been waiting to tell him would change the boy's mood in a hurry. Regrettably, the problems between him and Eleni couldn't be fixed as easily.

"Your eyes look as sleepy as mine feel." He pulled the covers up to Ari's chin.

"We walked all over Athens, huh?"

"I think so." Stasio chuckled. "Do you like being a tourist?"

"Yes," Ari said quietly. The lukewarm response didn't sound at all like his nephew.

"Stasi? What are we doing tomorrow?"

The question was a transparent one. What Ari really wanted to know was if Eleni was going to spend the whole day with them again.

Stasio didn't have an answer to that. It all depended on the outcome of his talk with her later this evening.

He took a deep breath. "We're going to fly to my home on Andros. Someone's going to be there you've wanted to meet for a long, long time."

His nephew hadn't been expecting that revelation. Suddenly he sat straight up in bed, acting very much like the boy Stasio knew so well. His dark eyes shone with a new light. *My mommy?*

"Yes, your mommy."

When the news sank in, Ari scrambled out from under the covers and jumped to his feet. A second later, he was hugging Stasio hard around the neck.

"Does she know her little boy is coming?"

Stasio gave him another squeeze. "Yes, and she's so excited I bet she won't sleep all night waiting for you to get there."

By Stasio's calculations, she and Rachel would have cleared up all their misunderstandings hours ago and were probably discussing Ari right now.

"But what if she doesn't like me?" He asked the question in such a wistful voice Stasio felt a swelling in his throat.

"Do you know what?"

"What?"

"She's afraid you might not like *her.*"

"But I love her!"

"She loves you, too. Tomorrow you'll find out just how much. That's why you've got to get to sleep as soon as possible so we can leave early in the morning."

"I can fall asleep in one minute," Ari promised. Immediately he climbed back under the covers and closed his eyes. "I'm almost asleep. Stasi? Are you going to Eleni's house now?"

"No."

"Oh."

"You must have heard her ask me, but you know I wouldn't leave you."

"Will she be mad?"

"I think she's a little mad at herself for not coming on the ship with us."

"We had fun on the ship with Rachel, huh?"

"Yes."

Fun. I hope to God that's all it was.

"I'm going downstairs now to say good-night to Eleni. As soon as she's gone, I'll be coming up to bed. My room's right next to yours. If you need me during the night, just come in. You don't have to knock."

"I love you, Stasi."

"I love you too. Just think. Tomorrow you won't need to look at your pictures because your mother'll be right in front of you." He bent to kiss the child's fore head. "Goodnight, Ari."

He switched off the lamp but left the door open so Ari could see light in the hall. A strange house could be uncomfortable for a visiting adult, let alone an impressionable child like Ari.

When Stasio entered the salon downstairs, he found Eleni lounging on a couch, a glass of wine in hand.

"At last," she muttered, raising both eyebrows.

He walked to the bar and poured himself something a little stiffer. "It would have been nice if you'd joined us. He loves a good story at bedtime."

"Maybe I'm not the bedtime-story type."

He studied her over the rim of his glass. It wasn't like Eleni to be this difficult.

"I've watched you with your own nieces and nephews often enough to know that's not true."

He made his way to a chair near the couch where she was sitting. "When you came to the ship, I assumed you were there because you wanted to meet Ari and get acquainted. Obviously that wasn't the case. What's bothering you, Eleni?"

She swallowed the rest of her wine and put the glass on an end table. "You lied to me from the very beginning of our relationship."

"Would you have had me tell you about Ari on our first date?"

"Yes! I told you everything about me. I had every right to expect you'd accord me the same privilege. Especially when the bond that exists between the two of you is so strong, you spend half of every month in New York."

"Aside from the fact that I have business there, he's Stella's boy, Eleni. It isn't as if I've been keeping another woman."

An image of Rachel flashed through his mind unbidden.

"Another woman I could handle," she said angrily, "but a flesh-and-blood nephew whom you love like your own son is something else again."

Stasio got to his feet and deposited his glass on the coffee table. "When we first started seeing each other, I had no idea where our relationship would go or how deep our feelings would run. Would you have expected me to divulge information to a relatively new acquaintance when I was holding back that same information from my own family?"

"Maybe not right away. But we've been together for two years! I only found out about him a week ago!"

"It was only recently that Stella's depression became so acute I realized she was still grieving for her child and had never stopped."

"You've been playing God with all our lives, Stasio."

He brows furrowed. "That sounds like one of Nikos's favorite lines."

"So it is. But he's right!"

At least once before, Nikos had interfered in something that was none of his business, and he'd destroyed the friendship between Stella and Rachel.

"When did you and Nikos find time to discuss all this?"

"A few days ago. I might as well tell you now that we've had several conversations about it over the phone. I finally asked him to meet me at the villa so we could both talk some sense into Stella."

Livid with anger, he demanded, "What sense would that be?"

"That she should leave things alone and let Ari grow up in New York with the foster parents who love him and have been raising him."

"You had no right to do that!"

"I thought you gave me the right when you asked me to marry you. This is a family matter that could tear everyone apart if it's not resolved."

"It sounds to me like you and Nikos have been playing God yourselves. Not to mention tearing things apart. Maybe I've been wrong and you don't have one shred of maternal instinct in you. Otherwise you'd have some comprehension of the hell Stella's been living through since she made the decision not to keep her baby. You'd feel some compassion for her.''

Stasio shook his head slowly. ''If you knew my sister the way I do, you'd understand that she sacrificed her own happiness for me. To my deep regret, I didn't figure it out until a long time afterward.''

Eleni's chin lifted. ''What are you talking about?''

''Stella never wanted to give up her child. But she knew she'd need help raising him and couldn't bring herself to burden the family.

''With Father gone and Nikos leading his own life elsewhere, she realized I was the only one around. She decided she couldn't ask that of me, couldn't interfere with my life. So she gave up her child for my happiness and his ultimate good.''

''And left you with a greater burden than ever, which you willingly assumed.''

''Ari's a joy, Eleni!''

''When we have a child, which one are you going to love most?''

Stasio couldn't believe what he was hearing. ''I'll love them both!''

''How do you think our child will feel if he or she isn't as *perfect* as Ari and discovers you love your nephew more?''

He shook his head again. ''Is that what you really think? Don't you love *your* nieces and nephews?''

''Of course. But I don't want to be their mother.''

''I don't want to be Ari's father. I want to father my own children. But if—heaven forbid—Stella doesn't marry, then I want to be a father figure he can continue to count on.''

''Couldn't Giorgio provide that support?''

''He does provide it. He and Anna will continue to

love Ari until they die. Is it possible to give a child too much love? I don't think so.''

''But your constant presence in Ari's life has set a pattern. He'll always demand your attention, even if Stella gets married. Doesn't it bother you that the man who loves your sister will have to compete with you?''

''Compete? What in God's name does that mean?''

''It means you could win the father-of-the-year award.''

''You say that as if it were a condemnation.''

''Not at all. Don't you know there's no man to compare to you as a father, let alone as a fiancé and lover?'' Her voice trembled. ''But your relationship with Ari could cause problems in Stella's marriage. And in ours…''

She rose from the couch and slid her arms around his neck. ''If you could just look at the whole complicated picture from my vantage point, you might decide to postpone taking Ari to Andros tomorrow while you consider all the consequences.''

Stasio grasped her arms and gently put her away from him. ''I can't do that, Eleni. After the first of the year, he'll be put up for adoption, so we don't have the luxury of time. Stella gave birth to Ari and has the God-given right to her son. Try to put yourself in her place.''

Eleni's body froze. ''Then you insist on carrying through with this, no matter how much I'm begging you not to do it?''

He searched her eyes for some glimmer of understanding. ''Have we reached a total impasse, Eleni? Is that what this is all about?''

''I don't know,'' she answered in a tortured whisper. ''You seem different from before.''

''Before what?''

"Before your trip with Ari."

Lord. Stasio had an idea what was coming next. He'd hoped that if he ignored it long enough, it would all go away.

"Naturally I've been preoccupied and worried about tomorrow. It'll be Ari and Stella's first meeting. They're both frightened."

"I'm frightened, too, but for an entirely different reason."

"What is it?"

"I noticed how natural Rachel Maynard appeared with Ari. It's obvious they became friends during the trip. Did her ability to connect with your nephew make you speculate on *my* potential as a mother?"

"No," he responded truthfully. "I admit she has a way with children, but it's her connection to Stella that brought about her friendship with Ari."

"Stella?" She smoothed her black hair from her face. "Now I'm really confused. I thought she knew Nikos."

"She does. But she met him through Stella when they were away at boarding school in Switzerland. Before Nikos won the silver medal, he trained in Chamonix. Stella stayed with him at the chalet on a winter break. She invited Rachel to go with her." A disastrous decision as it turned out.

"So she and Stella are friends."

"They were. Once. But someone tried to destroy their friendship and they lost track of each other. That's why Rachel came by my office. She's on vacation and wanted to see Stella again, but didn't know how to get in touch with her."

Eleni flashed him a look of shrewd regard. "Did you know Rachel way back then?"

He drew in a deep breath. "I knew of her."

"So it's Stella and not Nikos she really wants to see?"

"Yes. In fact, I assume she's on Andros with Stella right now."

There was a brief silence before she said, "I've never heard either of them talk about her."

"A lot of life has been lived in the past six years."

"Then it's all the more extraordinary that she'd come to your office for help. Why did you invite her to sail with you?"

"When she told me that Nikos was the person who'd caused the damage to their relationship, I wanted to help make up for the hurt."

"*Nikos?* What did he do?"

"What didn't he do." For the next few minutes Stasio explained his brother's unconscionable behavior.

"Oh, Stasio—you know how boys are." She came to Nikos's defense as usual. "Most of the time growing up, an older brother can be thoroughly obnoxious. At times, mine were hideous to me."

"I doubt as hideous as Nikos. Neither Stella nor Rachel fully recovered from what he did. That's why Rachel wanted to see Stella again, to explain what had happened and try to salvage their friendship."

"And you believed her?"

"What other motive would she have?"

"Why, to see Nikos again, of course. She admitted as much in front of us."

"She did that because I didn't want any discussion of Stella in front of Ari."

"Stasio? Are you so blinded by your love of Ari, you can't see that the proverbial ugly duckling has changed into a swan? If I were Rachel and I'd heard a man say all those awful things about me, I'd come back to see him for the sheer pleasure of revenge.''

"Rachel's not like that.''

"All women are like that. Don't forget, she had a colossal crush on him. You heard her. His posters wall-papered her room. And Stella was right there to feed her intimate tidbits about her famous heartthrob brother.''

For reasons he didn't want to analyze, he hoped Eleni's theory was dead wrong.

"Well, she may be on Andros now, but she's going to be in for a disappointment if she's waiting for Nikos to show up.''

"Do you know something about Nikos's plans that I don't?''

"Only that he didn't want to be around for the fireworks, in case you didn't do the right thing, which would be to leave Ari in New York where he belongs.''

Knowing Nikos had no intention of coming to An-dros any time soon was the only good news Stasio had heard all day. Given the mood he was in right now, it would better if he didn't see his younger brother for a while.

"I happen to agree with him, Stasio.''

His jaw tightened. "You've made that abundantly clear.''

"Then maybe you need to understand something else. If you allow Ari to live with his mother, I won't marry you.''

The room reverberated with her pronouncement.

"Eleni—be careful what you're saying.''

"I don't feel like being careful anymore. Without me, you can't get married, which means you won't be able to obtain custody of Ari. I guess we're going to find out who you truly love.''

''This isn't a contest, Eleni.''

''Oh, yes, it is!''

She turned on her heel and ran from the room, sobbing. Stasio didn't go after her.

He was taking Ari to meet Stella in the morning.

Eleni had made threats before. It wouldn't surprise him if she called early in the morning and said she'd fly to Andros with him and Ari.

But if there was any chance she meant what she'd said, then he was glad he'd already contacted Costas.

Stasio was prepared to do whatever it took to insure that Stella had legal claim to her son by the first of the year.

''WHAT DO YOU THINK I should wear to meet him? A dress? A skirt and blouse? Jeans, maybe?''

''I suppose that depends on what you're going to do when he gets here.''

Rachel's thoughts flashed back to Stasio and Ari. They'd had so much fun on the ship trying to play shuffleboard. Because of stormy seas, most of the time they found themselves falling down on deck. She'd never laughed so hard.

When she related the incident to Stella, her friend said, ''After what you've just told me, I know it'll seem strange if we just sit in a room and make polite conversation with each other. I think I'll take him for a walk down to the beach.''

''That's exactly what I'd do. Put on a pair of comfortable jeans and a pullover. He'll think it's great that his mother is so youthful-looking and approachable. He won't be afraid to get dirty.''

"Oh, Rachel," she squealed. "I'm so excited, I feel sick. He's going to be here any minute!"

So is Stasio.

"I know. I have butterflies, so I can just imagine what condition *your* stomach's in."

Rachel sat on the bed in Stella's room. It was comical to watch her friend run around getting dressed. She threw things here and there. Not much had changed since Switzerland. Stella was still messy. Rachel loved it, loved seeing that she hadn't completely changed.

She delighted in being with her best friend again. They'd talked until four in the morning, sharing memories and catching up on events in the past six years.

But beyond that, Rachel chose not to tell her friend anything. In a few days she'd be flying back to the States. Stella didn't need to know about Rachel's initial plan of revenge or any of the reasons behind it. She didn't want to reveal either the immature reasons having to do with Nikos, or the frightening reasons having to do with her father's enemies.

And Rachel certainly wasn't about to admit her love for Stasio, not when he planned to marry Eleni within the month. Stella had enough to worry about, dealing with the son she'd never seen.

When the sound of rotor blades pierced the air they both turned toward the window facing the sea. Stella reached it first.

"They're here!" She clutched the windowsill. "I'd like to go down to the heliport, but maybe that's not a good idea."

"Why don't you walk to the end of the driveway and meet him at the gate?"

"Do you want to come with me?"

"Only a little ways. I wouldn't dream of intruding on your special moment."

Stella gazed at Rachel tearfully, then reached out to her for a long hug.

"Does my hair look all right?" she asked when she finally pulled away.

Stella's shoulder-length hair glistened in one smooth cascade from a side part. "It's perfect. Just the way you look in Ari's pictures. *Ne t'en fais pas.*"

"All right. I'll stop worrying. I guess this is it. Let's go."

Last night Stella had taken Rachel on a tour of the villa. The only word for it was fabulous. Arm in arm, they'd walked on marble floors with irreplaceable area rugs from the ancient Ottoman Empire. The glow of firelight from the fireplaces in some of the common rooms lit the dark, wood-beamed ceilings. A fifteenth-century tapestry from Constantinople hung on one of the whitewashed walls.

The archways and nooks filled with icons whispered of a rich heritage. The patina on every piece of dark handmade furniture gleamed.

Everywhere she looked there were flowers in wonderful Byzantine pots and hanging plants in exotic baskets that had been woven on the various Greek islands.

Stella had let her inside Stasio's private library, where he kept his personal art collection. The rest of the walls were covered in bookshelves.

Perhaps if you'd lived here all your life, you would take its beauty for granted. But Rachel had only been a guest for twenty-four hours and couldn't imagine the enchantment ever diminishing.

According to Stella, Andros was home to the wealthy shipping families. Life tended to be a little more elegant here than on the other islands. As a result, the locals could seem somewhat snobbish, even arrogant on occasion. If Rachel came up against it during her sightseeing, Stella warned her not to let it bother her.

One thing Rachel had always admired about Stella was the fact that she was so down-to-earth. Never once had she acted spoiled, even though her family was purported to be worth millions. No one seeing Stella in this incredible ambience would understand that all the riches in the world couldn't make up for the loss of one little boy who belonged in her arms.

"Good luck," Rachel whispered. She squeezed Stella's hand before they parted on the front steps. Any minute now, the estate car would be pulling past the gate at the bottom of the hill.

She watched Stella run down the driveway like a young girl. From the villa steps, Rachel would be able to see what was going on without forcing herself on anyone.

It wasn't long before a black car appeared. When it stopped, she watched Stella approach the back door.

Rachel waited breathlessly for something to happen.

Soon she saw Ari climb out. He and Stella stood looking at each other. They didn't touch. Rachel could tell a serious conversation had begun, but from this distance she couldn't hear individual words. Ari nodded his dark head several times while Stella's identically dark head was bent toward him.

Mother and son.

In another minute, she saw Ari trustingly slide his little hand into Stella's. Together they started walking past the gate to the street, which would lead them to the port below.

The picture blurred for Rachel as she tried to swallow a sob.

CHAPTER NINE

WHEN SHE COULD SEE CLEARLY again, Stasio was strolling up the driveway. Alone.

Rachel thought her heart would fail her.

His happiness was reflected in his eyes and the curve of his mouth. He looked younger.

Was it any wonder? After six years of waiting and worrying, he'd brought Stella's son to her.

Stasio drew closer.

Later, when Rachel was alone and recalled this moment, she would be mortified at the way she'd grasped the hands extended toward her without any thought of hesitation.

Driven by a compulsion stronger than her will, she let her gaze travel over the tan chinos and white turtle-neck until it locked with black eyes so alive and intent she couldn't look away.

"Tell me everything. Please. I can't stand it."

His laughter vibrated in every cell of her body. "Ari was so shocked to see her waiting for him at the gate, wearing jeans and a pullover just like his, he forgot to be nervous and scrambled right out of the car."

A smile lit up her face. "What did he say first?"

"Hello. I'm your little boy, Ari."

"Oh, Stasio."

By now his eyes were suspiciously bright. "My sister said, 'I'd know you anywhere. You're my son, and I've missed you so much.'"

"What did Ari say?"

"'I hope you weren't too sad, Mommy. Missing someone makes people sad.'"

"That sounds just like Ari. He's so sensitive to the feelings of others."

"He is," Stasio agreed. "After that, I lost count of his questions. When she asked him if he'd like to see the remains of some buildings that were buried beneath the sea, that did it. He took hold of her hand and off they went."

"Did he ask for your permission first?"

Stasio shook his head. "No."

"That's because he felt her love in his heart. It's going to work, Stasio. I know it is."

"I know it, too." His voice was low, a little hoarse.

The entire time they'd been talking, her hands were still in his. Embarrassed, she pulled them away. He seemed reluctant to let them go. Ari's return had trapped them in a tumult of emotions difficult to define or contain.

"I don't need to ask how things went yesterday. I knew my sister would forgive you once she knew the truth."

"She was wonderful. We took a long walk, up to that beautiful little church on the hillside, and we talked it all out. Then we spent the rest of the day talking some more—until four this morning. It felt like we'd never been apart."

"And now you're installed at the villa instead of the *taverna*."

Heat crept into her cheeks. "Yannis wasn't supposed to tell, but I guess that was asking the impossible."

"You guess correctly." Another smile appeared, one that mesmerized her with its beauty and joy.

"I have to tell you something, Stasio. Being with Stella again makes me feel happier than I've been in a long time. She told me the same thing. We both have you to thank for making this reunion possible."

"I should be the one thanking you."

When she looked at him, she saw that his eyes were drawn toward the harbor. "Today there's a subtle difference in Stella that has nothing to do with Ari," he said. "My sister is more confident than she was the last time I saw her. That's your influence. Nothing matters quite as much as knowing there's one person in the world you can truly count on."

He said this in a faraway voice. She wondered why Eleni hadn't come to Andros with him.

"I agree. All it takes is one." After a slight pause, Rachel continued, "Stella tells me you and Eleni are going to be married in the church we visited yesterday."

She didn't know what she expected by way of reply, but she wasn't prepared for the fierce look that entered his eyes. "That's right."

The terseness of his remark was a far cry from the easy tenor of their conversations aboard ship. Maybe he was still upset that Eleni hadn't joined him for the crossing, and hadn't forgiven her yet. Engaged couples were famous for having quarrels before the wedding.

It certainly wasn't any of Rachel's business. She regretted having brought up the subject.

"I think Stella and Ari will be gone for a long time, so if you'll excuse me, I'm going to go in and see about my laundry."

"We have maids to do that."

"I know, but I still need to sort things out for them."

"That can wait. I want you to come inside with me. I have a present for you."

She shook her head. "You've done more than enough for me already. I couldn't accept it, whatever it is."

"Actually, it isn't from me."

Curious, she followed him up the steps and into the villa. They walked through the foyer and down the arched corridor to the library, where she'd been last night.

"Please." He motioned to a damask love seat near his desk. From his back pocket he produced a CD, of all things, and handed it to her.

"It's from Mrs. DeMaio. I had strict instructions to give it to you as soon as I saw you. As you can see, she added a note with her address, and hopes you'll write to her. You performed an invaluable service for her, you know."

"Nonsense. I was happy to do it." Stasio would never know how thankful Rachel had been for any excuse that forced her to stay away from him.

Avoiding his searching gaze, she glanced down at the title. "Portuguese Love Songs By Felipe DeMaio." Her head came back up. "This is a recording of her husband's."

"That's right. She gave me one, too. It's nice to meet a woman with romance in her soul."

Rachel couldn't help smiling. "You noticed."

"Of course. When I consulted with her and the ship's doctor, she told me not to fuss. 'Go on,' she said, 'Dance the rest of the night away with that beautiful wife of yours.'"

Schooling herself not to react, Rachel said, "Until

we could set them straight, I believe a lot of passengers assumed the three of us were a family.'' *I almost forgot we weren't married myself.*

''I'm sorry we never had that dance together.''

''It's a good thing we didn't. With the storm, we probably would've had as much luck as we did playing shuffleboard and ended up sprawled on the dance floor.''

''You don't think I could have saved you?'' came the unexpected question. He was sounding more like the Stasio she'd known on the ship. She couldn't keep up with his mercurial moods.

''I have no doubt of it. After all, your sister says you can perform miracles.''

Once more a shadow fell over his face. ''Let's hope that's true.''

While she sat pondering his last cryptic remark, the sound of a wonderful Latin beat suddenly began. Soon a man's passion-filled voice poured out a haunting ballad.

''Dance with me.''

She lurched on the seat. Had he really asked her that?

''You mean *now?*''

''Yes. I was denied the privilege aboard ship—remember? The sea is calm today. I promise we won't fall.''

She stared up at him in disbelief.

''Humor me this once? For Mrs. DeMaio's sake? Surely we can't let her present go to waste. Think how happy it'll make her when we send her our thank-you notes and tell her we enjoyed her gift as she meant for us to enjoy it.''

Even as he said the words, he came around the desk and reached for her. Rachel's heart had begun a low pounding. By the time he'd gathered her in his arms, a heavy thud resounded in her ears.

For so long, she had dreamed of being this close to him, and the first contact of their bodies electrified her. But it wasn't enough to hold him and be held. She wanted to touch him, to run her hands over the breadth of his shoulders. To caress his face.

Sometimes on the ship when he wasn't aware of it, she'd watch him at the railing with Ari. Then, too, she'd felt the urge to brush his dark lashes with her fingertips or touch his jaw where she detected the faint shadow of his beard.

As he drew her close, her head fit beneath his chin as if it belonged there. With her face pressed between his neck and shoulder, she could smell the soap he'd used in the shower. Never in her life had she been more aware of the differences between a man and a woman. She thrilled to every swaying motion of his lithe, powerful body. The slight pressure of his hand splayed across the back of her sweater made it easy to follow his lead. She wanted this moment to go on and on.

Rachel could thank Carl for those ballroom dancing classes he'd insisted she take at the institute. Nikos Athas, he'd said, would expect his wife to make him look good on the dance floor.

Nikos.

His name brought another attack of guilt.

I'm a fraud, Stasio, her heart cried.

If you'd known me before I entered Michelangelo's, you would have passed me by, or at the most felt a modicum of pity. I'm not who you think I am, and I didn't come here for the reasons you think I did.

Though she'd already abandoned her desire for revenge, Rachel's shame over her ignoble plan seemed to be growing stronger. She needed someone to talk to about it.

That person could only be Carl Gordon. After the promise she'd made to keep him informed, she should have called yesterday. She decided she'd phone him in the early afternoon. Greece was a half day ahead of Pennsylvania time.

Not that he could really do anything except act as her father confessor while she admitted her sins. They were legion. She couldn't believe she had preyed on the goodness of two innocent people she loved.

Stella meant the world to her. As for Stasio, her feelings for him were so deep, so overwhelming, she couldn't even imagine a relationship with any other man.

This was no schoolgirl crush, she knew that now. What she felt for him wasn't going to go away. But she had no right to any part of his life, no right to think about him, or to harbor any hopes, any dreams.

She rationalized that after watching the way Ari responded to Stella, Stasio was feeling euphoric and needed some way to release his emotions. Rachel happened to be on hand so he'd turned to her for a moment of celebration. Obviously he saw nothing personal in it. She was Stella's old friend.

But Stella's old friend knew it was insane to be dancing with him.

He and Eleni were going to be married within the month. If Eleni saw them like this, she'd have every right to think the worst. Rachel couldn't handle that transgression—almost a complicity in betrayal—on top of all the others.

The second the song ended, she pulled away from him. To her relief, he let her go with a thank-you and a smile she interpreted to mean *I needed that. Now you can run along and do your laundry, play tourist. Have a good day.*

Before she reached the door, he handed her the CD. "Don't forget this." Without looking up, she took it from him, muttered a thank-you and left.

The housekeeper happened to be at the other end of the corridor. When she saw Rachel come out of Stasio's study, her curious glance was so unsettling Rachel practically flew to the other part of the villa, where she slept in a guest room next to Stella's.

After she reached the safety of her four walls, she chastised herself for behaving like a woman caught flagrante delicto. Which, of course, she *had* been. That was why she stood there on legs as insubstantial as mush, breathing hard and scarlet faced.

"ELENI? IT'S NIKOS. I just got back from a trial run and saw that you'd called. Were you able to work your charms and get my brother to rethink his plans?"

"No. I'm afraid my charms have never worked on Stasio when it came to something I really wanted. For now and forever, Ari's a closed subject."

"I was afraid of that," he muttered.

"At this point, all I can hope for is that Ari's too attached to his foster parents to want to live with Stella."

"They have five years on my sister. There's no way Ari will want to leave them. Where's Stasio now?"

"He and Ari flew to Andros a couple of hours ago."

"Why the hell didn't you go with them?"

"Because it wouldn't do any good. When Ari's around, Stasio scarcely knows I exist. I'll go this evening when I won't have to fight for his attention."

"You have to hang in there, Eleni."

"What do you think I've been doing for the past two years!" she cried out in exasperation. "You know very well this whole thing has been a fait accompli from the beginning." After a hesitation, she said, "I think you know something else, too."

"What are you talking about?"

Eleni sucked in her breath. "How long has Stasio been seeing Rachel Maynard behind my back?"

"Who?"

"Rachel Maynard, the redheaded American who went to boarding school with Stella."

After a long silence Nikos let go with a burst of uninhibited laughter. "Good Lord, Eleni. I don't know how you happened to hear about her, but believe me, no man would be interested in that scheming little parasite, least of all my brother."

"Don't lie to me, Nikos," she said in a shaking voice. "This is too important."

The laughter subsided. "I swear I'm not lying. What's this all about?"

"Suppose you tell me. Do you deny that she spent some time at the villa in Chamonix with you and Stella years ago?"

"I'm not denying anything."

"Then she really *was* there with you?"

"Yes. She made certain Stella brought her along."

"Are you aware that Stasio has maintained a relationship with her ever since?"

"Come on, Eleni. That's impossible! He doesn't know her. He never even met her."

"Really. Then how come he knew all about your little affair with her?"

"My *what?* Eleni, you're not making any sense. Rachel Maynard was a pathetic-looking creature. A loser. My ski buddies thought the same thing. I told Stella to get rid of her or no guys would come near.

"That's why she gave up the baby, you know. So she could have another chance at life. With Rachel hanging around for whatever she could get out of my sister, that wasn't about to happen. If Stasio intimated I went to bed with her, it means Stella told lies behind my back as a form of revenge."

"According to both Rachel and Stasio, she lost track of you—and I guess Stella—during the intervening years. That's why she went to Stasio's New York office—to get your address so she could look you up while she was on vacation."

"That's preposterous!"

"If you're telling me the truth, my worst fears have just been realized."

"What do you mean?"

"I begged Stasio to fly back to Greece instead of taking the ship. He made up some excuse about not disappointing Ari, but now I know the real reason. Rachel had the stateroom next to Ari's on the *Neptune*. That suite would only be given to someone he cared about. When I walked in on them, they were having an intimate breakfast together."

Another silence ensued. "Rachel Maynard was on the same ship with Stasio?" He sounded totally incredulous.

"Don't cover for your brother, Nikos. After the hell he's put me through over Ari, I couldn't take it. Are you going to pretend you don't know she's his guest at the villa on Andros?"

"You mean *now?*"

"I mean Stasio made arrangements for his pilot to

fly her to the island yesterday morning, purportedly to stay with Stella.''

''I swear on my mother's grave I know nothing about this!'' Nikos's voice rang with conviction.

But Eleni knew that, as the old saying had it, blood was thicker than water. It was more than possible Nikos would defend his brother against Eleni rather than have her find out the truth.

If Stasio had been having an affair with the Maynard woman over a five-year period, that would account for his long delay in asking Eleni to marry him.

Maybe she'd been wrong about his obsessive attachment to Ari. Could it be that all this time he'd been using his nephew as a screen to carry on his relationship with the American woman? Two weeks out of every month!

Was Stasio really capable of doing something like that? Maybe she'd been wrong about him. Maybe, after all, he *was* like so many of the other men she knew. Unable to remain faithful even though he was engaged.

Did he plan to use the excuse that Rachel was his sister's friend so he could continue their affair after he and Eleni were married?

Eleni had a feeling she'd never get those answers out of Nikos. But Stella would know the truth about Stasio.

After Eleni's fight with him last night, she'd run out of the room in tears and phoned for her chauffeur to take her home. Somehow, she'd thought Stasio would come after her before morning to prove she was more important to him than anyone else.

But she'd waited in vain. Not only had he not come for her, he hadn't even tried to call her and beg her to fly to Andros with him and Ari. After the illuminating conversation with Nikos, Eleni thought she knew why.

"Nikos? I have to hang up now. I've got some packing to do before I leave for the island."

"You're not the only one."

"What do you mean?"

"I'm going to leave after tomorrow's race and join you on Andros as soon as I can get there. The Rachel Maynard I once knew looked like a short, plump Little Orphan Annie. Surely we couldn't be talking about the same person! I'll see you when I see you."

"CARL?"

He frowned. It sounded like Erica, but she was coughing so hard, he couldn't be sure. "Yes?"

"We've got an emergency on our hands. A chemical leak in the area. Our entire block is being evacuated. Leave everything as it is and come downstairs now!"

"What about the others?"

"Everyone's been notified. Police vans are waiting to drive us to the hospital. Hurry!"

"I'm on my way."

Even as Erica was talking, Carl had shut down the computer. There was too much sensitive material in the files to leave them open. With that accomplished, he grabbed his briefcase and hightailed it for the stairs.

Before he'd gained the foyer, he could smell noxious fumes and hear the sirens. When he opened the front door, it looked like a war zone outside.

Fire and police personnel wearing gas masks were herding people out of their homes and into vehicles. A half-dozen gas company trucks were parked up and down the street. Uniformed workers wearing masks had already started running a jackhammer in front of the institute, obviously looking for the source of the problem.

Carl pulled a handkerchief from his pocket and covered his nose and mouth. By the time he'd climbed inside the police van and they were off, not only had he started coughing, but his eyes were watering profusely.

Two of the workmen from the gas company watched the last load of occupants drive away before they hurried up the steps into the building.

"Dammit all to hell, T.J. I would've bet my medals Rachel Maynard was hiding in here."

"What do we do now, Colonel?"

"This place seems to be some kind of glorified hotel. I thought it was an all-women facility, but six or seven men came out, too."

"It's a weird setup. No sign on the building."

"It's bound to have a computer. Let's find ourselves one and get into the system. We're looking for anything on Rachel Maynard or Carl Gordon."

T.J. opened a door off the main foyer. "Colonel? I found one in here. Whoever left the room forgot to turn it off. This is going to be a piece of cake."

"All right. Let's do it. We only have a few minutes before somebody asks us what we're looking for in here when everyone's supposed to be outside."

"I realize that, Sir. Hey—here's a list of names by the side of the computer. Carl Gordon is at extension 220."

"I wonder where the hell his office is?"

"I'll keep pressing the button for his intercom. You walk around till you hear it."

"Good plan. In the meantime, break into those files!"

"Yes, sir."

It took Sean longer than he wanted to make a sweep

of the first floor. When he couldn't hear anything, he swore a stream of invective and raced up the staircase to the second floor. Halfway down the hall he heard the buzzer and found the room in question.

He pressed the button on the telephone apparatus. "T.J.? I've located his office—Room 220. We should've figured *that* out. The computer's been turned off, though. Have you found anything on Rachel Maynard?"

"No. Everything's in code. If you didn't know otherwise, you'd think the place was a CIA training facility. I'm going to need a lot more time than we've got to crack it."

"Damn. We're almost out of time already."

"Turn on the computer and see what you get."

Sean sat down at the desk and flipped the switches. There was a command to press the enter key. The second he complied, the screen turned a royal blue color and a sound beeped so loudly it hurt his ears.

"Illegal entry has been noted. Illegal entry has been noted." The same sign kept flashing.

"Hell and damnation!" Sean muttered before shutting off the computer.

"What was that, Colonel?"

"Damn thing's been booby-trapped." Furious, he rifled through the few items on the desk and in the drawers. Whoever this character was, he didn't want anyone looking in his files. There were no clues left lying around.

"I'm coming back down." If he couldn't get what he wanted one way, he'd get it another.

T.J. was waiting for him. "It looks like we'll have to resort to the other plan, after all. I was hoping it wouldn't come to that."

"You and me both. But the general said do whatever it takes to get the job done. Did you bring the stuff the doc sent in the pouch?"

"Yes, sir. It's in the back of the van."

"All right. After we drive to Maywood Hospital, we'll change into hospital gowns. Once Mr. Gordon tells us where to find Rachel Maynard, we'll give him a little present for his cooperation. He won't know what hit him, any more than that bastard Draco did."

"I don't want to be blamed for killing anybody, Colonel."

"What's stuck in your craw, T.J.? He's still alive."

"But how do we know something won't go wrong like it did with her father?"

"Because the doc says it won't! Look, I've been doing you a lot of favors, T.J. Don't screw up on me now if you want those new bars. You hear what I'm saying?"

"Yes, sir."

"All right, then. Let's get the hell out of here."

CHAPTER TEN

AFTER THE ENCOUNTER with Stasio in the library, Rachel had gone to her room and hadn't ventured out since. She didn't care what construction anyone put on her absence. After being in his arms, she couldn't face him again so soon. Besides, this was a family reunion in the most literal sense. And Rachel was an outsider who didn't wish to intrude.

When one of the maids announced lunch, Rachel had asked her to inform the family that she wasn't hungry and preferred to rest until dinner. The truth was that although nothing had happened yet, she couldn't shake off the feeling that the person looking for her was getting closer. She knew he had skilled accomplices on her trail.

What she needed was a chance to unburden to Carl. She'd called him on his extension at the institute and left several messages, but he hadn't returned them. Maybe he'd taken the day off.

Before she'd left Michelangelo's, he'd given her his home phone number and made her promise to use it. "In an emergency," she'd told him, never believing that one would arise.

How wrong could she have been!

"Please be home, Carl," she murmured as she reached for the phone again. But before she could start to punch in the numbers, there was a knock on the door.

She half turned, hoping it wasn't Stasio. She was just too vulnerable right now. Any more time alone with him, and she didn't know how she could keep from showing him what he meant to her.

"Yes?"

"It's Ari."

She frowned. What on earth would he be doing at her door? He was a dear little boy and they'd become good friends on the ship. But here on Andros he had a mother and an uncle who doted on him. Rachel couldn't imagine why he was seeking her out.

"Come in!" she said, putting back the receiver. The call to Carl would have to wait.

He entered quietly and shut the door, but he didn't run over to her the way he normally would.

Something was wrong, on this day of all days.

Uncertain what to do, Rachel sank down on the side of the bed. "Does your mommy know you're in here?"

"No."

"Does Stasio?"

"No. I told them I had to go and do something by myself."

She mulled over his answer for a minute. "Sometimes I say that to people when I want to be alone to think. Is that what happened to you?"

"Yes."

It was a very tentative yes.

She remembered the conversation they'd had in Stasio's office the first time she'd met Ari. It prompted her to ask, "Are you scared of something?"

He nodded.

Now she was getting somewhere.

"What are you scared of, sweetheart? Are you missing Anna and Giorgio?"

To her surprise, he ignored her questions and said, "Did you see the helicopter?"

Rachel blinked. A little while ago she'd heard the sound of one, but she hadn't attached any importance to it. She imagined dozens of wealthy natives on Andros commuted that way from the mainland.

"No. Why do you ask? If you don't like them, you don't have to ride in one. Just tell your mommy you want to take the ferry instead."

"I loved the helicopter!"

"Oh! I see." But she didn't.

Unexpectedly, Ari darted over and sat down on the bed next to her. "Eleni's coming for dinner. In the helicopter."

The knowledge that Stasio's fiancée would be arriving any minute ought to have been the answer to Rachel's cry for help. But the news brought a fresh wave of despair. As for Ari...

She stared at him, trying to understand. "Are you scared of Eleni?"

He nodded. "She doesn't like me."

"You said that once before. Ari, what happened in Athens? Did she *tell* you she didn't like you?"

He was so intent on his own perception of things, she needed to understand the basis of his fear so she could disabuse him of it.

"No."

"Then why do you say that?"

"She told Stasi she wouldn't marry him if I live with my mommy."

Rachel couldn't prevent a gasp. "When did you hear her say that?"

"Last night."

Rachel took a shuddering breath. "What happened?"

"I couldn't sleep. I went downstairs to find Stasi. He was with Eleni. She was real mad."

"Does Stasio know you heard him and Eleni talking?"

"No. I got back in my bed."

And you've been suffering ever since....

While she worked out what to do, she asked, "Did you have a wonderful time with your mommy today?"

His face brightened, causing a complete transformation. "Yes! She says she can take care of me now. She wants me to live with her all the time because she loves me!"

"Do you want to live with her?" Rachel asked unnecessarily.

He nodded. "I love her. She said I could visit Anna and Giorgio whenever I want, and she said they could come and stay with us. And guess what?"

"What?"

"Stasi is my mommy's brother!"

"That's right. Which makes him your *uncle* Stasi instead of your godfather."

He nodded. "And I have another uncle, Uncle Nikos, who's going to teach me how to ski!"

"That sounds just perfect. Did you tell your mommy you want to live with her more than anything in the whole world?"

His happy face crumpled. "No. I'm scared to."

Ahh... "Because you're afraid that when Eleni finds out, she won't marry Stasio, and you don't want him to feel bad."

He nodded again. "But don't tell my mommy."

The trauma of being torn like this would be too much

for a mature adult, let alone an innocent child who only wanted to love and be loved.

"Come here, sweetheart." She pulled him onto her lap and wrapped her arms around him. She rocked the little boy for a long time. Rachel craved the comfort as much as he did.

Out of the mouths of babes...

What on earth did Stella's desire to live with her own son have to do with Eleni's decision to marry Stasio?

He'd mentioned something about Eleni needing time to deal with the fact that he was an uncle. Why?

"Will God get mad at me if I don't like Eleni?"

I hope not, otherwise He'll be mad at me, too.

"No, sweetheart. God understands our pain."

"Do I have to eat dinner with Eleni when she comes?"

"I'll talk to your mommy about it. You stay in here. I'm going to go find her and tell her where you are. If it's okay with her, the three of us can eat an early dinner in my room. We'll have a party."

"Goody!"

"I'll turn on the TV. You watch it till she comes for you. Okay?"

"Okay."

Much as Rachel didn't want to get involved in complicated family matters that weren't her concern, Ari's confession had left her no other choice.

Stasio needed to know the truth so he could ease Ari's fears. Otherwise, not only Ari's but Stella's nightmares were just beginning.

No sooner had she closed the door of her room than she saw a devastated-looking Stella a little farther down the hall. Her friend was in agony, and no wonder. Ari hadn't told her yet that he'd come to live with her.

Instead, he'd run off with a vague excuse. He'd been gone for ten minutes already, and Rachel could imagine that Stella had interpreted her son's actions in the worst possible way.

She hurried toward her friend and put both arms around her trembling shoulders. "It's going to be all right, Stella. I promise. Ari adores you, but there's a problem that has to be resolved with Stasio first. It has nothing to do with you, Stella, I swear it! Right now he's waiting for you. I told him that if you approved, the three of us could eat an early dinner in my room tonight. Wash your face, and then go to him."

There was a lot of sniffing while Stella nodded. "You can't tell me what the problem is?"

"No. Ari told me something in the strictest confidence. I have to talk to your brother. This is something only he can deal with."

"He's downstairs on the covered patio with Eleni."

"So she's arrived?"

"Yes. Just a few minutes ago. They're having a drink."

"I'm afraid this can't wait, Stella."

"If it has to do with Ari, neither Stasio nor I would want you to wait." Her voice trembled as she spoke. "Go down past the library to the double doors on the right. They open onto the patio."

"I won't be long. In the meantime, pretend everything's fine and just enjoy your son."

"Thank you, Rachel. I honestly don't know what I would've done if you hadn't come to Andros when you did. Ari thinks you're wonderful. I'm so glad he could turn to you."

"I am, too."

My reasons for coming here were all wrong, Stella.

*But if I can be of any help now, do any good for your
dear little boy, then I'll be grateful for that much salve
to my conscience before I leave.*

"I GOT HERE JUST IN TIME. It's started to rain." Eleni
turned her back to the view and leaned against the bal-
cony. "Aren't you glad to see me?"

She made a picture in her stunning black-on-white
print dress, her long black hair flowing over one shoulder the way Stasio liked it.

"I'm always glad to see you. You know that. But
last night you said something that changed the com-
plexion of things."

With her head cocked to the side, she said, "Did it
ever occur to you that I said what I did out of jealousy?"

"Yes. But to be jealous of a little boy isn't rational,
Eleni."

Stasio had lain awake the rest of the night thinking
about it. If Eleni couldn't make this sacrifice for Stella
so his sister could claim the son she'd never wanted to
give up, if Eleni couldn't forgo a fancy wedding in
order to avoid unwanted publicity, if she couldn't join
him aboard ship in order to get acquainted with Ari—
then it appeared he'd made a grave mistake in judgment.

Or maybe he'd expected too much of Eleni. Maybe
it was too much to expect from any woman. But the
fact remained that Stella and her son were a big part
of his life.

Today was only the first day of their reunion. Ari
was having to deal with a lot of emotions. Stasio assumed that the reason he'd run out of the room a little

while ago was to call Anna and Giorgio and talk everything over with them.

Ari knew their number and had memorized the country and city codes, as well. Stasio had given him permission to call them whenever he felt like it.

His sudden departure had crushed Stella. But as Stasio had reminded his sister, this was all going to take time. She had to be patient and let Ari come around on his own.

Eleni spoke in a high, strained voice. "I'll admit it's galling to know that if you had to make a decision right this minute, you'd choose to be Ari's father rather than my husband."

"We've been over this ground too many times, Eleni. I've never denied that I have fatherly feelings for Ari. Try to remember the situation that brought him into this world wasn't of my making."

"But you're not sorry it happened."

"How could I be sorry when he's such a wonderful child?"

"You just don't understand!"

"Maybe neither of us fully understands."

"Or maybe you're keeping something else from me."

The guilt that had first appeared during Rachel's visit to his office seemed to be alive and doing well. The guilt that came from his attraction to another woman. To Rachel...

"Tell me what's on your mind, Eleni. I want to hear it."

"All right." She pushed herself away from the wall and walked toward him. "Have you been having an affair with Rachel Maynard?"

He'd been waiting for that question. "No."

Her mouth turned up at the corners, but her eyes weren't smiling. "Nikos defended you, but then that's what men do, even brothers who are normally at odds with each other."

"I asked you to marry me."

"But it took you a long time, didn't it? And you've known Rachel ever since Stella was at school with her in Switzerland."

"I don't appreciate having my motives misconstrued. But you're still my fiancée, so I'll tell you this once. I never laid eyes on Rachel until she came to my office."

"How do I know you're not lying? Men do it every day to their wives and fiancées. When we first started dating, I had to say goodbye to you every two weeks and wait another two for your return to Athens. If I ever suggested joining you in New York, you put me off."

"I've told you the reason, Eleni."

"But is it the truth? How do I know you haven't been seeing that American woman behind my back? What's to prevent you from seeing her after we're married? You have the perfect excuse since she's your sister's best friend."

Good Lord.

"I thought Ari was my competition. But maybe all along it's been Rachel. Yes, I'm jealous," she cried out. "When I walked into your stateroom and saw the three of you together, it was like looking at a cozy little family. Like I didn't belong there at all."

He could hear her pain. He closed his eyes tightly for a minute. He was in pain, too. Everything had gone wrong. Everything was so damn complicated, especially now that his feelings for Rachel were part of the equation.

It had been the biggest mistake of his life to dance with her, but at the time he'd felt the compulsion so strongly, he'd had to act on it.

"If you'd come on the ship, you would have been the one eating breakfast with Ari and me."

"Oh, I'm sure your nephew would have made sure Rachel joined us. Her name came up so often during our walk around Athens, I was under the impression Ari had spent time with the two of you long before your trip. Why do you think I was so quiet?"

He exhaled the breath he'd been holding. "Rachel's an easy person to get to know, Eleni. She's a natural around children. She's a genuine, compassionate woman. That's probably why she and my sister hit it off in Switzerland."

"So you're still denying any relationship with her?"

"I swear it, but evidently you refuse to believe me. If there can't be trust between us now, then how can we hope to have a solid marriage?"

"I don't know." Her eyes filled with tears. "I just want you to love me. I thought you did."

"I do. But maybe love isn't enough. Some other vital ingredient seems to be missing where you and I are concerned. There's always a new issue. At first it was my work and the time I had to spend apart from you. Then it was Ari. Now it's Rachel."

"You make me sound like I'm some kind of...of unreasonable monster."

"Not at all. The trouble lies with me. I don't seem able to make you feel secure."

"How can I feel secure when I'm always going to

wonder if you asked me to marry you in order to gain custody of Ari?''

''If that had been my plan, don't you think I would have married you during the first year of our courtship?''

Her eyes looked wounded. ''Then it means you weren't even sure you wanted to marry me until ten days ago.''

''I've never made a secret of the fact that marriage is the one thing in my life I could never enter into lightly.''

Her features froze. ''I knew I wanted to marry you the first night we went out together, but you didn't want to make our relationship legal.''

''I had to be very certain first.''

''Some people would say two years of waiting has more to do with *uncertainty*.''

''It doesn't matter what other people say. We're talking about our relationship, which has been stormy at times for one reason or another. I want my marriage to endure.''

''You think I don't?''

''Last night you said things that could make it impossible for us to even get to the altar.''

''You're twisting everything.''

''No.'' He shook his head. ''When two people marry, they don't marry only each other, they marry each other's families, with all their attendant problems.''

''You mean, love me, love Stella and Ari.''

''Yes. And the same goes for me. When your brother's business went under and he had little mouths to feed, I helped him start another business.''

''He should never have come to you. I told you not

to listen to him. We both know he was never cut out for the antiques business in the first place. He got in way over his head."

"That may be. But his wife and children were innocent victims. I wanted to help them because they're your family, and families stand by each other. Now he's running a successful freight business, which he enjoys much more."

"I know, and I'll always be grateful to you for that. But the situation with your sister is quite different."

"How?"

"You and Stella are much closer than my brothers and I. You'd do anything for her."

"That's because we lost our parents. Nikos handled the hurt in his way. Stella and I clung to each other. You still have your parents. The two situations aren't comparable."

"That's my point. I have this feeling that when I'm your wife, you'll still do anything for her but not for me."

"Eleni?" He rubbed the back of his neck, weary of the battle. "Perhaps you can see now why I haven't been ready to jump into marriage. After two years, we're only starting to address the real impediments to our happiness."

"Kyrie Athas?"

At the interruption, Eleni made a sound of protest. He turned to the housekeeper. "Yes, Melina?"

"If I could have a word with you?"

He faced Eleni again. "Why don't you go to the sitting room and get warm by the fire while I find out what she wants. Later on, after dinner, we'll finish talking."

He thought she meant to argue with him, but then she seemed to think better of it and merely nodded.

"I promise not to be long." He took her by the shoulders, kissed her forehead and followed Melina through the doorway into the corridor.

"Despinis Maynard wants a word with you in the library."

No matter how precarious the situation with Eleni, he couldn't quell the hammering of his heart when he heard that Rachel was waiting for him.

"*Efcharisto,* Melina."

In a few strides, he entered his favorite room and shut the door. Rachel had been standing in front of the paintings, but she turned when she heard him.

A fire had been lit in the hearth. In the shadowy light of the room, her hair gleamed like pure flame. She was wearing a simple dark brown skirt and a long, body-skimming sweater. Nothing could have suited her coloring or her figure more.

His gaze sought hers across the room. He'd never seen her look so solemn. That, in itself, was alarming because he suspected this was about Ari. "Melina said you wanted to see me."

"Yes. I'm very sorry to have interrupted you when I know you were talking to Eleni, but this was too important to put off till later."

He braced himself for what was coming. "I thought Ari and Stella were getting along so well. But a little while ago, he left the room and never came back. It devastated my sister. Does he want to return to New York already?"

"No. It's something much more serious."

He felt as if someone had just dealt him a vicious

blow to the gut. "Tell me," he demanded, moving toward her.

For the next few minutes, he listened to her account of the conversation with Ari. Every revelation increased his pain.

"*Lord.* I had no idea he'd overheard us."

"None of this is my business, but since he confided in me, I knew you'd want to relieve his suffering. You're the only one who can."

Their eyes caught and held. "Thank you for being honest with me and bringing it to my attention immediately."

"You're welcome. I want Ari to be happy and secure. I'm crazy about him."

"He feels the same way about you, thank God. Otherwise we could all have remained in our individual hells without knowing why."

"I think eventually he would have told either you or Stella."

"I don't know. Even so, too much damage would have been done. I'm indebted to you, Rachel."

"Then we're even."

Her radiant smile captivated him. He had to clamp down hard on his emotions, which were too deep, too intense, to let him remain alone with her any longer.

"I hope it's all right that I told Ari he could stay in my room and have dinner with me and his mother."

Considering Eleni's feelings, it was providential. If things had been different, Stasio would have loved to join them. "I'm sure he's excited about that. Tell him I'll be up to say good-night afterward."

She nodded, then hurried out of the library. When she'd gone, he grasped the mantel with both hands and stared into the flames.

The situation with Ari had reached crisis proportions. So had his relationship with Eleni. In the beginning the one had absolutely nothing to do with the other, but somewhere along the line they'd become inseparable in his mind. Not anymore, though...

Tonight he was seeing things clearly for the first time. He had Rachel to thank for unknowingly acting as a catalyst to clarify his thinking.

Although he'd always cherish what he and Eleni had shared, they didn't have the firm foundation needed to support a lasting marriage. The insecurities plaguing her would always be there. In time, she would manufacture new ones. Eleni would never change from the person she was into someone else.

He would never change, either.

For both their sakes, he had to let her go.

When they'd finished dinner, he would take her back to Piraeus. By the time he'd delivered her to her front door, she would know it was over.

As soon as he'd said his final goodbye to Eleni in Athens, he'd meet with Costas and find out what his attorney had to tell him.

Stasio flattened his hand against the edge of the mantel. After going to such unprecedented lengths, he refused to let the law of either country tear mother and son apart. There had to be a solution. They would simply have to find it.

"YOU KNOW WHAT? I think my little boy's tired after such a big day. Let's go into Mommy's room. I have a surprise for you."

"You do? What is it?"

"You'll find out in a minute."

Ari turned to Rachel. "Do you want to come and see it?"

"I'd love to, but first I have to make an important phone call. Will you show it to me in the morning?"

He nodded. "Good night, Rachel."

"Good night, Ari. Sweet dreams."

At the door he waved goodbye once more before following Stella from the room.

Since confiding in Rachel, he'd been acting more normal again, much to Rachel's relief and his mother's joy.

Stasio still hadn't made an appearance. He loved Eleni; naturally they had a lot to sort out, since she seemed to resent Ari so much. Until they could resolve their differences, they couldn't make plans for their wedding. It meant they might be up all night talking.

Now that Rachel was alone, she decided to try to reach Carl. His number was in the address book she'd left on the table. After picking up the receiver, she punched in the digits and waited.

"Hello?"

"Hello? Is this Mrs. Gordon?"

"Yes?"

"This is Rachel Maynard calling from Greece. I know it's late, but I'm one of your husband's old clients from Michelangelo's. I'd like to speak to him if I could. I tried him at the institute earlier, but there was no answer. Is he home by any chance?"

"Yes, he is. Just a minute."

Thank heaven, he was there. She waited impatiently for him to come on the line.

"Rachel?"

"Carl! It's so good to hear your voice."

"Same here. You've kept me in suspense, you naughty girl."

"I couldn't call before."

"That's all right. But now that you're on the phone, I want to hear everything that's happened to you so far."

"It'll take a long time."

"I haven't got anything else to do."

"I know that's not true. How come you weren't at the office? Has your schedule changed?"

"No. There was an emergency at work."

Rachel grimaced as he told her the details.

"I didn't inhale as many fumes as some of the others. By the time we reached the emergency room, I felt all right and called for a taxi to go home."

"I'm glad you're okay. What a bizarre thing to have happened!"

"I agree. Now enough about me. How's our plan progressing?"

"Too well." She couldn't keep her voice from trembling. "Except that I haven't even met Nikos yet and I've already fallen in love with his brother. Stasio's so wonderful, I didn't know a man like him existed. If he ever found out why I came to his office in the first place, he'd never forgive me. Neither would Stella, and I wouldn't blame either of them." She broke down sobbing.

"Whoa...Rachel! Wait a minute! Hold on there, young woman. Take a deep breath and start all over again."

She fought for control. "What I've done is wrong, Carl. Revenge is wrong. It's evil. And you were right about Nikos. I was never in love with him and never could be. But none of it matters because what I've done is evil.''

"That's twice you've said that word. Now, listen to me, my dear. You don't have one evil bone in your body, so I don't want to hear you talk that way again.

"When you came to the institute, you were a very depressed woman. Setting some lofty goals helped pull you out of the worst of it. There's nothing evil in trying to better yourself and make the most of your assets.''

"I agree with you so far.''

"Tell me one thing,'' he interjected. "Were you honest with Stella? Does she know why you ended your friendship with her?''

"Yes.''

"Did she forgive you?''

"Yes. She couldn't have been more understanding. It's made us both very happy. We're better friends than ever.''

"What's evil about that?''

"Well, nothing, but—''

"No buts, Rachel. You accomplished something very important. Don't you realize that some of your depression stemmed from that ugly experience in Switzerland?

"Nikos's part in the whole affair isn't nearly as important as the fact that you turned your back on a friend. It isn't in your nature to do something like that. Therefore you internalized that guilt over the years. Doesn't it feel wonderful to have gone to her and set the record straight?''

"Yes.'' Tears trickled down her cheeks. "Oh, yes.''

"As for Nikos, I knew you'd never end up with him. He's not your type. But your anger over what he did was a healthy emotion. For one thing, it forced you to reevaluate yourself. For another, it helped you get to the point that you could become friends with Stella again.''

"But you don't understand! I used Stasio to find Stella. He's such a remarkable man, and he's been so generous. That's why what I've done is *horrible*.''

"Not horrible. Admit you're just feeling guilty because you fell in love with him, and it wasn't in your plan. I was hoping you might. He's much more your type.''

"Carl!'' she cried out. "Were you deliberately matchmaking for me?''

He chuckled. "No. Not deliberately—but if I were?''

"Then you overlooked one slight detail.'' Her voice shook again, despite herself.

His laughter stopped. "What was that?''

"Eleni Souvalis.''

"Who?''

"Stasio's fiancée. They're getting married over the holidays.''

"Stasio Athas is engaged?''

"Yes.''

"I couldn't have missed a detail that important.''

"You didn't. He's just made it official.''

"Nevertheless, I'm paid to know about things like that.''

"I don't see how you could. He's been forced to keep everything hush-hush because of Ari.''

"Who's Ari?''

"It's a long, sad story.'' Over the next few minutes, she told Carl everything.

"As I recall, there's a newspaper picture in my files of Stasio Athas and an unidentified woman walking down a street in Athens. I'll describe her to you and you let me know if she's this Eleni.''

"You don't need to do that.''

"I want to. I'm curious. My wife says that's my middle name. Give me a minute to get into my office computer from this one.''

Rachel smiled as she pictured him at his desk. He was a good friend. She felt a lot better just talking to him.

"Uh-oh,'' she heard him say. "Uh-oh.'' The second time he sounded upset.

"What's wrong?''

"Someone's been trying to get into my computer.''

She blinked. "How do you know that?''

"I had a device built in for exactly that reason. It tells the time and date of the attempted break-in. Whoever was trespassing did it while I was at the hospital today.''

"I thought everyone was evacuated.''

"They were. The only people around were fire and police personnel, gas company people. I wouldn't put it past some tabloid paparazzi to pay one of the people who works here to get information on a client. It's happened before.''

"That's criminal!''

"Rachel? Give me your phone number and I'll call you back in a day or two. I want to get my private investigator going on this before everyone's back at Michelangelo's tomorrow.''

"All right.''

After she'd given him the information, he said, "By the way, do you still not want to be found?''

Ice filled her veins.

"Rachel?''

"H-has someone been trying to reach me?"

"Yes. A Colonel Dodd."

Oh dear God, no.

"He says he's a good friend of your family. Is he the one you said might be looking for you?"

"Yes." Her fingers twisted the telephone cord. "He was my father's best friend—or so I thought."

"Apparently he phoned Dr. Rich, who in turn phoned me. I immediately alerted Erica, and she told the colonel nothing when he came over to the institute inquiring after you."

"Carl?" she cried in a frantic voice. "Listen to me!"

"I'm listening."

"He and whoever helps him were the ones who tried to break into your computer. I'm sure of it!"

After a brief silence, "What does he have on you, honey?"

"I have knowledge of a cover-up, Carl, possibly stemming from the White House. I'm positive Sean's working under orders from someone at the Pentagon.

"The base doctor told me my father died of a heart attack. But I know he was murdered because he had kept the negatives of some classified photographs of Mars.

"On his deathbed, Daddy started to tell me about them, where he'd hidden them…. When I said I'd give them to Sean, Daddy reacted so violently, I realized something was horribly wrong. I asked him what he wanted me to do with them, but h-he died before he could tell me anything else." She had to swallow a couple of times. "Because of Daddy's reaction, I never said a word to Sean.

"After the funeral, I tried to pretend everything was normal, but I was so scared and in so much pain, I couldn't sleep. That's why I called Dr. Rich for medication.

"Sean and Ruth kept phoning and dropping by to offer their support, but I couldn't forget the horrified look in Daddy's eyes when I mentioned Sean's name.

"After a couple of months, Sean started pushing to come over to the house and help me clear out Dad's things. He was so aggressive about it, I realized he must be after the pictures...and had probably been the one to murder Daddy.

"I was terrified because at that point I didn't know who to trust. I called Dr. Rich again and asked him to prescribe a tranquilizer to help me function so I could work out what to do.

"Instead of that, he suggested I enroll at Michelangelo's. As soon as he told me about the institute, it sounded like a godsend. Without telling a soul about my plans, I put my things in storage, quit my job and left for Pennsylvania where Sean couldn't find me.

"But three months ago, I tried to reach my old boss. His radio program had been blocked out again by the Air Force—and I found out he'd had a stroke. He's living with relatives in California now.

"Carl—Manny was in perfect health before his stroke. So was my father. It's clear to me that Sean killed Dad and did something horrible to Manny. I'm afraid you're the next person on his list.

"I knew it was only a matter of time before he caught up with me. No doubt he's been watching the institute. When he couldn't find me, he staged that emergency, and now he's after you!

"You can't go back to work tomorrow, Carl! You'll be injured or killed. I couldn't handle it."

Carl made a grunting sound. "I wish you'd told me

this a lot sooner. At last I have the full explanation for the goal you set to marry Nikos. It wasn't just revenge or some kind of adolescent infatuation. It was safety more than satisfaction, wasn't it? The protection of the financially and politically powerful Athas family is no small thing. It all makes sense. So does the guilt you've been carrying around.''

''Then you believe me?''

''Except for that one lie of omission, you're the most honest person I ever met. Yes, I believe you. No amateur set up that stunt today. It forced the evacuation of an entire city block.''

''Then get your wife and family and go someplace safe. Please, Carl!''

''I'll worry about me and mine. What about *you?*''

''I was planning to stay in Greece for a while with Stella, but now that I have proof Sean's not going to stop until he finds me, I'm going to leave tomorrow. There are too many people here I love. The last thing I want to do is endanger their lives.''

''Where will you go?''

''Los Angeles, where I can lose myself and maybe find out about Manny. If he's still functioning at all, he'll help me come up with a plan.''

''You need to be under the witness protection program while the situation's investigated. I'll see what I can arrange.''

''Carl?'' she cried out in shock. ''Who are you?''

''A friend, I hope. But to answer your question, I used to work for the FBI as a psychologist. After putting in twenty-five years, I decided to get out and enjoy a normal life with my wife and kids. Since I needed a job where I could keep a low profile, Michelangelo's turned out to be the right spot for me.''

"No wonder you're so brilliant at what you do."

"Those are kind words. Let's just hope I can be of help to you now. I'm going to give you a phone number. When you get settled in California, call me. The person who answers will relay your message and we'll go from there."

She wiped her eyes. "Thank you for everything, Carl. But please don't underestimate Sean."

"I won't. What's even more important is that you get out of Greece as fast as you can."

"I will."

"I'll expect to hear from you in a few days." The line went dead.

CHAPTER ELEVEN

THE MOMENT STASIO STEPPED inside the bedroom, both Ari's and Stella's heads whipped around. They'd been poring over the scrapbook Stasio had kept for Stella from Ari's birth.

His sister was already a changed person. The light that pain had extinguished from her eyes years ago was back, brighter than before.

More than ever, Stasio was determined that Ari would belong to Stella by the year 2000. He would do whatever it took.

"Stasi!" she called out.

"I came to say good-night."

"Mommy's been showing me pictures. I looked funny when I was born."

"I think you looked beautiful." Stella's voice broke.

"Boys aren't beautiful, huh, Stasi?"

"That's right. We're just good-looking and intelligent."

At that comment Stella burst out laughing.

"I'm glad I found both of you in here. Eleni and I are going out on the yacht tonight. Since I have business in Athens early in the morning, I won't return to Andros until noon.

"But as soon as I get back, I thought we could all drive to Gavrion, where we'll hike up to the old Byzantine watchtower."

"The one people used for a signal when pirates came?"

His nephew never forgot anything.

"That's the one, Ari."

"Have you been there, Mommy?"

"Once, when I was about your age. It's kind of spooky. You have to bend really low to get in, and then you have to climb all these steps to get up to the top, where you can see out. You'll love it!"

Ari made happy sounds, his eyes shining like his mother's. Stasio had a hunch Rachel would love it, too.

"Afterward, if we're not too tired," he added, "we can drive to the beach at Batsi and go paddleboating."

"I won't be too tired!" his nephew exclaimed.

Stella hugged him. "There's a nice place to eat dinner right there at the harbor. They serve berry jelly and vanilla ice cream that's so good, you can't get enough."

"Yum!"

Several things were apparent to Stasio. Ari couldn't have cared less that Eleni was leaving. Even more important, although Stasio would be absent from the villa until tomorrow, his nephew seemed perfectly content to remain with Stella. Already the mother-son bond had made Ari feel secure.

Thankful for this much progress, he bent down to kiss them. Tomorrow on the walk up the mountain, he'd have that talk with his nephew and reassure him about Eleni. He'd make sure Ari realized there was no reason to feel guilty or anxious because of Eleni.

"Get a good sleep, you two. We'll need all our strength for the big day ahead of us."

"Good night, Stasi. I love you."

"I love you, too."

When he'd left them, the overpowering urge to stop by Rachel's room took him as far as her door.

Though he could hear nothing from her side, he didn't think she was asleep. All he had to do was knock. And then what? Tell her he'd come to say good-night?

He'd already done that on the ship, when he'd used the excuse that he'd wanted to inform her of their early breakfast in his stateroom.

Tonight he had no justification for his actions.

After forcing her to dance with him earlier today, she would know that a simple good-night wasn't all he wanted. Lord, he felt like a trembling schoolboy who'd become so enamored he was sick with desire, unable to concentrate on anything or anyone else.

There'd been other women in his life before Eleni. But none, including his fiancée, had taken possession of his mind and body the way Rachel had.

One minute he'd been in his New York office agonizing over the outcome of Stella's first meeting with Ari, not to mention Eleni's less than enthusiastic acceptance of his nephew in their lives.

In the next, Rachel had entered his world like one of those UFOs Ari couldn't stop talking about. By the time she'd joined him aboard ship, he'd known deep in his psyche that this woman had already changed his life irrevocably.

The observations Eleni had made, about what she'd seen and felt as she came to his stateroom during that breakfast with Rachel, only confirmed it.

There was no way around the fact that during the ocean crossing, he'd fallen in love with Rachel.

The difference between his feelings for her and all the other women he'd known in his life made him realize his heart had never been involved before. It couldn't have been, or he would have married Eleni long before now.

It appeared he was his father's son, after all. His parents' marriage had been a love match. When his mother died, she took his father's heart with her. At the time, Stasio hadn't experienced that depth of emotion himself and hadn't been able to understand his father's suffering. But now he did...

Unfortunately, that understanding filled him with a new emotion. One of pure, unadulterated fear that Rachel's feelings weren't affected in the same way.

He knew she didn't mind being in his company. When he'd persuaded her to dance with him, she seemed to enjoy it. But what he needed to find out was how she'd respond if they spent time alone, when she couldn't use Ari or Stella as a shield.

But in order to learn the truth of her feelings, he'd have to take care of another matter first. Eleni was waiting....

AT SIX IN THE MORNING, Yannis drove Rachel out the gates of the villa. She couldn't leave Andros fast enough. After waking from a nightmare near three o'clock, she hadn't been able to get back to sleep. It was worse than any she'd experienced since her father's death, because this time the menace struck at someone other than herself.

In her dream she'd been on a ship, looking for Manny. She couldn't find him. The ship had many doors, but every time she opened one, she found the room empty. Searching frantically, she came to a room at the end of the deck.

When she opened the door, she discovered herself in

an office of sorts, where she saw Manny's body lying on the floor. She ran over to him, desperate to find out if he was still breathing. But when she turned him onto his back, it was Stasio's beloved face that wore the look of death. Unspeakable pain pierced her heart.

She'd experienced two painful losses with the deaths of her parents, but losing Stasio constituted a new depth of agony she couldn't endure. She wished herself dead, too, and let out a scream.

The sound brought Stella running into the bedroom to see what was wrong. It took a full minute for Rachel to realize it had only been a nightmare.

"Oh, Stella. I'm so sorry I woke you. I was having a bad dream."

Stella eyed her anxiously. "It sounded much worse than that."

In an attempt to elude her friend's curious eyes, Rachel buried her face in her hands. "You know how strange they can be sometimes."

"You were calling Stasio's name."

Her heart raced unmercifully. "That's because in my dream we were on a ship looking for Manny. He's the man I told you about who had the stroke."

"You mean Draco, your boss."

"Yes. When I looked in this one room, he was lying there as if he were dead. I turned to Stasio and screamed!" she lied.

"How awful. You must care a great deal more for Manny than you realized."

Rachel nodded. "We had a very close relationship. Last night, I phoned a mutual friend in the States and learned that Manny's not doing well. Obviously he was on my mind more than usual when I went to bed."

Forgive me for lying to you, Stella. The only person

I talked to last night was Carl. But there are life-and-death reasons I can't tell you the truth…and I don't dare admit to you that I've fallen in love with Stasio.

"I'm sorry you've had bad news, Rachel."

"So am I." *Believe me, so am I. You'll never know.* "Under the circumstances, I don't think I could enjoy a vacation right now. I have this feeling Manny needs me. I've got to go to him."

"You mean right away?"

On one level the disappointment in Stella's voice was gratifying to hear. But on another, Rachel was terrified. Every second she spent on Andros meant she was endangering the lives of the people she loved.

"Yes. Tomorrow if possible. I hope you'll understand and won't think the worst of me."

Stella's face fell. "Of course, I wouldn't think that. First thing in the morning I'll phone Stasio and ask him to make arrangements for the helicopter to fly you to Athens."

"What do you mean? Isn't he here with Eleni?"

"They decided to spend the night on the yacht."

Rachel had to stifle a groan. No doubt, by sunrise the two of them would have worked out their problems, and Stasio's plan to adopt Ari would go through as scheduled. Though none of it was Rachel's business, she couldn't stand to think about it just now.

"I'm glad he's not here to be bothered. I was going to say I'd prefer to be driven to the port at Gavrion, where I can take a ferry back to Rafina."

"Why would you do that when the helicopter is so much faster?"

"Because the flight from Piraeus made me feel ill." Another lie. But she didn't dare risk seeing Stasio again.

Knowing him as well as she did, she realized that if he heard about her plan to leave, he wouldn't let her go without giving her the proper send-off, even if it meant putting himself out to escort her personally to the airport. The one thing she couldn't handle was saying goodbye to him.

"Rachel! I had no idea."

"I didn't want you to know. After all your family's done for me, won't you please let me take care of my departure and expenses in my own way? It's only a two-hour ferry ride. I have a schedule. I'd be grateful if Yannis could drive me at six so I could make the first crossing. I've already booked my flight from Athens for late afternoon."

She hadn't really booked it yet, but it didn't matter. She would make arrangements from Rafina.

Stella stared back with a mixture of bewilderment and sadness. She finally nodded. "Of course. He's always in the kitchen by five-thirty, having breakfast with Melina. You can ask him yourself."

"Thank you. Please say goodbye to Ari for me. I'll be leaving before he's up. Tell him I'll send him some cool UFO stuff as soon as I can."

"He'll love that, but he's going to miss you as much as I already do."

Stella threw her arms around Rachel. "I wish you didn't have to go, but if this man needs you…"

Maybe he does. When I get to California, I'm going to find out.

"I hate leaving like this, Stella. But I'll always be thankful you were open to me so I could explain what happened all those years ago. Now I can go away happy because we're friends again."

"Best friends!" she cried out.

"I promise I'll let you know where I am as soon as I get there. You have to promise to write and send tons of pictures. I want letters from Ari and huge, long letters from you."

"I promise. Nothing's ever going to separate us again." If only that was true. "Maybe when Manny feels better, you could both come here for a vacation."

"You're the dearest, most generous soul alive, Stella. I'll keep your invitation in mind. Take care, and thank Stasio for me."

"I will. Call me and let me know you've arrived safely in California so I won't worry."

"I promise. Now go back to bed before Ari wakes up and discovers you're gone. We don't want him to be frightened on his first night home."

Stella's eyes filled. "I hope this *will* feel like home to him soon."

"It already does, my friend. Otherwise he would have asked Stasio to take him back to New York."

"You think so?"

"I know so. Don't forget I spent a week with him on the ship. Trust me on this one."

"COSTAS?" IN HIS ATHENS office, Stasio sat forward and leaned both hands on his desk. "What are you saying? Can the boy be returned to Stella? Or failing that, can I become his legal guardian?"

Seated across the desk from Stasio, the older man who'd been the Athas family attorney for over thirty years spread his large hands in a gesture Stasio had seen many times before. It could mean anything.

"It's *possible* you could be granted guardianship, but the judge may not feel it's in the best interests of the child. After all, Ari has lived with loving foster parents for five years—foster parents who want to adopt him.''

Costas shook his head as he looked directly into Stasio's eyes. ''Think about it. Why would an American judge allow you, a single man, to take the child from an emotionally stable environment to a foreign country to live with the birth mother Ari's only known for a few days? You're not the boy's father, and Stella has no husband. I think the judge may look at those factors and decide Ari is better off staying where he is.

''I could be wrong, of course. The judge might be swayed by the fact that you've maintained constant contact with Ari since his birth, and that you can provide extraordinary financial means to give the boy every opportunity he might need or want. Then there's the fact that Anna and Giorgio are already in their fifties. Your age and Stella's *could* work in your favor.''

Stasio had spent a hellishly long night ending his engagement with Eleni. He felt physically and emotionally drained. ''The more you talk, the more I sense Ari slipping away from Stella and me.''

The older man's bushy eyebrows furrowed. ''I'm sorry, but you wanted the truth. Stasio, I know how much you love the boy, how much you want him united with Stella. Under the circumstances, I don't see that you have any choice but to marry Eleni. Surely it's not too late....''

Stasio gazed at his long-time friend for a moment. ''If I were in love with Eleni, I would find a way.''

Costas grunted. ''For such an intelligent man, you never figured out you weren't in love with Eleni until now? I could have told you that two years ago!''

The older man was one of the few people Stasio

respected. When he spoke, Stasio listened. "Was it that obvious?"

"Only to me. If Eleni had been the right woman for you, you would have married her within months of meeting her. Unfortunately, this doesn't solve the problem for Ari and Stella.

"As I suggested from the beginning, why not find the man who fathered the boy and explain the situation? He and Stella could be married for the sake of the child, then divorced later if their personal relationship didn't work out."

"No." Stasio shook his head. "That's not an option because Stella's like me. She's no longer in love with Theo and she'd never use him that way."

"What about Nikos?"

"No woman has meant enough to him to get him to settle down."

"Then it's likely Ari's foster parents will be adopting him, and we'll have to hope they allow Stella liberal visitation rights."

Stasio pushed himself away from the desk and got to his feet. "After all my plans, I can't believe it's come down to this."

"There's always a way around the problem, if you get my meaning," Costas interjected, "but you're not the kind of man to stoop to such tactics."

You don't know me as well as you think you do, Costas. I thought of a solution long before you did. To my shame I haven't been able to think of anything else.

When the phone rang, Costas stood up. "Go ahead and answer it, Stasio. I'll let myself out. I wish I could have brought you the kind of news you were waiting for. If I can be of further help, let me know."

"Thanks, Costas. I'll be in touch."

Once the other man had left the room, Stasio reached for the receiver. The caller ID indicated someone was calling from Andros. "Stella?"

"No. It's me, Ari!"

Just hearing his nephew's voice made him smile. "Good morning, Ari. How did you sleep?"

"Fine. How soon are you coming?"

"Right now. I finished my business earlier than I expected."

"Goody!"

"Is everyone dressed for the hike?"

"I am."

"Rachel, too?"

"Rachel's gone."

His heart skidded to a stop. "What did you just say?"

"Draco called her up. Mommy said he needs her, so she went back to America this morning. I wish she didn't have to go. Mommy's real sad. So am I. Hurry home, please?"

"Put your mother on the phone, Stasi."

"Okay. Just a minute."

Stasio was still reeling from the news when Stella came on the line. "I guess Ari's already told you."

"When did the helicopter take off?" he demanded without preamble.

"She doesn't like helicopters. Yannis drove her to the ferry at six this morning."

The revelations were too shocking to comprehend. He glanced at his watch. If she caught the first one, it would be docking at Rafina within the next fifteen minutes.

"Stasio? You're so quiet. What's wrong?"

"Tell Ari I'll be home as soon as I can."

"But—"

"I have to go, Stella."

He'd never cut her off like that before, but time was of the essence.

Minutes later he climbed into the helicopter, which was ready for takeoff.

He could still feel Rachel's soul reaching out to him from those fabulous blue eyes when she'd told him she wasn't in love with Draco.

If that was a lie…

CHAPTER TWELVE

"Ms. MAYNARD?"

Rachel was about to follow some people down the gangplank when she heard her name called out. She'd lived with paranoia for such a long time, anything and everything was suspect in her mind.

Intellectually she knew Sean couldn't have caught up with her already. But her reaction was always an emotional one.

She swung around to discover who it was. A man in an official-looking uniform motioned her over to the railing.

"Yes? Is something wrong?"

"If you'll come with me please." He spoke English with a heavy Greek accent.

"Why?"

"Kyrie Athas would like a word with you."

Heart pounding, mouth dry, she merely nodded. Stella must have told Stasio her plans. That had to be why he was phoning her aboard the ferry.

The man picked up her suitcase and led her to a steward's cabin below the main deck.

"Stasio!" she gasped the second she saw him standing inside. She hadn't been prepared to see him again.

His hands grasped her upper arms to steady her. He shoved the door closed with his foot while his eyes searched hers relentlessly. She could tell he was upset.

"Years ago you turned on my sister, then disappeared from her life. When you came to my office, I bought your excuse and made it possible for you to be with her again. Now I see the same pattern repeating itself." His eyes glittered dangerously.

Rachel started to shake, but that only seemed to anger him. His fingers tightened over the material of her suede jacket.

"How can you hurt Stella all over again, disappoint Ari, and steal out of my house during the small hours of the morning without the slightest compunction for anyone's feelings? What kind of woman are you?"

"I—I know what it must look like—"

"No," he said in a quiet, controlled voice. "You don't have the faintest idea. Once before I asked you a question. Now I'm going to ask it again, and this time I want an honest answer."

"What is it?" she whispered, averting her head.

"Are you in love with Draco?"

"No!"

I'm in love with you. Can't you feel it?

"Look at me and say it."

Rachel couldn't understand why he was so interested in Manny. Slowly she raised her head. "I love him in my own way, but I'm not *in* love. There's a huge difference."

His body tensed. "Be that as it may, you told Stella he needed you. I thought he'd had a stroke and his family was taking care of him. Why are you suddenly rushing back to him when you came here expressly to be with Stella? What in God's name has changed since yesterday?"

Oh, Stasio. If only I could tell you.

"I—I feel I'm in the way." It was the truth. There

wasn't a villa big enough to contain herself and Eleni when they were both in love with the same man. But that wasn't the reason she was getting out of Greece today.

"You're lying to me. I can feel it." He still hadn't let her go.

"This isn't the right time for a visit, Stasio. Not when Ari's just getting acquainted with Stella, and y-you're making marriage plans."

She heard his sharp intake of breath. "There's not going to be a wedding. Last night I called off our engagement."

Rachel almost fainted at the news. She was glad he had such a tight hold on her. "I don't understand."

"It's over. I, too, know the difference between loving someone and being in love. A marriage between Eleni and me would never have worked."

Forgetting not to look, she stared into his eyes to read the truth.

"So that's why you took her on the yacht last night?"

He nodded.

All this time she'd thought—

"I—does she, I mean is she—"

"She's devastated. And I'm very sorry about that. I'm fond of her and would never have caused her pain. But there's no other way things can be right now."

"Naturally she'd be devastated. According to Stella, she's been in love with you for a long time."

"The same way Draco's been in love with you?"

Having learned he was free, Rachel couldn't bear to be this close to him without touching him, kissing him. She pulled out of his arms and backed away.

"Our situations aren't the same. I was never engaged

to Manny." After a slight hesitation, she whispered, "Stasio? If you're not getting married to Eleni, what will happen to Ari?"

"He'll be adopted by his foster parents unless—"

"No!" she cried. "Stella would never be able to handle that now."

"I agree, and I have a solution. I was coming back to Andros to make you a proposition. Ironic, isn't it, that Ari would call to tell me you'd already left to fly back to the States without so much as a goodbye to me?"

She put a nervous hand to her throat.

"Stella said you left by ferry because you got sick on the helicopter. That's a lie, Rachel. My pilot told me you loved every minute of the tour he gave you."

Despite her fear for the safety of his family, Rachel had the grace to blush. "I'm sorry. But you have to believe me when I tell you I asked Stella to say goodbye for me. She would have told you. Surely you realize that after all you did to help bring about my reunion with your sister, I'll always be in your debt."

A strange tension emanated from Stasio. "I wonder if you really mean that."

"About being in your debt? You think I'm lying now?" Her voice rose on the last word. How could she defend herself...and persuade him to let her leave?

"If you're not lying, prove it."

She swallowed hard. "How?"

"By becoming my wife."

The world reeled for a moment. "What did you say?"

"When you came to my office seeking my help, you had no idea there might be a price to pay. I'm asking you to marry me so I can adopt Ari for Stella. After a decent interval, we could divorce. I would make it worth your while.'' There was a slight pause. ''I know you love them.''

Her breath caught. *I would marry you for any reason.*

''I do love them enough to marry you. For everyone's happiness I'd become your wife in a heartbeat. But when I first approached you, Stasio, you had no idea the price *you* might have to pay—the price for simply knowing me. I'm afraid it's too high. That's why I'm leaving.''

A shadow darkened his face. ''After admitting that, do you honestly think I'd let you go anywhere without knowing the whole truth?''

''No.'' She took a long, shaky breath. ''You deserve it. In fact, I spent the night writing you a long letter of explanation so you could take the necessary precautions.''

''What precautions?''

''Stasio, please listen. In the letter, I enclosed some information about my father in case you wanted verification. I planned to post it at the airport.'' Tears welled in her eyes. She couldn't hold them back. ''It explains everything, particularly how my staying in Greece would put your family in the gravest danger. I know you have the power and the means and you'll try to protect everyone you love—but sometimes that's not enough. If anything happened to you, I'd want to die.'' She looked down at the floor and spoke in a low, almost inaudible voice. ''When you read it, you'll realize what an evil person I really am.''

His brows dipped ominously. ''Why don't you let me be the judge of that?''

With shaking hands she pulled the envelope out of her purse and handed it to him.

He studied it for a moment before putting it in the pocket of his navy suit jacket. "Come on. The ferry's starting to load for the return crossing. We'll fly to Athens and go straight to the villa where we can be alone to talk."

"But I have a plane to catch—"

"To hell with the damn plane. Let's go." He reached for her suitcase and put a firm hand at her back to usher her from the room.

With the mood he was in, she didn't dare protest.

STASIO HELPED RACHEL board the helicopter and strapped her in. When he was seated, he gave his pilot a signal and they lifted off the pad. Consumed by curiosity, Stasio pulled her letter from his pocket and started to read.

Dear Stasio,

You'll probably think this letter sounds as crazy as my belief in UFOs. But it's the truth as I know it. I'm telling you everything so you'll take the necessary steps to protect yourself and your family.

My father didn't die of a heart attack. He was murdered by his supposed best friend, Colonel Sean Dodd. While Dad was taking his last breath, he told me about some sensitive photographs he'd been hiding. He kept the negatives. Before he died, he managed to tell me where he'd hidden them, but I never did find out what he wanted me to do with them.

Good heavens. Were those the pictures she'd shown Ari?

There's a group in the government who want these negatives and they won't stop till they get them. Sean is acting on orders from higher up. Sean's wife used to mention a General Berman, and I'm convinced he could be the one issuing those orders. He has connections to the White House. Again, I need proof which I don't have yet.

Not long after Dad's funeral, I quit my job and went into hiding. One day I tried to reach Manny. I found out he'd had a stroke. That seemed unlikely. Manny was in perfect health. It meant Sean was trying to find me. When Manny wouldn't tell him anything, he put him and his broadcasting network out of commission.

I felt guilty and terrified. Finally, I decided to lose myself in Europe, where I was convinced Sean would never find me. I had reached a low ebb in my life and wanted a friend desperately. I wanted Stella. That's why I came to you.

Good Lord!

But last night, with one phone call to a friend in Pennsylvania, everything changed. I realized that Sean's getting closer and closer to finding me. Soon he'll trace me to Europe. After what he did to my father and to Manny, I know he's capable of hurting you and your family. I can't let it happen. As I said before, I realize that you, more than most people, can afford protection. But there's always a risk. That's why I left this morning.

Please don't underestimate the danger, Stasio. Stella told me you have security, but I beg you to add to it. Do whatever you need to keep all of you safe. That includes Eleni, of course, but Nikos particularly. Sean knows I was in Switzerland with him. He might try to use Nikos or Stella in some way to get to me. Don't trust anyone.

I just have to pray that when Sean's intelligence reports back that I'm no longer in Europe, he'll leave you alone. If I thought any of you could be hurt because of me, I couldn't live with myself.

Knowing you and your family has been one of the great privileges of my life. I'll cherish every moment in my heart.

God bless you all.
Rachel.

At this point Stasio couldn't look at her.

She was up against something no person could battle alone, yet her only thoughts had been for his safety and his family's.

His protective instincts were so overpowering right now, he wanted to fly them to some corner of the universe where he could be alone to love her, where nothing could touch them.

One day he hoped to do just that. But for now, he needed to deal with her fears. Reaching for the next page, he began perusing her father's resumé.

Colonel Charles (Chuck) Maynard is Commander of the 98th Range Squadron, 98th Air Base Wing, Headquarters Air Warfare Center, Red Crater Air Force Base, Las Vegas, Nevada.

He is responsible for the maintenance and operations of Red Crater Complex, 3.5 million acres of land and 17,000 square miles of airspace. He commands three detachments, and holds the responsibility of insuring operational and support matters, which are coordinated with MAJCOMs.

He entered the Air Force in 1974, gaining his commission as a Distinguished Graduate from the AFROTC.

He was married to the former Liliane Brace of Piedmont, California, who passed away in 1986. They had one daughter, Rachel.

Stasio scanned the list of Maynard's academic achievements and assignments, noting that among the dozens of different places he'd served was Hahn Air Base in Germany, where he'd been an F-16 Instructor Pilot and Chief Flight Commander.

In 1991 he'd been Mission Director of Al Minhad Air Base in the United Arab Emirates during Operation Desert Storm.

Stasio whistled, absently tapping the paper against his cheek. Rachel's father had led a very distinguished career. But his work had made it necessary for her to attend boarding school throughout her adolescence.

The kind of loneliness she'd had to live with for the greater part of her life made what Nikos had done even more despicable in Stasio's mind.

His gaze dropped to the bottom of the page.

Awards and Decorations:
Kuwait Liberation Medal
National Defense Medal
Meritorious Service Medal
Southwest Asia Medal
Combat Readiness Medal
Air Force Achievement Medal
Air Force Commendation Medal

"Stasio? We've landed."

Rachel must have called to him several times. The rotors had already stopped whirring.

"So we have."

He put everything back in the envelope and pocketed it for future reference.

"I know you're angry because you're so quiet," she murmured as he helped her out of the helicopter onto the roof of his office building.

Rachel, Rachel. Don't you know my anger's not directed at you?

There was so much to say, he felt as if he might explode. For that very reason he didn't speak until they'd descended the few steps to the top level of the building and entered the elevator. "You're right. I'm feeling pretty violent at the moment and I'd rather not talk about it until we reach home."

After the ride to the lobby, he hustled her into the waiting company limo with her luggage and told the chauffeur to drive them to the villa.

Since he had no idea how long his talk with her was going to take, he reached for the car phone and punched in the numbers to speak to Stella on Andros.

Melina answered. Apparently his sister and Ari had decided to go on the hike without him. They weren't expected back until late afternoon. Her message filled him with relief.

He had Rachel to himself for the day.

STASIO SAT AT THE HEAD of the table, with Rachel in the chair next to him. A maid served them in the formal dining room of the Athas town villa.

Rachel observed that no matter how upset he was, his feelings didn't seem to affect his appetite. He appeared to relish their brunch of lamb wrapped in phyllo and leek croquettes.

"That tasted good," he murmured. "I never was one for conversation on an empty stomach."

Rachel, on the other hand, had been too distraught to eat. Out of courtesy she made an attempt to swallow some of the delicious-looking cheese salad. Inwardly she kept reliving the moment when Stasio had proposed marriage.

Of course, it had been a last, desperate attempt on his part to insure Ari's legal place in the Athas household. But that was before he'd read her farewell letter. How bitterly he must be regretting his impulsive proposal. Her intrusion into their lives had endangered the entire Athas clan.

She didn't think his silence on the subject was meant to make her suffer. Stasio wasn't that kind of man. If anything, he was already conceiving a plan to guarantee the family's safety.

"When I asked you to marry me," he began unexpectedly in a low voice, "I had a lump sum payment in mind. After what I learned in your letter, I'm prepared to underwrite any monies needed for legal counsel to represent you and look into your father's death."

Rachel caught her breath. Once upon a time, those words had represented her ultimate goal at Michelangelo's. Only they were supposed to have been said by her husband, Nikos. He was the one she'd intended would pledge his protection and his money, along with his undying love.

"I couldn't let you do it."

"Not even for Ari and Stella?"

"Stasio, I don't want your money!" she cried out, jumping up from the table. "All I care about is your safety. Sean's a murderer! But if you f-feel—" She hated it when her voice trembled like that. "If you feel you can provide enough security to protect everyone while I'm on the premises, then of course I'll marry you whenever you say. I love Stella and Ari. I want to help. They're mother and son and should be together.

"Besides," she continued quietly, "your family has always been wonderful to me. I was Stella's guest at your home in Chamonix six years ago, and your guest on the *Neptune*. This can be my way of repaying you for your generous hospitality."

"That's all I wanted to hear," he said in an oddly satisfied tone.

"Yes, well…after the adoption's final and we feel enough time has lapsed, we can divorce quietly and I'll go back to the United States. I have a friend there who's going to help me."

"If it's not Draco, then *who?*" he fired back.

"His name is Carl Gordon."

"Another man who's in love with you?"

"No!" She shook her head because she couldn't understand why he kept dwelling on the subject. "Carl's happily married. He's an ex-FBI agent who works at this place where I was hiding out."

"What place was that?"

She moistened her lips nervously. *Dear God.* She couldn't tell him about that. Maybe later, but not right now.

"I'd rather not talk about it if you don't mind."

"At some point we're going to have to," Stasio

commented cryptically. "But for now, I'm content you've agreed to marry me. For security reasons, I want us to be married in the next three days."

Three days? Rachel stood there in a stupor.

"Why don't you go into the salon with your coffee and I'll join you after I've phoned Costas."

"Who's he?"

"The attorney handling the adoption. He'll want to meet with us at my office later. We have papers to sign.

"On our way there, we'll stop by the jeweler to buy rings. If I'm not mistaken, there's a shop right around the corner where you can purchase a wedding dress. We'll take everything with us when we leave for Andros this afternoon. Tonight, we'll meet with the priest and sign more papers."

"Can we get married so soon? Aren't there wedding banns to post or something?"

He flashed her a half smile. "Costas will arrange a special license for us."

Stasio moved in the kind of exclusive circles where such things were a matter of course. Clearing her throat, she said, "Can I ask a favor?"

His eyes narrowed on her mouth. Her body started to tremble again—but for an entirely different reason. "Of course. What is it?"

"Can we buy a dress for Stella and a little black tuxedo for Ari? He'll look so handsome in one. Our wedding is really for them. Let's make it special."

From this distance, the expression in his eyes was difficult to make out. But there was a husky tone in his voice when he answered, "You must be reading my mind."

She knew her suggestions had pleased him. Needless to say, his proposal had made her happier than she'd ever been in her life. By marrying Stasio, she and she alone would make it possible for Ari to be with Stella. A way had been provided to compensate for the bad thing she'd planned at Michelangelo's—the revenge, the manipulation.

She knew Stasio wasn't marrying her for love. How could he be? He'd only broken his engagement to Eleni a few hours ago. Even if he'd decided he couldn't marry Eleni, the loss of their relationship would live with him for a long time.

Rachel had no right to expect anything from Stasio. She wasn't asking for his love. She only hoped she'd be forgiven for loving him in secret, for enjoying the weeks or months with him until she had to leave Greece for good.

Please, God. Keep everyone safe while I'm here. Don't let Sean bring harm to any of the people I love.

"MOMMY? I CAN HEAR the helicopter!"

"Sweetheart, it could be anybody coming to Palaiopolis." But Stella hurried over to the window to join him anyway.

They'd both had a wonderful time hiking to the watchtower. Ari had loved the pedal-boating and they'd eaten two orders of ice cream before coming home. But now they were back, the villa felt empty. Stella hadn't been prepared for Rachel's hasty departure early that morning. It had taken away some of her joy. She and Ari had stood at this same window, both close to tears, and watched her leave. Now they were standing here again, anxiously awaiting Stasio's arrival.

All day she'd wondered if her brother had caught up with Rachel. He hadn't been thrilled with the unexpected news, either.

Stasio had been different since his return to Andros. She knew that after spending seven days on the ship with Rachel, he must have realized why Stella had become best friends with her years ago.

There was no one like Rachel. No other girl at the school had her maturity and kindness. Her sense of fun, her intelligence. Ari adored her. Obviously Manny, whom Rachel referred to as Draco, adored her too, and wanted her to come home.

Stasio must have noticed all those qualities of hers, or he would never have invited her to be his guest on the ship. Because he was a man, he would have noticed other things about her, as well....

Stella felt guilty for thinking this because it seemed so disloyal to Eleni. Somehow, she had to put the awful confrontation with Stasio's fiancée out of her mind. For all Eleni's faults, Stasio still loved her. It wasn't Stella's place to judge her brother's choice of wife.

Heaven knows Stella was no judge of character! Theo had told her he'd always love her. That avowal was put to the test when he learned about the baby— and immediately left Athens. Stella had been such a gullible fool.

But as she felt her son's warm little body move closer and hug her hard around the waist, she could never be sorry that in loving Theo, Ari had been the result.

Stasio had saved him for her. If her brother could sacrifice six years of his own happiness so Stella could have her son, then she could stand by Stasio and learn to love Eleni. She'd just have to try harder, that was all.

In time, Eleni would learn to accept Ari and not see him as a threat to her happiness with Stasio. Stella could tell that her brother was more than ready to have a child of his own. If he and Eleni got pregnant right away, surely Eleni would become so focused on their own child, her fears would vanish.

Deciding a little levity was called for, Stella gave Ari's shoulder a squeeze. "How about a game of checkers, my little love? Whoever wins gets to tell the other person a bedtime story."

Ari's face brightened. "I know a lot of stories!"

"So do I. My checkers game is over there in that cupboard on the middle shelf. It's the yellow box."

"I'll get it!" he volunteered. Galvanized into action, he dashed across the room.

She sat down on the bed and patted the place next to her. "Bring it over here." When he'd done so, she asked, "Which color do you want?"

"I like black." There was a pause. "But if you want it, I'll take red."

Stella smiled down at her son. "I'm proud of you for being so generous. As a reward, you take the black checkers."

"Goody!"

Twenty minutes later, they were finishing the last game of their two-wins-out-of-three competition when she heard footsteps in the hall. The door to her bedroom had been left open.

"Hello? Anybody home?"

As her spirits plummeted, Ari's head bobbed up. "Who's that?" he whispered.

She leaned across the board and whispered back, "It's your uncle Nikos."

CHAPTER THIRTEEN

"WE'RE IN MY ROOM, Nikos!" she called to her brother.

"Who's we?" he demanded. His entrance always made an impact. In fairness to him, he *was* sinfully handsome, always dressed to perfection. This evening he wore a smoky-green silk sweater over black trousers.

The color emphasized his startling tan. His long dark hair contributed to the flamboyant quality his fans loved.

The flaw in his nature that made him difficult and contrary wasn't readily apparent at a first glance or even a second. But as Stella had learned over the years, it was there, and it could hurt.

She wanted to love him the same way she loved Stasio. Unfortunately, his personality kept everyone at a distance, particularly those who cared about him the most. The unpleasant encounter in Athens a few days ago was a case in point.

Ari scrambled off the bed and stared up at him in awe.

"Nikos?" She got to her feet. "This is my pride and joy. Meet my son, Ari." She put a hand on his back. "Ari? Say hi to your uncle."

"Hello, Uncle Nikos," came the bright voice. "I've seen a whole bunch of your pictures. You won a silver medal, huh?"

Had her son but known it, praise was one of the keys to her complicated brother's heart.

Nikos's face broke into the dazzling smile he was famous for. "I sure did."

"Can I see it?"

"I left it at home."

"Don't you live here?"

Nikos flashed Stella a message that said he was surprised by her son's question. "No. My home is in Switzerland."

"How come?"

"Because I can ski outside my back door."

Ari's eyes lit up. "Will you teach me how to ski?"

Such a flattering question took her brother by complete surprise. "There's no snow here."

"Mommy says we can come to your house. If you'll let us," he added in a quiet voice.

Ari's charm was working, even on Nikos who'd been prepared to send him packing without ever meeting him. For once, her brother was at a loss for words.

"I'm sure Nikos can find some time when he's not skiing to give you a few lessons—huh, Nikos?" She consciously imitated her son.

She could tell her brother was deep in thought. Finally he nodded. "Of course."

"Goody! Do you play checkers?"

He put his hands in his pockets. "Not for a long time."

"Do you want to play with me? You can choose the color."

Stella averted her eyes. She was waiting for his answer, curious to find out if her brother had grown too selfish, too hardened by his own inadequacies and his talks with Eleni, to accept a child's innocent gesture of friendship. Not just any child, of course. Ari was blood.

"I like black."

She exhaled the breath she'd been unconsciously holding.

"I do, too, but I'll play with the red. Mommy?" Ari turned to her. "Is it okay if Uncle Nikos and I play right now?"

"I think that's a terrific idea. I'll run downstairs and get us something to drink. Nikos? Do you want a beer?"

"If we have any."

"We do. Your favorite brand. This is your home, too. I always make sure there's plenty on hand for you."

Their eyes met again. Once more, his held that guilty look of surprise. She suspected it was because he knew he'd been so cruel to her earlier in the week. "Thanks. Where's everyone else?" he asked out of Ari's hearing.

"I'll tell you as soon as I come back."

She fled from the bedroom, not willing to enter into a discussion that would spoil this very important moment between him and her son. For everyone's future happiness, she wanted—needed—Nikos to bond with him.

She hurried down the stairs and through the villa to the kitchen. After rummaging in the refrigerator for two Oranginas and a beer, she grabbed a bag of pretzels from the pantry shelf and started back toward the stairs.

But she came to an abrupt halt when she saw Rachel and Stasio in the foyer, their arms loaded with shopping bags and luggage.

"Maybe I'm hallucinating," she muttered, mostly to herself.

Stasio's deep chuckle assured her the two of them were very real. His dark eyes shone like Ari's when he was excited about something. It sent chills up and down her spine.

"What's going on?" She looked from him to Rachel. "You're supposed to be on your way to California!"

"There's been a change in plans," he informed her.

"But what about Draco?" She was still addressing Rachel. "I thought he needed you."

"I needed Rachel more," Stasio interjected. "She'll visit him at a later date."

His quiet statement filled her with a fresh sense of wonder. The tone in his voice alerted Stella that her brother was in the grip of some profound emotion.

"Where's Eleni?" she blurted without thinking.

"In Athens. We called off our engagement last night."

What?

"Don't worry about the adoption. It's still going through as planned."

When Stella could find her voice again, she whispered, "How?"

"Today I asked Rachel to marry me, and she did me the great honor of saying yes."

Afraid to believe anything so absolutely fantastic, she focused her attention on Rachel.

"Please tell me this isn't a joke!"

"It's all true," Rachel assured her. Putting one of the packages on the floor, she held out her left hand for Stella to see. A brilliant solitaire diamond glittered on her ring finger.

"You're really marrying Stasio?"

"Yes." Those fathomless blue eyes of Rachel's never lied. They weren't lying now.

"We fell in love on the ship and decided we needed to do something about it." Stasio's simple declaration had the sound of truth.

From the beginning, Stella had questioned his motives for inviting Rachel to travel on the *Neptune* with him and Eleni. When she really thought about it, she realized it was just as out of character for Rachel to accept his invitation as for him to issue it. Her friend had always been independent to a fault. The visit to Chamonix had occurred at Stella's urging—and look how *that* had turned out.

When Rachel met Stasio in his office that afternoon, it must have been love at first sight for both of them.

Stella clutched the stair railing with her free hand. For two of her favorite people in the whole world to have found each other like this— she just couldn't believe it.

"We've already signed the papers with Costas," Stasio explained. "Everything's official. Our marriage will take place in three days. By the time our vows are said, Ari will be yours."

"We bought something for him to wear at the ceremony. Look at this!"

Rachel's excitement was contagious. Stella watched in almost feverish anticipation as her friend put down her packages and opened one of the boxes. She lifted a young boy's tuxedo from the tissue.

"Oh, Rachel!"

Down went the drinks before Stella, half laughing, half crying, reached for her soon-to-be sister-in-law. "I'm so happy, I'm about to burst."

"I feel the same way."

Stella was listening with her heart as well as her ears. Rachel's tear-filled response couldn't possibly be an act.

They really were in love. She could feel it.

They were getting married.

Rachel was going to be Stasio's wife.

"Wait right here. I have to tell Ari you're going to be his aunt. He'll be absolutely thrilled! And Nikos will be speechless for once in his life."

"Nikos?" The mention of their brother produced a strange look on Stasio's face.

Like Stella, Stasio had his reasons for being upset with Nikos, who'd aligned himself with Eleni over the situation with Ari.

"Yes." She gathered up the tray of drinks. "In all the excitement I forgot to tell you he arrived here a little while ago. He's upstairs playing checkers with Ari. I'll get both of them and be right down."

"Don't bother. We're coming up. Rachel needs to get settled in her room."

How odd to think that Nikos Athas was upstairs.

Six years ago, a much younger Rachel would have been witless with excitement to know she'd be seeing Europe's most dashing heartthrob in the next few seconds.

Now, today, the adult Rachel felt distinctly unaffected.

Quickly she put the miniature suit back in the box and bundled everything in her arms before following Stella up the stairs, with Stasio in close pursuit. Rachel was so madly in love with him, she didn't have to act the part of the besotted bride-to-be.

In his office earlier today, he'd told her they'd have

to convince Stella they were in love. Otherwise his sister wouldn't be able to handle the guilt of knowing her best friend had stepped in for Eleni at the last second to insure that Stasio could adopt her son.

Rachel agreed with him. It had to look like the real thing in word and deed. To the depths of her soul, it *was* the real thing.

Because she was making it possible for Ari to be adopted, she felt no guilt for playing a role she would covet until the day she died and beyond.

However, her guilt over the family's safety was another matter. But when she'd brought it up to Stasio again, reminding him that Sean was carrying out the orders of a dangerous enemy, she knew she'd irritated him.

"I've told you to let me worry about that. Our family has been threatened by this sort of thing ever since my father went into politics years ago. It's nothing new, believe me.

"What this Sean is doing is covert. That means he and General Berman—if that's who it turns out to be— live in fear of exposure and can only work in secret. I have my own resources for dealing with this kind of situation.

"While you were trying on wedding dresses, I made some phone calls to put the necessary security in place. Once we're married, we'll meet with officials in my government who were close friends of my father's. They'll begin an investigation of your father's death through diplomatic channels. You have nothing to worry about, Rachel, so let this be the end of the discussion."

She'd dropped that particular fear, but immediately

brought up another one. Exactly how was she supposed to behave around his family?

"Just follow my lead and everything will fall into place without problem."

Easy enough for Stasio to say, but at least she had no fear that he'd expect her to go to bed with him. He'd barely left Eleni's. In fact, it wouldn't surprise Rachel if, after they were married, he continued to see Eleni from time to time.

Two years of a physical relationship would make it difficult to walk away and never experience that fulfillment again. But it would kill Rachel to know he'd slipped out to see Eleni while he was still married to *her*.

Stasio had been vague about how long he and Rachel would have to wait before they divorced. She assumed six months at the most. For her own emotional survival, she couldn't live with him that long. The first time he went back to New York, she would go with him and then fly on to California.

Everyone would understand if she said she was going to visit Draco. When she never returned to Andros, Stasio could handle the explanations in his own way and mail her their divorce decree.

Getting out of his life would leave him free to pursue his own dreams—and find a woman he loved.

Getting out of his life would save him money, as well.

According to Carl, the Athas family was one of the wealthiest in Greece. But wealthy or not, it was still Stasio's hard-earned money keeping everyone safe. Because of her!

She had no idea of the kind of costs involved in providing security on the scale he was talking about.

She didn't want to know. Guilt over that alone was enough to make her want to leave Greece at the earliest possible moment.

When they reached the guest bedroom she'd vacated only this morning, Stasio put everything on the floor, then slid an arm around her shoulders. "I'm going to give the priest another call to let him know we've arrived on Andros. I'll be back in a few minutes." With a kiss to the side of her neck, he strode from the room. On his way out the door, he stopped to give his sister a quick hug.

She knew Stella had been watching them. Somehow Rachel had found the strength to keep standing, even though her body had started its inevitable reaction when he'd pressed his lips to her heated skin.

Now that he'd gone, Stella was beaming. "Put your things down and come to my room. I can't wait to see the look on Ari's face! As for Nikos…"

They stared at each other, exchanging silent messages.

"After what he said about me, I have to admit there've been a few times lately when I wished he could see me now."

Stella nodded. "He's going to see you, all right— and he's going to have a heart attack!"

"Have I changed so much?"

Her friend sobered. "No. You were always beautiful to me. But, of course, you've grown up and slimmed down. Besides, I'm a woman and I see you through a woman's eyes.

"But a man, and a brother in particular…that's different. Nikos was always attractive to women. He never had to work at it to keep them around. As a result, he's never stopped to analyze his behavior, which has sometimes been very cruel. But since you know all about that, we won't say any more on the subject.''

"No," Rachel agreed. "That's in the past where it belongs."

"But not forgotten?" Stella's eyes were suspiciously bright.

Rachel sucked in her breath. "Today Stasio asked me to marry him. He's made me so happy, I can barely remember what anything else feels like. Especially those negative emotions."

The part about being happy was the truth. It was why she could lie to her friend with impunity.

"Thank God you two found each other!" Stella cried. "You're so perfect for Stasio."

Smiling through the tears, Rachel followed Stella to her room farther down the hall.

When she walked in, Rachel immediately noted changes in Nikos. She had to admit they were all good. At a glance, the years had made him more attractive than ever.

"Rachel!"

It was Ari's happy cry that brought Nikos's dark head around. While Ari jumped off the bed, upsetting the checkers in his haste to greet her, Nikos simply stared at her for endless moments.

She was wearing a simple black wool suit, tailored and sophisticated. When she'd changed into it to go shopping, Stasio told her she had wonderful dress sense because her use of understatement brought out the glory of her hair.

The fashion consultant at Michelangelo's had put it a little differently. "With your voluptuous figure, my dear, understated clothing not only makes you look classy, but much more alluring to the opposite sex."

She hoped that was what Stasio had really meant, though he hadn't put it in quite those words.

Although he wasn't marrying her for love, she still wanted him to be proud of her. To the world, she would be Mrs. Stasio Athas. She wanted to look the part for him.

Was it less than a month ago that she'd wanted to look the part for Nikos?

Maybe it was because of Stasio's proposal of marriage, Rachel didn't exactly know, but as she continued to look at his younger brother, she felt emboldened enough to say, "Don't tell me you don't remember me, Nikos. The American Army brat?" She lightened her teasing with a smile.

"I thought if nothing else, my 'orange' hair would give me away. Oddly enough, I never did join the circus. Perhaps even odder from your point of view, I'm going to be marrying your brother in a few days. I guess you were wrong about his opinion of military trash. But that's okay. I won't hold it against you since we're going to be in-laws soon and I'm prepared to love you…as a brother.

"Life's ironic, isn't it? I used to have a terrible crush on you. Who would've thought that six years later I'd end up in love with Stasio—and about to become your sister-in-law?"

Probably no speech delivered by Rachel had ever given her more pleasure. She could hear Stella in the background attempting to stifle her laughter. Ari, looking puzzled, still had his arm wrapped around his mother's waist.

There was a charged silence as a ruddy color stained Nikos's tanned cheeks.

Well, well, he did have a conscience.

Slowly he got to his feet.

"Nikos!" She laughed. "I was only kidding you. Don't look so serious. How about a hug?"

She walked toward him and gave him a warm embrace. His body was rigid. Looking up into his handsome troubled face, she said, "It's been a long time. Please don't blame yourself for something I overheard years ago.

"Anyway, we're all adults now, and I love Stasio very much, so I couldn't bear for there to be any animosity between us. Tell me you're happy to see me."

"I'm happy!" Ari piped up.

With a smile, Rachel turned to him. "So am I, darling."

"Stasio brought you back, huh?"

"Yes, he did. We're getting married in that little church up on the hillside. Nikos and you and your mommy are going to be there in the front pew. And guess what? Anna and Giorgio will be there, too. And guess what else?"

"What?" His eyes shone like stars.

"Stasio and I bought you something special to wear for the wedding."

"You did?"

"Yes."

"Where is it?"

"In that box."

He stared at it, then he stared up at her. "I love you, Rachel."

"I love you, too."

A thoughtful expression crossed his face. "Is Eleni sad?"

Such a grown-up question for a small boy. His innate

empathy for others was one of Ari's most endearing traits. Rachel had trouble swallowing.

"I think so. We'll have to hope she feels better one day soon. Sometimes people love each other but it doesn't work out for them to live together.

"Eleni is a lovely person. If she weren't, your uncle wouldn't have loved her for so long. In time, she'll meet a man who's right for her and they'll get married."

"I'm glad you're going to marry Stasi. 'Cause on the ship he told me you made him happy."

Those words filled her with a warmth that radiated throughout her whole body.

"I felt the same way about him."

"He got mad when you kept reading to Mrs. De-Maio."

Oh, Ari, Ari. "He did?"

"Yes. He said he wanted you to read to *him* in bed."

Scorching heat rose swiftly up her neck into her face. She didn't dare look at Stella.

The comment uttered in all naiveté broke Nikos's long silence. "Ari? I think you'd better stop. She's blushing. Rachel never could hide her embarrassment."

"Stasi says that's 'cause she's a redhead."

"She's definitely that," Nikos muttered.

For the first time since she'd known him, Rachel felt Nikos's gaze wandering over her face and figure in the way she would have died for six years ago. The expression in a man's eyes was unmistakable when he found a woman attractive.

"Come on, Ari," Stella said. "Let's go into Rachel's room and see that new outfit."

"How long have you known my brother?" Nikos asked quietly after Stella and Ari had gone out the door.

"About ten days."

"Why do I have a hard time believing that?"

"I realize this has come as a shock to you. It came as an even greater one to me!"

"Shock doesn't quite cover it. Eleni must be suicidal."

Rachel shuddered. "I hope you're joking."

"If you're telling the truth, what kind of power does Stasio have over you that he could get a perfect stranger to marry him? All to make sure he can adopt Stella's son…?"

"You live in French Switzerland, Nikos. You know the saying *coup de foudre?* Love at first sight?"

His eyes narrowed on her face. "I'll concede you've turned into a breathtaking woman. Stasio would have to be blind not to notice."

"Thank you." She smiled. "Coming from you, that's a real compliment."

"But don't take me for a fool. Eleni was convinced you've been carrying on an affair with him. Now that I've seen and heard you, I believe it."

"Eleni's wrong, and so are you."

"You don't think your marriage is going to stop him from seeing her, do you?"

No. I don't think that, but I'm not going to give you the satisfaction of gloating over it.

"We'll be making vows before God to love and cherish only each other," she answered instead. "Your brother is an honorable man. He wouldn't make such an oath if he didn't know he could be true to it."

She could say that and mean it because when Stasio *did* fall in love, it would be the forever kind.

"You haven't changed, Rachel. When you came to Chamonix, you pretended to be a naive little innocent living in a fairy tale. But you knew exactly what you were doing when you chose to befriend Stella.''

"I did," Rachel said defiantly. "Stella was—and still is—the sweetest, nicest, kindest person I've ever known."

He gave her a patronizing nod. "Beautifully said. And now you're beautifully grown up and back in her life, the way you always intended." Nikos shrugged contemptuously. "Do you honestly expect me to believe it was a mere coincidence that you arrived at the exact moment Stasio needed someone to fit into his plans?"

"You made up your mind about me years ago, Nikos. I'm not asking you to believe anything."

"That's good, because I don't. Your timing was too perfect. The love-at-first-sight business won't wash."

"Why are you so passionate about this? Could it be that you're worried because despite the countless number of women you've known, you've never actually been in love? So you don't want to believe it could happen to anyone else. Least of all, your brother."

His expression turned to thunder. "Don't try to psychoanalyze me!"

"Then try not to walk around with such an enormous chip on your shoulder. You have the potential to be a wonderful man, you know. I don't want to sound condescending. But I do know that until you take yourself seriously, you're not going to take any of your relationships seriously, either."

He blinked. "What in the hell is that supposed to mean?"

"I thought that by now you'd be your own man, rather than working for a company like Brousillac. Somehow, I could see you establishing your own ski schools throughout Europe and the States. You're one of the best skiers in the world, and you have an Olympic medal to prove it. But that should only have been a starting point. For the life of me, I can't understand why you haven't capitalized on such a talent.

"It could work for you in a hundred different ways and be infinitely more satisfying than selling someone else's equipment. You, Nikos Athas, have something millions of men would give anything to possess—and you don't even know it."

"She's right."

Rachel turned around to see Stasio standing in the doorway with his hands on his hips. She'd been so intent on her conversation with Nikos, she hadn't even realized they had an audience.

The two brothers nodded to each other.

"Good to see you, Nikos. I'm sorry to interrupt, but Rachel and I have an appointment. We won't be long. When we get back, it would be nice to assemble the family and talk about the wedding."

"Why the rush, Stasio? I thought your original plan was to be married over the holidays. It hasn't even been twenty-four hours since you ended things with Eleni."

Stasio's eyes held an enigmatic gleam. "Haven't you ever heard the phrase 'love waits for no man'? Rachel and I need to be married *now*. I want her to be my wife as soon as possible."

If only that was true

"I had no idea you were such a romantic." Nikos's mocking comment couldn't hide the fact that he was shocked and puzzled by his brother's behavior.

Rachel couldn't blame him. Stasio was giving a masterful performance of a man in love.

"I guess there are still things to be learned, even between brothers."

Rachel wanted to tell Nikos they were acting quickly because of safety concerns. Stasio had convinced her that a marriage in the next few days would solve two immediate problems. The sooner she was Mrs. Stasio Athas, the sooner his people could fine-tune the security measures they were putting in place. As well, there would be less chance of Sean Dodd prematurely learning her whereabouts from the press.

But Stasio had also explained that he didn't want to tell any of this to the rest of the family yet. Not only would it alarm Stella unnecessarily, it would give Nikos more ammunition to go on playing devil's advocate for his own selfish reasons.

Rachel could see Stasio's point on both counts and agreed with him. The only thing to do was brave this out in front of Nikos. Their marriage was for Stella and Ari, the worthiest of causes.

Having established Ari's adoption as their top priority, the wisest course for Rachel was to remain silent and let Stasio handle this. She had infinite trust in his judgment. *She loved him.*

"Have you even considered how this is going to hurt Eleni?"

"I'm not in love with her. Is there any alternative? Could you imagine anything crueler than to lock us both in a marriage without love on both parts?"

His questions gave Nikos pause. For a moment the mask seemed to fall away. "Then why didn't you break up with her a long time ago?"

Stasio's dark head was bowed. "Because I didn't know I wasn't in love with her until I met Rachel."

His words inscribed themselves in every cell of her body.

"Nikos…" His voice sounded oddly grave. "When you meet the right woman, you'll remember this conversation and you'll understand." He turned to Rachel. "Shall we go, darling? The priest will be waiting."

The unexpected endearment fell so easily from Stasio's lips, Rachel was caught off guard by it. Before she left the room, her glance happened to meet his brother's. He flashed her a private smile reminiscent of the old Nikos. She could almost hear him saying, "You're not fooling me. Besides, you were in love with me six years ago. I can have you anytime I want and we both know it."

CHAPTER FOURTEEN

"So where do we go from here, Colonel? She's not in there, and we haven't seen Carl Gordon go in or out of the place in a couple of days."

"I don't know how Rachel did it, but she can smell that I'm after her and she tipped him off. I thought for sure we had him cornered at the hospital. Bloody hell, T.J.!"

"Colonel, if we saw him come and go from this place all last week, then she warned him off some time after we pulled the gas-leak stunt. Otherwise, he would've come back to work."

"Yeah? So what are you getting at?"

"Well, she had to have a way to contact him."

"You know, T.J.? Sometimes your brilliance astounds me. Of course she had a way, you idiot!"

"All I'm getting at is that they probably used the phone to make contact. As I see it, if we could get hold of the phone bills coming to this address, we could get a list of every call he's made locally or long distance. One of them will lead us to her."

"I'm not so sure. Rachel's sly. She's managed to elude us so far."

"Didn't you find Dr. Rich by going through Colonel Maynard's phone bills?"

"That was one man's phone records, T.J. Do you

have any idea how many hundreds, maybe thousands, of calls originate from this place every month?''

''Yes, but since we know Carl Gordon wasn't on to us until we had the building evacuated, we can assume he and Rachel probably had very recent phone contact. We'd only need to see the bills for the last month or so, right? She probably spoke to him a few times *before* the gas leak, and we could try finding her number that way.''

The Colonel grunted.

''Was that a yes or a no?''

''It means your idea's the only one we've got, and General Berman's waiting for those negatives. Let's get busy.''

''Yes, sir!''

''STASIO, DARLING?''

''I'm afraid not, Eleni.''

''Nikos! Thank heaven it's you! Have you heard what's happened?''

''Why do you think I'm calling?''

''Your brother ended our engagement last night.'' He could hear her swallow back a sob. ''You and I know why, don't we? He's been having an affair with her for who knows how long.''

''No. I'll swear on my mother's grave that he never laid eyes on Rachel until she went to his office just before they sailed.''

''How can you go on defending him?''

''If I were on his side, would I be talking to you now?''

There was a prolonged silence. ''It's a nightmare.''

''It's a very clever setup. Machiavellian, even.''

''What are you talking about?''

"Something's not right here. You and I both know it. Rachel has duped my brother. Stasio actually believes he's in love with her."

"You think I don't realize that?" she cried out. "He's been a different person since that trip."

"She did her research very carefully. But after the things she said to me tonight, she unwittingly gave herself away."

"What do you mean?"

"I mean I know her arrival at Stasio's office was part of some grand design orchestrated down to the last detail by Rachel herself. There aren't any coincidences here. She doesn't operate that way."

Eleni made a sound of protest. "You didn't talk like this about her earlier. You said she was some sort of obese, pathetic creature unworthy of a man's notice!"

"If you recall, Eleni, I was describing her outward appearance. I never said there was anything wrong with her brain.

"Back in Switzerland years ago, I spotted her right away as a conniving little opportunist who cold-bloodedly befriended Stella as soon as she found out how much the family was worth.

"When she realized my sister wasn't much of a student, Rachel started doing her homework for her. If I brought Stella back late from a weekend trip, Rachel would ingratiate herself by covering for her in front of the headmistress. As a reward, Stella invited her to Geneva on a weekend trip, all expenses paid.

"Once Rachel found out that being Stella Athas's best friend brought monetary perks, she seized every opportunity to become indispensable to her.

"After watching all this happen, I had to do something to break them up. Since I knew Stella would defend Rachel to the death, I made sure Rachel heard every word I said to my sister. I admit I was a bit of a bastard but I had to insure a permanent separation.'' He took a deep breath. ''Obviously I did a better job than I thought.''

''How do you mean?''

''Do you remember *The Count of Monte Cristo* by Dumas? What is it they call that book? The classic tale of revenge?''

''Yes?''

''Rachel is the female version of Edmond Dantes. She never forgave me for ending her relationship with Stella. Over the past six years she's been plotting her own revenge.

''I knew she was smart, but I never realized just how cunning. From the beginning she wanted me. I'm sure her teenage fantasy was to end up married to me.

''I saw the look in her eyes tonight. She still wants me. But she realized Stasio was the one who controlled the money and held the power. She decided to go for him instead.''

''I don't understand how this could have happened!''

''It's simple. She's been watching our family for a long time, Eleni. To give you one example, she can tell you everything about my work for Brousillac. If I didn't know the truth, I'd actually be flattered by her interest in my career.

''Hell— she brought up ideas for my future that made a lot of sense. The point is, they couldn't possibly have been spontaneous. What she had to say about my life took a lot of thought and deliberation.

''It's clear she knows private details about everybody in the Athas family. Stella, Stasio, Ari…she's been aware of our every move.

"I'm positive that showing up at Stasio's office with the excuse that she wanted Stella's address was all part of a carefully calculated charade. Before approaching him she underwent a total transformation, then made herself out to be one of my victims." He twisted his mouth. "That combination was irresistible to Stasio."

"Maybe you're right about her motives, but she had to be beautiful to begin with, Nikos."

"I sure as hell didn't see it at the time."

"That's because she was a lot younger then, and your suspicions about her got in the way. But none of that matters now. What I can't figure out is how she could've known I'd decide not to go on the ship with Stasio. I didn't know myself until we fought over the phone and I threatened him."

"Of course she couldn't have known that," Nikos broke in. "Unfortunately, your absence played right into her hands. She learned long ago that Ari was the key to Stasio's heart. A whole week to befriend the boy and make my brother fall for her—and all without any interference from you? She must have rubbed her hands with glee! I told you not going on that trip was a big mistake."

"If all this is true, then we've got to do something to make Stasio see it. I can't lose him, Nikos!"

"I'm afraid it might be too late. They're with the priest right now."

"*What?*"

"Stasio's determined to marry her in three days' time."

Eleni gave an agonized cry. "How could he do this to me? How could he humiliate me this way?"

"In all fairness to my brother, he's not in a rational frame of mind right now. This monumental change in him can be laid squarely at Rachel's feet,'' Nikos muttered.

"We've got to find a way to stop them!"

"It won't do any good to go through Stella. Rachel got her hooks into my sister years ago. As for Ari, he thinks the sun rises and sets with her.''

"Then talk to Costas. He's the one person Stasio listens to. If you could persuade him that Rachel's a con artist, he could prevent the adoption from taking place or at least postpone it until you expose her as a fraud.''

"That might work, but he can't prevent Stasio from marrying Rachel if that's what my brother wants to do.''

"Are you saying Stasio's so crazy about her, he'll go ahead with the ceremony, Ari or no Ari?''

Nikos chewed on his lower lip. "I don't know. To be honest, I've never seen my brother act this way before. There's something about him...."

"Thanks a *lot*, Nikos.''

Her pain put him on the defensive, as if somehow this were all his fault.

"You think *I* like the situation? If something isn't done, that little gold digger's going to be my sister-in-law. It would be her ultimate revenge against me, wouldn't it?'' He shook his head. "I couldn't stand having her become part of the family.''

"Then do something about it!''

"I intend to,'' he said in an absent tone.

One idea took root in his mind. There was nothing Stasio detested more than a liar with an agenda. All Nikos had to do was confront his older brother with undeniable proof.

"When?''

"Tonight. But first I need to do some reconnoitering of my own before Rachel and Stasio get back. I'll call you in the morning."

"I'm counting on you, Nikos. Don't let me down."

"Don't worry, Eleni. I have a plan. Talk to you later."

He hung up the receiver.

"Two can play at this game, Rachel Maynard. You think it's all going your way. You can think again."

Without hesitation he walked from his suite to the other side of the villa, where his sister's bedroom was located. The first order of business was to mend fences with Stella, repair the damage he'd done in a couple of well-intentioned—but perhaps ill-advised—conversations, the most recent one at the house in Athens last week.

Reparations were necessary if he was going to elicit any information about Rachel. He wanted to know where she'd been living and what she'd been doing for the past six years.

It wouldn't be easy to win back Stella's trust. He'd definitely need help. For that he would use his nephew.

Tomorrow would be soon enough to get close to the little boy. Ari had spent an entire week on the ship with Rachel. All Nikos had to do was act the loving uncle with a little more aggression and he could solicit the information he required to build his case against Rachel.

As for Rachel herself, Nikos knew exactly how he'd approach her—if Stasio gave him the chance.

Nikos had yet to learn if his brother had spent every night in her bed while they were on the ship. Now that Stasio was home on Andros, would he steal to his own room before sunrise for propriety's sake, or was her magic too powerful for even his brother to resist?

No matter how far Nikos reached back, he could never remember Stasio losing his head over a woman before.

Knocking on Stella's door, he called out, "Are you still up?"

"Come in, Nikos."

"Hi." After he'd entered, he glanced quickly around the room. "Where's Ari?"

"He's in the tub playing with some new toys I bought him."

"Good. I'm glad we're alone for a few minutes."

A wary expression crossed her face. The older she was getting, the more she reminded him of their mother. He wished there was no resemblance. That look troubled his conscience.

"Stella, I realize that if I were to apologize to you for the way I treated you in front of Eleni, you still wouldn't be able to forgive me.

"The truth is, I'd like your forgiveness. But I understand how you must feel. I just wanted to say that I can see why Stasio's always loved Ari. I've only spent an hour with him, yet already I feel an attachment I can't explain." Oddly enough, in saying the words, he found they were the truth.

"You always could beat me at checkers, Stella. All I had to do was glimpse that impish smile of his when he was winning our third game in a row, and it was like déjà vu."

Stella's head was bowed. She hadn't said a word but he knew she was listening.

"I know I haven't been the kind of brother who was there for you, like Stasio.

"My problem is, I never really tried to develop more of a relationship because I was too concerned about myself. I still am. I'm selfish—I admit it. I'll probably never change. But I have eyes, and I can see that you and Ari belong together.

"He may love his foster parents, but he obviously loves you, too. Far be it from me to cause either of you any further grief. I guess what I'm trying to say is, I support you in your decision."

"Thank you," she said in a quiet voice, still not looking at him. "It means more than you know."

"You're welcome. As for Eleni, I have to admit I've always liked her. From the beginning she made a point of being nice to me. She even came to some of my ski races. Maybe that's why I've been in her corner and didn't stop to think of Ari's importance in your life." He paused. "You have to admit Stasio took an awfully long time to propose to Eleni. It hurt her a lot."

She nodded. "I often wondered why she bothered to hang on."

Many times Nikos had asked the same question.

"Well, now that their engagement's been called off, it's a moot point."

"You're right," she asserted, lifting her head. "He's in love with Rachel."

"At first I thought that whole situation was ludicrous. Then I heard something in Stasio's voice that led me to believe he might not be lying, after all."

"He isn't!" she said vigorously. "Nikos... Since you're speaking frankly, would you mind telling me what it was about Rachel that you despised so much?"

Before he could answer, she went on. "Have you considered what will happen after she and Stasio are married? How will any of us be able to pull together as a family if you're as cruel to her now as you were then?''

He rubbed the back of his neck. ''Your question's valid. In Switzerland I felt she was using you. I'm sorry, but from my perspective she seemed obsessive where you were concerned, going out of her way to perform the smallest service for you, rushing to do your homework for you, and so on. I didn't think it was healthy.''

Stella flashed him a sad smile. ''I was the unhealthy one. Several months after my arrival, she found out I was contemplating suicide.''

Nikos stared at her.

''I never told anyone, especially not Stasio. But Rachel knew. Instead of probing or asking embarrassing questions, she just let me cry. She understood what I needed because she'd been through heartache of her own. I clung to her because she was so kind to me. The fact is, she accepted me as I was. She helped me in so *many* ways. Nikos, Rachel is and was my *friend*.''

Nikos felt himself incapable of response. He had no idea what to say.

Stella continued. ''The first few times you came by the school for a visit, she forced me to go with you, even when my depression kept me from wanting to do anything. But she knew you were good for me and could make me laugh.''

Good Lord. He'd never guessed any of this.

''In time her friendship brought a measure of peace to me. She helped pull me out of that darkness so I could live with the pain of giving up Ari.

''Sometimes we'd hike to a field of narcissus high above Lac Leman and read our favorite books out loud to each other. Other times we'd sit there and talk for hours.

"You figured heavily in our conversations. We'd speculate on your future, all the things you could become because of your charisma and great athleticism. She imagined you would become an ambassador for Greece the way Jean-Claude Killy did for France. With that smile of yours, she said, you couldn't lose.

"Anyway, we discussed everything, including our own futures. I never had much more ambition than to be a wife and mother. Rachel wanted to join the American Air Force and eventually become a pilot. Because of her father's experiences, she had more stories to tell about space than you could believe.

"It was while I listened to her tales that she got me started eating again. She'd bring surprise treats in her backpack. Chocolate, mocha yogurts, fresh fruit. Out of our sadness, we created a happy little world for ourselves there in Montreux, Rachel and I.

"After everything she did for me, you can't imagine how thrilled I was when you told me I could come to Chamonix and bring a friend. It meant I could pay her back a little for all the emotional support she'd given me."

Nikos stood there in a quandary. He'd never known his sister to lie. But the picture she'd painted of Rachel was such a far cry from his own interpretation, he didn't know what to think.

"I'm sorry I ruined it for you, Stella," he whispered.

"Sorry enough to apologize to Rachel?"

"At the first opportunity, I'll talk to her." It would take more than Stella's say-so to change his mind about Rachel's true agenda. Maybe she *was* innocent, once.

But if that was so, why had she waited so many years before trying to find Stella again?

None of it made sense to Nikos unless, as he'd assumed from the beginning, she wanted the money and notoriety that came with being Mrs. Stasio Athas.

"Nikos?" Ari cried in delight. "I didn't know you were here."

He turned his head and smiled down at his nephew, who'd run into the bedroom with a blue towel hitched around his lean body, wet hair plastered to his head. He reminded Nikos of a much younger Stasio out swimming beyond the rocks.

Stella rushed toward him with a clean pair of pajamas.

"Did you come to play another game of checkers with me before I go to bed, Uncle Nikos?"

"There's nothing I'd like more, even if you did beat me. But it's getting late. How'd you like to spend some time with me tomorrow instead?"

"Goody!"

Stella glanced up at him in surprise. "Really?"

"Since there's going to be a wedding right away, you'll probably be busy helping Rachel all day. I thought Ari and I could go down to the port and do some fishing."

"Can I, Mommy?" His eyes shone as he begged for her permission.

She swooped down and kissed the end of his nose. "That sounds like fun."

Turning to Nikos once more, she said, "If you're sure…"

"Of course. It's been ages since I left the ski circuit to spend time with my family."

The mention of the word "family" seemed to please

his sister. He could tell by the soft look in her eyes. So far, so good.

"Tell me something, Ari. Are uncles entitled to a hug good-night, or do you only give them to mothers?"

Ari laughed. "You're silly, Uncle Nikos." He ran toward Nikos and into his outstretched arms. "What time are we going fishing tomorrow?"

"How about after breakfast?"

"What time is my breakfast, Mommy?"

"About eight o'clock."

Nikos put a hand on his nephew's shoulder. "That settles it. We'll leave at eight-thirty."

"Goody! Mommy?" he cried excitedly. "Can I call Anna and Giorgio before I go to bed? I want to tell them I'm going fishing with Uncle Nikos!"

Nikos watched to see if the mention of Ari's foster parents upset his sister. To his amazement he detected no shadows as she said, "I think that's a wonderful idea. I bet they've been waiting to hear all your news."

When Ari had hurried over to the phone, Stella turned to Nikos. Tears had sprung into her brown eyes. "Thank you for making Ari feel part of the family."

"He's very easy to like." It was the truth.

As for Rachel...

He glanced at his watch, wondering what was keeping her and Stasio. They'd been gone a couple of hours already. The visit to the priest would only have taken twenty minutes at the most.

Actually he could think of something they might be doing, but for some odd reason the picture of Rachel in his brother's arms bothered him a lot more than he wanted to admit.

CHAPTER FIFTEEN

RACHEL LEFT THE SANCTUARY ahead of Stasio and walked toward the low retaining wall. There was no rain tonight. From the church grounds, the lights of Palaiopolis twinkled like sparkling jewels thrown down the mountainside to the sea.

"I thought this place looked like fairyland from the helicopter. Tonight I have to pinch myself to believe any of it's real."

Her breath caught as she felt his hands slide up her arms from behind and draw her back against him. His chin rested in her hair. Despite the thickness of her wool suit jacket, she could feel his warmth. His nearness set her body trembling with excitement, with happiness, with hope.

"Tonight is the first time I've had any peace since Stella came into my bedroom late one night and told me she was expecting a baby. We were still grieving over Father's death. Nikos couldn't handle the silence at the villa. He'd left to party with some ski buddies in Austria.

"I envied him his ability to compartmentalize his grief and work off the worst of it through drinking and physical activity. I'm afraid I'm not like that. During a crisis, I tend to brood and bury myself in more work.

"When I learned my sister had a child on the way, with no husband to love or support them, I felt helpless.

There was Stella looking to me for answers. But for once in my life, the situation was beyond my experience.

"I talked at length with her doctor. Together we discussed her options, but no solution seemed right. By the time she chose to give up the baby for adoption, I found I couldn't. In some way, the baby had become important to me.

"What appalls me now is that I was so blinded by my own feelings, I couldn't see that Stella had made the decision she did so *I* wouldn't be burdened. Because of me, she missed out on those vital years of Ari's life."

Rachel turned in his arms and looked up at him. "Don't do this to yourself, Stasio. Only God has the power to look into the soul of another human being and know what's right for him or her."

"Do you know how many times my brother has accused me of playing the role of God?"

Without conscious thought, she let her hands slide up the front of his suit jacket. "Nikos abdicated his responsibility," she reminded him. "Someone had to help Stella. You did the best you could with the facts as you knew them. Most importantly, you made your decision out of pure love for your sister and her baby.

"Because you kept Ari from being adopted by anyone else, he now has his foster parents *and* his birth mother in his life. As for your sister, she's united with her son. Her grieving has come to an end. Those are priceless gifts only you could have given to them."

Stasio's dark eyes penetrated hers. "Rachel," he whispered. His head descended and she felt his mouth seek hers.

Rachel had been kissed before, but she'd never been

in love. The driving force of his passion produced sensations like nothing she'd ever experienced in her life. Her mouth, like her heart, melted into his, helpless to do otherwise. She slipped her arms around his neck to bring him closer, the way she'd wanted to when they'd danced in the library.

There was so much to tell him, so much she needed to show him, her mouth and body exploded with excitement. For too long, she'd had to hold in her feelings. Now, unbelievably, Stasio had lifted her from the ground so their faces were level.

It was as if he'd just given her permission to do whatever she wanted—to kiss his dark hair, his eyes, his cheeks, his lips, over and over again.

Her body molded to his as if it had a will of its own. She had no idea how many times she cried out his name. She was so overwhelmed by her feelings, time and place had no meaning. Not until she was suddenly blinded by the headlights of a car coming up the hill did she realize how out of control she was.

Though it passed by without stopping, leaving them to their privacy once more, the moment had given her pause to reflect that they were still on church grounds.

Mortified by her behavior, she buried her face against his shoulder and asked him to lower her to the ground.

Without saying a word, he did.

It had only been a kiss to Stasio. He was a man who for the past two years had shared a physical relationship with Eleni—or so Rachel assumed. She could imagine how much he was missing Eleni, even if he'd decided against marrying her.

The blame for this incident rested squarely on Rachel's shoulders. She was the one who'd turned a kiss of gratitude into a torrent of unbridled passion. The whole situation had left her shaken and out of breath.

"I haven't been kissed like that since college," she felt compelled to explain.

"What about Manny?"

"I didn't have that kind of relationship with him. It seemed wrong to kiss him unless I meant it. Since I didn't want him to get the wrong idea, I made sure he never got the opportunity."

"Then I can assume you meant it with me."

"Well, yes!" she blurted, her face hot with embarrassment. "For one thing, you're not liable to take it the wrong way!"

His deep chuckle always resonated to her bones, but tonight it also irritated her.

"As a meaningful kiss, then, how did it feel?"

"You know how it felt!" came her cross retort. "I loved it. I was completely out of control and behaved like…like a wanton."

"In case you hadn't noticed, I'm not complaining."

"Of course not. You wouldn't. And you'd never tell me if it left a lot to be desired because you're a gentleman. So let's forget the whole thing, if you don't mind."

He took her arm and they started walking toward the street where he'd parked his Maserati. "Will *you* be able to forget it?" He opened the passenger door for her.

"No. I'm sure I won't."

He threw back his head and laughed. "An honest woman. Whatever you do, Rachel, don't change."

I'm not all that honest, Stasio. You still don't know how I plotted to get Nikos to marry me. That's one secret I hope never comes to light. If you knew the truth, you wouldn't like me anymore.

I know you'll probably never love me, but I want you to like me.

STASIO FOUGHT TO KEEP his hands steady on the wheel. Tonight he'd just had his baptism of fire. Talk about kissing! He felt as if the two of them had invented it.

If she could respond to him like this during their first encounter, he didn't know how he was going to wait until she was his legally wedded wife.

Thank heaven he only had to endure two more nights alone. If that kiss had gone on a second longer, he wouldn't have been able to control himself.

Rachel believed they'd be getting a divorce down the road. He would only allow her to think that until they'd said their vows. Once he'd wrung the confession from her lips that she was as in love with him as he was with her, everything was going to change.

She *did* love him. Even before tonight, he'd known it in his gut. Their kiss had said everything they couldn't say yet, for too many reasons. But the time was near when they'd hold nothing back. Not words, not love.

He wanted to take her away on a long honeymoon. But until the men trying to harm her were in custody, he needed to be on the premises to protect everyone he loved.

"I was hoping to get the family together to start making definite plans for the wedding. But it's too late for tonight." The priest had been delayed because of an emergency in the village, and it was now almost ten o'clock.

"I agree. I'm sure Ari's asleep. No doubt Stella is,

too. Now that she's a mother with an active little boy, her life is no longer her own.''

Stasio cast her a covert glance. ''Are you tired?''

He noticed the way her breasts suddenly rose and fell before she answered with a vague yes.

You're lying, Rachel. You feel as alive as I do.

''Well, tomorrow will be soon enough to take care of the arrangements.''

''The priest was very sweet.''

''He's an old friend of the family.''

''The one who taught me Greek was more forbidding.''

''How old was he?''

''Maybe the same age as Manny. Early sixties.''

''Then he probably forced himself to be gruff to withstand your considerable charms.''

She turned to him with a smile. ''You think that explains it? He was relentless when it came to pronunciation.''

''Sometimes your accent and intonation sound completely Greek. He taught you very well.''

She faced the front of the car again. ''Thank you, but there's still so much to learn. Ari has taught me quite a lot already.''

''Thanks to Giorgio and Anna, his Greek is flawless. Speaking of them, I'll call New York as soon as we reach home. The company jet will be standing by to fly them over tomorrow night.''

''What do you think their feelings are right now?''

''They've been upset since the day I told them Stella was ready to claim him.''

''Of course. But when they see her and Ari together, they'll realize this was right, and they'll feel differently.

Stella's so loving and generous, she'll win them around. I'm sure of it.''

"I agree. If anyone can do that, she will.''

"Stella confided to me that if they'll come, she wants them to move back to Greece. No matter how much Ari loves her, she feels it would be better for him if they're around too. She's very aware that they've invested almost six years of their lives in him, and she'd hate to deprive them of watching him grow up.''

"My sister possesses a lot of my mother's wisdom. But as you know, Giorgio and Anna were against the idea before. They do have a business in New York…''

"Well, of course, it'll have to be their decision. But do you think they're resisting because they haven't met Stella yet?''

Stasio felt as though Rachel were already his wife. They could discuss anything. She always made sense and he inevitably felt better after their talks.

"You may be right. Whatever happens, we'll work something out.'' He reflected for a moment. "It's also possible they'll change their minds about coming back after this separation from Ari.''

"He's such a delightful child. I'm not even related to your nephew and already I'm dreading the thought of leaving him when I have to go back to the States.''

You're not going anywhere, my love. Later, after we're married, if you still want to visit Manny, we'll go together.

"Are you hungry? Thirsty? There's a *taverna* not far from here with a live band. We could stop for a little while before we go home.'' He needed to hold her again. That kiss had not only left him unassuaged, it had made the fire burn hotter.

Glancing over, he watched her clasp her hands nervously together. Normally she was more composed. He stifled a groan of satisfaction. She was debating whether to say yes or no.

"If you're going to make that phone call, I think we'd better get back right away."

"Have you forgotten the seven-hour difference? It's only midafternoon in New York. There's still plenty of time to make contact."

"Well, to be honest, I was really thinking about Nikos."

The mention of his brother sent an unprecedented stab of jealousy through Stasio's heart. *After all this time, do you still have feelings for Nikos?*

"What about him?" he asked.

"Since he's rarely home, I thought maybe he'd enjoy your company, especially if Stella and Ari are already in bed. Unless, of course, he's seeing a woman."

He detected a curious tremor in her voice. Maybe she realized she'd sounded too eager just now. His hands tightened on the steering wheel.

"I don't think so. So far, his taste hasn't run to Greek women."

Rachel smoothed a lock of hair away from her face, giving him another glimpse of her youthful profile. "That's probably because he hasn't met anyone who could live up to your mother's image."

"You're very perceptive," he murmured, growing more and more disenchanted with the trend of this conversation. "As for his waiting up for me, that remains to be seen." It would be a first for Nikos. "But as usual, you're right. He's flown all the way from Switzerland. The least I can do is be there."

He heard her sharp intake of breath. "Stasio? If I've offended you in some way, I'm sorry. Naturally I'd love to go to that bar with you. I just sense that because I told you those things about Nikos—and what he said six years ago—it might have strained your relationship with him.

"Before I confided in Stella, I made her promise she wouldn't hold it against your brother. The last thing I ever meant to do was cause any kind of rift in your family."

"You haven't. I'm sorry if I gave you that impression."

Lord, I hope that's all this is about, Rachel.

But for the rest of the short drive back to the villa, he kept remembering a certain conversation with Eleni.

"You can't see that the proverbial ugly duckling has changed into a swan? If I were Rachel and I'd heard a man say all those awful things about me, I'd come back for the sheer pleasure of revenge."

"Rachel's not like that."

"All women are like that...."

The tires screeched as he drove through the gates to the villa. All appeared quiet as he pulled to a stop in front and handed Rachel from the car. The housekeeper happened to be in the foyer as he opened the front door.

"*Kalispera,* Kyrie Athas. Despinis Maynard."

"*Kalispera,* Melina," they both answered at the same time. This produced a smile from Rachel.

"Is my brother around?"

"*Ochi.*" No.

The news shouldn't have pleased Stasio, but it did. "Do you know where he went?"

"He didn't say. Your sister and the little one are asleep."

"Good. I guess you heard there's going to be a wedding on Thursday."

Melina nodded.

"We'd like you and your husband, Yannis, to be part of it," Rachel spoke up in her best Greek. Stasio was proud of her continual attempts to converse in his native tongue.

"Stella regards the two of you like an aunt and uncle. And Ari thinks you're wonderful. He says he likes you better than Barbara."

"Bar-ba-ra?" the housekeeper questioned with a confused look on her wizened face.

"Yes. She's his foster parents' housekeeper."

Stasio watched Melina's face. Usually she wore a rather stoical expression. But now she smiled, at first rather uncertainly, and then with sheer delight. Tears followed before she excused herself and ran off to tell Yannis.

Rachel turned an excited face to Stasio. "I think it made her happy."

"You think so?" Stasio chuckled, feeling the dark cloud lift. "You mean you don't know for sure?"

"Oh, Stasio…" Her blue eyes had an electric quality. "I just want everything to be perfect. Stella was so desperately unhappy when we first met. I didn't understand why. Now that I do, I want our wedding day to wipe away every tear. This is for her—for Stella and Ari."

And it's for you and me. You don't know it yet, Rachel, but our marriage is going to last forever.

"I believe you'll get your wish."

"I hope so," she whispered fervently. "Now, if you'll excuse me, I want to phone Carl Gordon before I go to bed. I know your security people have already been in touch, but there are some personal matters I want to talk over with him."

"Go right ahead. I'll wait up for Nikos."

After a slight pause, she said, "Good night then, Stasio."

"Good night. Sleep as late as you want."

"I may do that. I really am feeling tired all of a sudden."

Stasio didn't doubt it. He reveled in the sight of her shapely legs as she hurried up the stairs. She expended enough energy to infect an entire roomful of people. That energy was contagious. He longed to gather all of it to himself.

RACHEL REACHED HER ROOM out of breath. The second she shut the door, she fell back against it.

I'm in trouble. After the way I kissed Stasio a little while ago, he has to know I'm in love with him. That wasn't part of the plan!

I can't make that mistake again. I'll have to make sure I'm always around other people.

Charged with adrenaline, she took a shower, prepared for bed and made a phone call to Carl. He wasn't at the office, so she left a message saying she'd try again tomorrow.

Still keyed up, she took a book to bed but couldn't concentrate. She gave up staring at the pages, and turned on the television so the noise would drown out the frantic pounding of her heart. After ten minutes, she turned it off.

She'd almost fallen asleep when she heard a tap on the door.

It wasn't Stella, who would have knocked, then entered immediately.

Another tap sounded. "Ari?" she called out. He was the only person she could think of who might pay her a nocturnal visit. She sat up in the bed. "Come on in, sweetheart."

"That's the nicest invitation I've had in a long time."

Nikos.

He walked all the way in and shut the door. "I'm sorry I'm not Ari. Does he make a habit of disturbing you?"

She pulled the covers up to her chin. "No. Of course not. He had a bad dream on the ship once and ran to my room because Stasio was asleep."

"I see," came the thoughtful comment. "I had a drink with an old school chum in town and returned later than I expected. I know it's almost midnight, but I was hoping we could talk without anyone else around."

He seemed to hesitate before he said, "If I don't apologize to you now, I probably won't be able to summon the courage again."

A visit from Nikos in the middle of the night, let alone a Nikos ready to apologize, was absolutely the last thing she would have expected. She'd assumed he would want to spend time with Stasio.

"Is it all right for me to be here?"

"Yes. But open the door. It wouldn't be proper otherwise."

He laughed softly as he did so.

"Thank you, Rachel. You never change. You're always generous," he murmured. Then, instead of finding a chair, he sat on the side of her bed, next to her.

Moving to the far edge of her double bed, she asked, "Which time are you apologizing for?"

She heard him take a deep breath. "I deserved that. Let me start by saying I've already apologized to Stella.

We had a long talk this evening. She told me everything.

"When she finished, I felt like a world-class jerk. I had no idea she was suicidal, or how instrumental you were in saving her life."

Tears welled in Rachel's throat as she remembered those painful times.

"She exaggerated, Nikos. All I did was give her a little sympathy and support."

"Apparently you did a lot more than that. And then I had to come along and break everything up—like a bad boy kicking in someone else's sand castle."

It was hardly a sand castle, Nikos, hardly as insignificant as that. But I suppose you're doing your best to apologize.

"I guess what I want to know is, how come it took you this long to reappear? Did I do so much damage you couldn't face me until now?"

She drew her knees to her chest beneath the covers. "The only damage you did to me, personally, was to hurt my feelings, but I got over that. Causing trouble between me and Stella was something else again.

"But even if you hadn't done what you did, Stella's life and mine would have gone in different directions. We just would have maintained our friendship long-distance, and maybe spent a yearly holiday together.

"To be perfectly honest, I didn't dwell on the past too much after I left Switzerland. Four years at university kept me pretty busy, and then I lived with my father while I established a career as a radio talk-show host."

"You're kidding!"

"Not at all."

"Tell me about it."

He actually sounded sincere. In fact Nikos seemed so intent on extending the olive branch, she didn't have the heart to ask him to leave her bedroom just yet. Her father had taught her that if a person made the attempt to apologize, then the injured party had an obligation to listen.

"What do you want to know?"

"Everything. What kind of a talk show?"

"We talked about UFOs. Aliens. Outer space. It was a lot of fun."

"Stella said you wanted to be a pilot."

"Don't all children think they want to be like their parents when they grow up?"

"Not all," Nikos muttered.

"You have a point. Why would you want to walk in your father's shoes—become a businessman and a politician—when you're such an amazing athlete?"

"You really believed in me, didn't you?"

"Of course. I still do."

A long silence ensued.

"Rachel...I've been friends with Eleni for years. I hated to see her hurt. That's why I gave you such a hard time earlier."

"I understand."

"I don't think you do. She loves Stasio."

"I know."

"Please don't be insulted by my next question. You've become a beautiful woman, and any man would be fortunate to marry you. God knows I'm not paying lip service here. All you have to do is look in a mirror.

"But Stasio's been in love with Eleni for two years. How did you happen to go to his office at the precise moment you did, and proceed to turn his world inside out within a matter of days?"

"If I tell you the truth, Nikos, and then you treat me like you did before, I swear I'll never be your friend or trust you again."

"Go on."

"First of all, you have to understand that Eleni is the person who killed Stasio's love. She refused to share him with his family. When he realized it would always be a tug-of-war, he broke his engagement to her. I had nothing to do with it.

"You've already guessed he's not in love with me. He asked me to marry him so Ari could be legally adopted."

"So you admit it!"

"Yes. But what you don't know is that I'm marrying him in return for something I need from him."

"You mean money."

"I know it looks that way. But no. I want something far more important. Unfortunately it has to be my secret for a little while longer. When enough time has elapsed, we'll get a divorce and I'll go back to the States to live and work.

"Whether you believe me or not, I won't be accepting one dime from Stasio. In the meantime, neither Stasio nor I want anything to ruin our wedding day because it's all for Ari and Stella."

For once, Nikos remained quiet.

She took a fortifying breath. "Now for the rest. I'm going to preface this by saying I'm not proud of what I'm about to tell you. But until I confess it to you, I don't think I'll ever be able to throw off the guilt."

"What are you talking about?"

"I wasn't quite truthful when I said I'd recovered quickly from my hurt feelings after Chamonix. The fact is, because of your cruelty to me and Stella, I wanted to hurt you back. I wanted revenge. When I arrived at Stasio's office without an appointment, I was ready to carry out my plan.''

''I *knew* you had one. What was it?''

''To find you and make you fall in love with me, the girl you'd once called a short, fat, ugly American Army brat with orange hair.''

''*Lord,* Rachel. Eleni said as much—she said you were after revenge—but I didn't believe her. I had no idea the hurt went so deep.''

''That's because I thought you were the best-looking, most exciting man I'd ever known in my life. I was crazy about you. Six months ago, I formed a plan—all with the intent of making you fall for me, maybe end up marrying me.'' There was no reason to tell him about her other agenda, her need for protection. ''Marriage to you would be my ultimate revenge. But there was one thing I hadn't counted on.''

''Stasio?''

She nodded. ''Stasio. I hadn't expected to like him, let alone fall in love with him. But I did. Those seven days and nights on the ship transformed my life. The truth is, I adore him, Nikos.'' She shook her head slowly. ''I know he still loves Eleni, even if he's decided not to marry her. What an irony, eh?''

After a hesitation, he murmured, ''I'm sorry, Rachel.''

He sounded as if he meant it.

''I'm sorry, too.'' She sniffed. ''But at least one good thing will come out of this. After our marriage, Ari will belong to Stella. In the long run that's all that matters.''

''That's not true. What a hell of a mess! Maybe there's something I can do.''

''No!'' Rachel cried out. ''I don't want you any

more involved than you are. This is *my* problem. I'll have to deal with the consequences in my own way. One day I'll be out of your lives for good. I'm just glad you came to talk to me tonight. Now that everything's out in the open, I hope your feelings toward me will be a little friendlier.''

"I hope for the same thing from you." He leaned over to kiss her forehead, then slowly got off the bed. "Good night, Rachel."

"Nikos?" she called out. "I've told you these things in confidence, so I'd appreciate it if you kept our conversation to yourself."

"You have my word."

CHAPTER SIXTEEN

RACHEL AWAKENED late the next morning, more at peace with herself since she'd confessed everything to Nikos—even the fact that she'd fallen deeply in love with his brother.

She wished she had permission to tell Stella and Nikos about Sean so they would understand the measures Stasio had taken to protect everyone. But the precariousness of the situation dictated that she remain silent.

The only thing she could do was hug every memory of Stasio to herself. After last night, she knew the taste of his mouth, the feel of his hard, powerful body. When she allowed herself to relive the rapture of being in his arms, she could hardly breathe.

But last night was a moment out of time. It would not be repeated. If she wanted his company, she would have to share him with everyone else.

Unwilling to waste another second, she dressed in a silky, cream-colored long-sleeved blouse and beige wool pants. After running a brush through her hair and applying some light makeup, she hurried to join everyone downstairs.

Whenever she anticipated seeing Stasio, a yielding sensation of delight radiated through her body. By the time she reached the dining room, her heart felt as if it had wings.

But her spirits plunged when she realized Stella was

the only one about. Not that she didn't adore her friend, but after thinking and dreaming about Stasio all night, she'd been living for the very sight of him.

Stella's worried face brightened a little when she saw her. "Good morning, Rachel. You look beautiful."

"I could say the same thing about you. Motherhood agrees with you."

They kissed each other in greeting before she sat down at the table next to Stella and reached for a tempting peach.

Rachel wanted to ask about Stasio but didn't dare. "Where's the cutest little boy in the world this morning?"

"He is the cutest, isn't he?" Stella murmured. "Nikos took him fishing over an hour ago. Can you believe it?"

"Actually, I can. Nikos came to my room last night and apologized for everything."

"That must have been some apology," she said as the maid served them eggs and coffee.

"It was. We got a lot of things straightened out. I feel so much happier."

"So do I. Nikos apologized to me, too. I don't understand what's happened, but a change has come over him. No one can be more fun or charming than Nikos when he wants to be."

"Maybe it's the 'Ari effect.'"

Stella smiled at the comment, but her smile faded just as quickly. "Oddly enough, Stasio seems to be the one out of sorts today."

Rachel closed her eyes tightly for a moment. "He loved Eleni for a long time. You don't forget all those memories in an instant."

"I don't think his black mood had anything to do

with her. I was hoping you could shed some light. You were with him till you went up to bed.''

The cup almost slipped from Rachel's hands. She feared Sean might have tracked her to Greece, and Stasio's security people had just apprised him of it.

"We got home late because the priest was detained," she said. "I went straight to bed. As far as I know, Stasio was going to wait up for Nikos."

"I wonder if they argued."

Rachel's hand tightened on the knife she was using to butter her roll. "Nikos didn't come to my room until midnight. He said he'd been out at a bar with a friend. As far as I could tell, he hadn't seen or talked to Stasio, but of course I could be wrong."

"Well, something's happened. Early this morning, Stasio came in here unshaven, looking like death, then he walked right back out with not even a word of greeting. The next thing I heard was the screech of tires. I've never seen Stasio this angry in my life. It frightens me."

"Surely you're exaggerating."

"No," she said. "No. He was furious about something. I hardly recognized him as my brother."

The roll Rachel had been eating turned to sawdust in her mouth.

Was it rage Stella had seen in his eyes—because Rachel's presence had brought this menace into their lives?

She couldn't remain at the table. Adrenaline forced her to her feet.

"Rachel," Stella cried softly. "I didn't mean to upset you. Maybe I'm just being paranoid because Anna and Giorgio are coming and I-I'm scared of what's going to happen."

"Anyone would understand your feelings, Stella, but I'm sure you don't have to worry. They sound like lovely people."

Stella joined her at the window overlooking one of the gardens. "That's the problem. When Ari sees them again, he may decide he'd rather live with them, after all."

"No. He's too happy with you. It's going to work out. You'll see."

"I hope so." Her voice sounded tearful. She paused, then managed a shaky laugh. "Oh, listen to me. Why don't we take a walk to town? It's nice enough. I want to buy a little present to give Ari after the wedding."

"That's a wonderful idea." After hearing about Stasio, Rachel couldn't have stayed inside the villa right now if her life had depended upon it. "Let's go."

They went back to their bedrooms for jackets, then hurried through the house and out the front door. As they stepped off the porch, Rachel saw a red sports car come through the gates at too great a speed. It barreled up the driveway.

"Nikos knows not to drive that fast. Something's wrong!"

The car came to a shrieking halt in front them. Nikos jumped out. "Is Ari here?" he demanded, his face a grayish color beneath his tan.

"No." Stella grabbed his arm. "What's happened?"

"I don't know." Nikos sounded anguished. "We'd been casting for a while, but no bites. There were several people stretched along the shoreline. He said he was going to go down by this one guy who seemed to be having better luck.

"I told him I'd catch up with him as soon as I found a different lure in my tackle box. I swear my eyes were only off him for half a minute. No longer. When I stood up, I couldn't see him. I started running, but he wasn't anywhere. Neither was the man. When I questioned the other people along the shore, they said they hadn't noticed anything.''

Stella's face had gone so white, it was frightening. "You mean he was kidnapped?"

"I don't have any other explanation," Nikos said hoarsely. "I went straight to the police and gave them his description. They're scouring the town now, but they suggested he might have decided to come home. The officer said children do things like that. So I drove here as fast as I could, praying he'd come back to the villa.''

Rachel felt sick to her stomach. Although Stasio had assured her his security men were in place, Sean Dodd had still managed to snatch Ari away. "Does Stasio know about this?"

"The police said they'd reach him and told me to go home in case Ari was here.''

"We've got to find Ari! I couldn't bear it if anything happened to my little boy now. Ari— Ari—'' She started to sway.

"Of course we'll find him. Come on, Stella.'' He put a loving arm around his sister and gathered Stella's limp body in his arms. Rachel watched him carry her into the house.

Unable to move, she buried her face in her hands, convulsed with fear and horror. *This is my fault. All my fault. If anything happens to Ari because of me, life won't be worth living.*

Please God. Don't let Sean hurt Ari. Please. If anyone's going to get killed, let it be me.

Saying the words to herself had given her an idea

and seemed to release her from the paralysis that gripped her.

She ran into the villa and dashed upstairs to her room. After locking the door, she hurried to the phone and picked up the receiver.

It was three in the morning at Red Crater Air Force Base. That didn't matter. This was a case of life and death. Rachel punched in the numbers and waited.

A tired-sounding voice answered after four rings. "Yes? Who is it?"

"Hello, Ruth?"

"Yes?" came the tentative response.

"This is Rachel."

"Rachel? After all this time! Honey, where've you been? We've tried looking everywhere for you. Sean even went to Pennsylvania hoping to find you. Are you all right? We've been so worried ever since you left and never told anyone where you were going."

Tears poured down Rachel's cheeks. Ruth Dodd was a good woman. Her emotion was genuine. She had no clue what an evil man she'd married.

"It's good to hear your voice, Ruth. I was wrong to have run off like that. I never knew just how wrong until today." She breathed deeply for a moment, trying to compose herself. "Listen, I'd love to catch up on all the news, but right now I need to speak to Sean. Can you put him on the phone for me?"

"Honey, I'm sorry. He's in the Middle East on some assignment for General Berman."

So it *was* General Berman orchestrating things!

"Do you have a phone number where I can reach him?" She brushed at the tears with the back of her free hand. "It's an emergency."

"I don't have a number to call him directly. But I

can phone someone right now who can get him the message and he'll call you back. He'll be so happy to talk to you! Your father asked us to look after you, you know. Give me your number.''

Rachel had to think fast. "Just a minute, Ruth." She jumped off the bed and grabbed her purse. She still had the phone number of the *taverna* where she'd taken a room the day before yesterday.

"Ruth? Here it is." She read off the number. "If Sean gets my message right away, have him call me at this number in twenty minutes. If it turns out he can't call me till later, the hotel proprietor will take a message and get in touch with me.''

"I'll do it as soon as I hang up. Where are you, honey?''

"I'm in Greece.''

"Greece. Oh, Rachel. I'm so happy you phoned. I'll get right on this. Don't be a stranger now. Please call me soon.''

She bit her lip hard. "I will. Thank you, Ruth.''

Without wasting another second, Rachel ran to the closet and opened her large suitcase. A specially treated envelope containing her father's negatives lay in the bottom.

Sorry, Dad, but I can't hang on to them any longer.

She took the envelope and her purse, slipped into a pair of sneakers, then flew out of the room and down the back stairway to the kitchen.

Yannis was trying to comfort his wife, who was in tears and wringing her hands.

As soon as she saw Rachel, she cried, "The little one has disappeared! Aiyee—''

"I know. I'm going to try to find him. If anyone asks where I am, tell them I'll be back soon.''

"But Kyrie Athas wouldn't approve of you going out alone!"

"I have to, Melina."

The older woman crossed herself before following Rachel to the back door. "This is not good. Kyrie Athas wouldn't like it."

"But I want to help," Rachel called over her shoulder.

"If anything happened to you, *Kyrie*—"

Rachel didn't wait to hear the rest.

At this point I don't care if anything does happen to me, as long as Ari's safe.

Yannis ran after her. "I will drive you where you have to go, *Despinis.*"

There wasn't time to argue. "All right. Thank you." She climbed inside the estate car and they were off. "Take me to the *taverna.*"

Through the rearview mirror his eyes showed surprise at her destination, but he merely nodded.

Minutes later, the car pulled up in front of the *taverna,* and Rachel scrambled out. "Thank you, Yannis. I'm going to stay here for a while. I'll call you when I'm ready to come back."

He seemed hesitant, then nodded again and drove away.

Rachel hurried up the steps, anxious to find the patron. He was all smiles when he saw her approach the bar. After she explained that she was expecting an important phone call, she asked for a room so she'd be able to talk to Sean in private. The patron obliged by giving her the same charming room as before.

She hadn't been inside ten minutes before the phone rang.

"Hello?" she said into the receiver.

"Well, well, Rachel. At last. You really are your father's daughter."

"Where's Ari?" she demanded. "Is he safe?"

"I figured if I took something you wanted, I'd be hearing from you. You must want the boy very badly to call Ruth in the middle of the night."

"I'll give you anything you want, Sean. The negatives are right here. All of them. Just let Ari go. He's an innocent little boy. Please tell me you haven't hurt him." Her whole body was trembling.

"I never wanted to hurt anybody."

"You killed my father. How could you do that to your best friend?"

"Chuck knew too much for his own good, but he wasn't supposed to die."

"You mean he was just supposed to have a stroke like Manny."

"That's right. That's what the injection was meant to do. But for some reason, Chuck didn't survive it."

"I want to talk to Ari," she said abruptly.

"Not over the phone. As soon as you hang up, catch a bus for Batsi Beach. Rent a paddleboat and head straight out into open water. If you tell anyone where you're going or what you're doing, neither you nor the boy will live another hour." The line went dead.

This time Rachel put the key and money for a two-night stay on the bedside table. Then she crept down the hall the opposite way and left the *taverna* through a back exit leading to an alley.

She looked like any tourist on holiday. Except for a few local men who stared and smiled at her, no one took any special notice.

She found the bus stop and waited, but her anxiety

over Ari made her restless and jittery. The first bus to finally come along was going the wrong way.

She paced nonstop until another one pulled up. In her best Greek she told the driver she needed to get to the beach at Batsi. He nodded and motioned for her to climb aboard.

Batsi was only a short drive from Palaiopolis. Less than ten minutes had passed before he dropped her off in the center of the town. After a brief walk she reached the beach, where she saw a paddleboat concession.

When she looked out at the dark blue sea, she could see only two paddleboats farther up the shoreline. Swallowing hard, she paid the rental fee for a paddleboat, then got in one and headed out of the bay.

Her progress was slow. She had no idea what was going to happen, but she didn't care. All she wanted was to find Ari. Once he was safe and Sean had let him go, nothing else mattered.

Sean hadn't given her a destination, but she knew she'd gone a long way past the point allowed. Fortunately the sea was calm. She had nothing left to do but pray harder than she'd ever prayed in her life.

Suddenly she could hear the sound of a motor. She glanced around and saw a speedboat racing in her direction. When it got closer without decreasing its speed, she thought it meant to run her over.

Obeying the urge to survive, she climbed up on the seat and dived deep into the water. When she surfaced for breath, she felt two pairs of hands pull her into the cruiser. No one said anything.

One of the burly seamen had already retrieved the envelope and purse from her boat. The other turned the cruiser around and they sped through the water, open throttle. When she looked back, the pedal boat had become a little dot on the horizon.

They rounded a headland where she caught sight of a large white yacht in the distance, slowly cruising the Aegean. She realized General Berman could arrange anything, anytime, anywhere. All he needed was a henchman like Sean Dodd to carry out his orders. She shuddered to think Ari was at the mercy of such men. No, not men. Fiends.

The speedboat drew right up to the yacht. Sean's silvery blond hair and clean-cut looks belied his dark side. Dressed like a wealthy American tourist, he stood waiting for her when she was forced out of the cruiser to climb aboard.

He made her feel sick as his cold blue eyes assessed her. He stared at her body, revealed by the wet clothes that clung like a second skin. "You've changed since the last time I saw you."

Too angry to be frightened for herself, she cried, "I brought what you wanted. I followed all your instructions. Now where's Ari?"

"He's in his room being a good boy."

Tears filled her eyes. "If you've hurt him—"

He flashed her a cruel smile. "There wouldn't be anything you could do about it. You've led me a merry chase, carrot-top. But it's over now. T.J.? Show her below."

The man who had retrieved her things from the paddleboat grabbed her arm and shoved her into a hallway. There was a narrow flight of stairs to negotiate.

"In here," he ordered, pushing her head down so she'd clear the small opening. The minute she went through the door, he pulled it shut, enclosing her in complete darkness. She heard the click of the lock.

Unable to stand up straight, she turned and pounded on the door with both fists. "Let me out! I want to see Ari! Let me out!"

"Rachel?" a little voice called to her in the darkness.

She blinked and stopped her pounding "Ari, darling? Is that really you?"

"Yes. Those bad men made me stay in here. I got scared because I couldn't see anything."

"I'm here now. Come to me, sweetheart."

Suddenly she felt a warm little body next to hers.

"Oh, Ari. *Thank you, God. Thank you.*"

She picked him up and held him in her arms. He wound his arms so tightly around her neck, she could scarcely move, let alone breathe. But she didn't care.

"You're wet!" Ari cried.

"All I care about is that you're alive." Between sobs she said, "Is there a place to sit in here?"

"No. They made me lie on the floor."

"That's okay. Come on. You can sit on my lap." She felt her way to the wall. They seemed to be in some kind of storage closet. She sank down and he tumbled into her lap.

"You're such a brave and wonderful boy. Do you have any idea how proud I am of you? Everyone's going to call you a hero after this."

"Did those bad men take you, too?"

"Yes. But now that we're together, we're going to stay together until Stasio comes for us."

"Stasi can do anything!"

More tears streamed down her cheeks. "You're right about that. He won't stop until he finds us and brings us home to your mommy."

"How soon do you think he'll come and get us?"

"Very soon."

"Did they take Nikos?"

"No. He called the police and then came to the villa to tell us what happened. That's when I went looking for you. Nikos loves you very much, you know. He's at the house with your mother. They're comforting each other until you get back."

"One of those men put something in my mouth and I couldn't make any noise. Uncle Nikos didn't see them put me in a car and drive away." He was on the verge of tears now.

"I know. He was frantic with worry because he was too far down the shore to protect you. But it's over now, and no one'll ever hurt you again."

"Why did they take me away?"

"Because there's a man who wants those pictures of Mars I once showed you. I got them and the negatives from my daddy. He wouldn't give them to this man, and I wouldn't either. So he came after me to get them. He knew that if he took *you* away, I'd tell him he could have the pictures."

"Did you give them to him?" he asked in a quiet voice.

"Yes."

"You love me a lot, huh?"

"A lot more than a lot!" She hugged him close.

"Why does he want them?"

"Because they're controversial."

"What does *contversial* mean?"

"It means some people think those pictures prove that there's life on Mars. If that's true, then the government wants to keep it a secret until they can learn more about it.

"My father believed there shouldn't be secrets that important. He said the whole world ought to know everything the government knows—about outer space or anything else—because the government's supposed to represent all the people.''

''Oh. Are secrets bad?''

''Not all of them.''

''I know one Uncle Nikos told me.''

''Then it's not a bad secret.''

''Do you want to hear it?''

''Did he ask you not to tell anyone?''

''No. He just said, 'Do you want to know a secret?' '' She smiled through the tears. ''If you want to tell me, go ahead.''

''He said you loved him first, but then he did something awful, and now you love Stasi.''

''It wasn't so awful, and we were both very young. Now we're all grown up and good friends.''

''I'm glad you're going to marry Stasi.''

''So am I. I love him with all my heart and soul,'' she whispered into his hair.

''I know another secret. My mommy hopes you have a baby real soon so I can have a cousin.''

Oh Ari, Ari. It's not going to happen.

''I bet your uncle Nikos will have a baby first.''

''He can't have a baby. You're silly, Rachel.''

That little laugh of his bubbled out. She was so happy to hear it, she started crying again. ''You know what? We're as snug as two peas in a pod.''

''What's a pod?''

''It's like a bed for the peas.''

''But it's so dark in here.'' A huge sigh escaped. It was too big for such a little boy. ''I hope Stasi gets us out soon.''

''He will.''

''Do you think my mommy's crying?''

"Yes. She loves you more than anything in the world."

"Do you think Anna and Giorgio are crying, too?"

"I don't think they've been told about this."

"I hope Anna doesn't find out. She cries real hard when she's sad."

"Women sometimes do that."

"Will you tell me another UFO story?"

"I was just going to ask if you wanted to hear one."

"Goody!"

CHAPTER SEVENTEEN

"MY MEN HAVE COMMANDEERED the vessel, Stasio."
It was the chief of police, who'd called the police boat
Stasio had boarded. "The Americans are in custody,
but they're refusing to talk. We'll hold them without
the possibility of extradition to the United States until
you're ready to move on the wrongful death suit of
Despinis Maynard's father."

"That's good news. But I have to know if you've
seen any sign of Rachel and Ari."

"Not yet. We're just starting to search the yacht
now."

"I'll be there shortly."

Until they were safe he would never know a moment's happiness again. He wouldn't, anyway, not after
he'd seen Nikos disappear into Rachel's room in the
middle of the night. When he didn't come out right
away, Stasio had left the villa to take a long walk. He
couldn't tolerate the thought of what might be going
on.

Early this morning, he'd come back home for his
wallet, then driven off only to receive a call from the
police that Ari had been kidnapped and Rachel was
gone. Shock had twisted his guts to shreds.

No matter what Dodd might have done to them, Stasio wanted to be there when Ari and Rachel were
found. He shut off his cell phone and signaled the skip-

per of the police boat to move alongside the yacht. Information from Greek Intelligence indicated it was owned by an American drilling company with a subsidiary in Greece. Evidently, a man matching Sean Dodd's description had been seen on board. It meant he'd been in Greece for several days, at least, and had known of Rachel's exact whereabouts.

When the harbor police learned that an unknown party had made arrangements to borrow it this morning, that sent up a red flag. Yannis had informed Stasio that Rachel had gone to the *taverna,* and from there to Batsi Beach to rent a paddleboat.

Once he'd alerted the authorities, all the pieces fell into place. After that, he told Stella and Nikos the truth about Sean Dodd's vendetta against Rachel.

In an emotional moment, Nikos had broken down, sobbing that everything was his fault. While he'd been at the bar drinking with his friend, one of Dodd's men must have heard their conversation, which was probably how he knew about Nikos's plan to go fishing with Ari the next day.

Stasio had shaken his head and told him that if anyone was to blame for the kidnapping, he was. If he'd told the family the truth in the first place, Nikos wouldn't have said anything he didn't want anyone to overhear.

Stella had gotten angry then, and told both of them to stop crucifying themselves. None of it mattered as long as they got Ari and Rachel back alive.

"We're here, Kyrie Athas."

"*Efcharisto.*"

Stasio stood by, then climbed off the boat onto the stairs leading to the deck of the yacht, which was now crawling with police from several different forces. Six harbor police boats circled it, while three police helicopters hovered overhead.

He approached the chief. "Have you found them yet?"

"No," came the grim reply. "We've searched all the cabins. They're empty. The hold didn't reveal anything, either."

"Then let's start looking in every storage and housekeeping closet till we find them."

They have to be on board, alive. I refuse to believe anything else.

Ten minutes later, they still hadn't found them. Stasio felt as if he had a boulder in his gut. He walked along the deck, his gaze traveling over every spotless inch.

Lord. Where were they?

Once again he went below. His eyes explored every line and seam. The chief followed him.

"We've been over this deck twice now, Stasio."

Maybe they really weren't on board. Stasio opened and closed more doors. By the time he'd reached the narrow staircase at the other end of the hall, he'd run out of ideas.

"They aren't here. I'm sorry."

"They have to be!"

As he turned to go up the steps and search again, he remembered that his yacht had the same kind of staircase at one end, with a small storage area hidden beneath it for extra rope. You entered it from a door hinged at the top. It was locked by a dead bolt near the floor rather than a key.

With a suffocating feeling in his chest, he vaulted around the side. Sure enough, there it was. The dead bolt.

"They could be in here. Aim your flashlight at the opening, Chief."

Muttering surprise that his men had missed it, the chief held his light while Stasio turned the dead bolt and lifted the door. Since the storage area was only four feet high, he had to get down on his haunches to see inside.

There was a sudden movement. He caught the gleam of red-gold hair before Rachel lifted her head. Her body covered Ari's, protecting him.

"Sean, you bastard," she screamed. "You'll have to kill me to get to him!"

In that moment, he loved Rachel Maynard more than he'd ever loved anyone in his whole life.

"Dodd and his cronies are on their way to a Greek jail, Rachel," he said in a barely controlled voice. "You don't need to be afraid anymore."

"Stasi!" Ari's shriek of joy rang through the yacht, warming his heart. "I knew you'd come!"

"Thank you, Stasio. Oh, thank you," he heard her tremulous whisper before she moved away from Ari so he could scramble out.

With one arm around his nephew, he used the other to pull Rachel beyond the opening. Once she could stand, he crushed her against his body. Nikos or no Nikos, she was his life!

"Are you all right?" he murmured into her hair. It smelled of her shampoo and the sea. Her clothes were damp. What had they done to her?

He wanted to love her. He wanted to kiss her. He wanted to hold her, and have the right to protect her. He wanted to tell her what she meant to him. He needed answers to so many questions, but they'd have to come later.

"I-I'm fine now." But she wasn't. She'd begun sobbing. He felt every trembling movement of her body as she clung to him. "H-how did you know we were here?"

"Yannis had orders to keep his eye on you. That part was easy. The worst moment came when we tore this yacht apart twice and still couldn't find you."

"Your husband-to-be would not give up, Despini Maynard." Stasio noticed the way the chief and his men stared at her in obvious appreciation. "He was the one who found you."

Stasio felt a sense of bleakness as he realized those moist blue eyes lifted to him in gratitude would never glow with the kind of love he felt for her.

"We knew Stasio would come, huh, Rachel? Stasi can do *everything!*"

The officers clustered around them threw back their heads and laughed.

"Come." The chief motioned. "We'll take you back to port in my boat. I'm sure we have some drinks on board for a brave boy about your age."

"But I was scared till Rachel came."

"So was I when we couldn't find you," the chief admitted.

Amen, Stasio murmured inwardly, bending down to hug the child.

Ari patted Stasio's cheek. "I'm hungry, Stasi!"

"Of course you are." *So am I.* "We'll go home right now. Cook's going to have your favorite dinner waiting. While we eat, you can tell the family everything that happened."

"That's going to take a long time!" Ari said as soon as they'd all moved to the upper deck.

He heard Rachel laugh despite her emotions, or

maybe because of them. There were several dark moments earlier today when he'd feared Sean Dodd might have silenced that wonderful sound forever.

Ari and the chief started to climb aboard the police boat, chatting like two old friends. Stasio, who still had his arm around Rachel's shoulders, couldn't take another step once he felt her arm slide across the back of his waist to detain him.

He darted her a questioning glance.

"How will I ever repay you for what you've done?" she whispered.

"You protected Ari with your life. That's payment enough."

"If I'd never come to your office, none of this would have happened." He heard that tremor in her voice again.

"If you hadn't come, we wouldn't be getting married and Ari would never belong to Stella."

She averted her eyes. "I've been thinking about our wedding."

"So have I."

"You never did say how long you wanted us to stay married."

"Does that bother you? Are you in such a hurry to be divorced?"

"No! Of course not. I just don't want you to worry tha—" She broke off talking.

"That what? That I might've misunderstood last night and have now concluded you're in love with me?"

Her head was still bowed. "I'm afraid I made a fool of myself. You would have every right to think it."

"I made no secret of the fact that I enjoyed kissing you, too. But we both know it's possible for two healthy, consenting adults to find pleasure in each other's arms without either party reading too much into it.''

''Exactly. I simply wanted you to know that I realize you'll be missing Eleni's company for a long time to come, so—''

''So you think I have plans to use you for a substitute, as I did last night.''

''No!''

Liar. Her facial color matched her hair.

''Rachel—I'm not in love with Eleni. I don't believe I ever was. We both drifted along until one day, I woke up. Contrary to what you're thinking, I never plan to see her, talk or be with her again unless it's purely accidental. If I still had any of those urges, any feeling for Eleni at all, I wouldn't be marrying you, not even for Ari's sake.''

She looked dumbstruck.

''Now that we have *that* out of the way, are you going to tell me you understand how I, like many men of the world, could be engaged one day, and make casual love to another woman the next because it's the nature of the beast?''

''Well...yes!''

''You're an extremely understanding woman. I, on the other hand, would *not* be an extremely understanding man if our roles were reversed.''

''I'm just trying to be reasonable,'' she said hotly.

''Reasonable. That's a very interesting word. It implies passionless, tepid, heartless, gutless.''

She was kneading her hands again.

''Is it because you're in love with another man that the idea of my dabbling in a meaningless flirtation wouldn't be abhorrent to you...hypothetically speaking?''

"I already told you I'm not in love with Manny! I don't understand why you don't believe me."

"I believe you. About Manny."

Her head jerked toward him. "What other man are you talking about?"

"The one you're in love with. The one you've loved for a long time."

She frowned. "There is no other man!"

"Then how do you explain my brother's visit to your room in the middle of the night?"

"Nikos came to apologize!"

"You two have a history that goes back six years."

"It was a teenage infatuation. Every girl has at least one."

Sucking in his breath, he said, "Yours lasted a little longer than the average, wouldn't you agree?"

He could tell she was having trouble swallowing. "How much did Nikos tell you about our conversation last night?" Her voice throbbed with anxiety.

Was that all it was, Rachel? Just conversation?

"Stasi? Rachel? Come on! The boat's leaving!"

"Ari's calling us. It's been a long day. I think it's past time we got him home to Stella."

"Yes, of course. She must be frantic!"

She's not the only one....

RACHEL WAITED UNTIL TWO in the morning before she crept over to Nikos's room on the other side of the villa. She'd had to wait that long for everyone to go to bed.

Though she'd had dinner with the family, she'd been

in such distress, she'd let everyone else do the talking. Ari contributed most of it, of course.

The kidnapping seemed to have bonded their family like nothing else could have done. A jubilant spirit surrounded the table. Every member of the Athas clan, particularly Stella, was in high spirits, at least for this one blessed night. Because Ari was back home and safe once more.

Rachel couldn't have been happier for them, or more thankful the whole terrifying ordeal with Sean Dodd was over. But she'd counted the seconds until she could excuse herself from the table and go to her room to grieve in private.

Throughout the meal Stasio had behaved with Rachel exactly as he'd been doing all along. To everyone else, she was his beloved fiancée, the woman he could hardly wait to marry.

She knew that Nikos had told him the ugly truth about her plan of revenge—although no one would have guessed anything was wrong. Stasio was too honorable to reveal her guilty secrets to the family. Instead, he'd waited until they were on the yacht to confront her, but they'd been interrupted.

Stasio was the kind of man who could never live with a lie. That was why he'd let her know he was aware of her scheme before they said their wedding vows.

Rachel, in turn, had been forced to play her part at the dinner table, but there was one thing she hadn't been able to bring herself to do, and that was look at Nikos.

She thought he'd hurt her in Switzerland, but it was a mere pinprick compared to this last act of treachery.

Spoiled, self-absorbed Nikos, whose jealousy of his brother had brought him to an all-time low.

How dared Nikos do that after she'd told him how she felt about Stasio?

Unlike Nikos, who'd knocked on her bedroom last night before entering, she didn't bother to announce herself. She simply barged in and turned on the light.

"Get up, Nikos! I want to talk to you."

He'd been lying on his side beneath the covers. At the sound of her voice, he jackknifed into a sitting position.

"Rachel? What's wrong?"

She could hardly contain her rage. "You're not going to get away with this!"

He shoved some hair out of his face. "What are you talking about?"

"You're coming with me to Stasio's room. Now!"

A dumbstruck expression broke out on his face. "Why?"

"If you won't cooperate, then I'll bring Stasio in here. The choice is up to you."

After a pause, he said quietly, "I'll come."

"I'll wait for you in the hall."

Ten seconds later he emerged from his room wearing a black-and-purple striped robe. She marched down the hall toward Stasio's suite, then turned to face Nikos.

"Tell your brother we're here to talk to him."

She thought Nikos would give her an argument. To her surprise he walked ahead of her and rapped on his brother's door.

"Stasio?"

"Come in, Nikos. I'm not asleep."

"Rachel's with me."

A long silence followed. Then in a curt tone, he said,

"If you two have come for my blessing, consider it given. Good night!"

Nikos's head swiveled toward Rachel, his face twisted in anger and confusion. "His blessing? What the hell's he talking about?"

"You ought to know."

"Well, I damn well don't!"

He pushed open the door and stormed into Stasio's bedroom. Rachel walked a few steps behind. Her bare feet curled luxuriously in the pile of a thick area rug. The room was a symphony of earth tones with a dominant black geometric motif running throughout.

Stasio's eyes flashed the second he saw her lingering near the doorway, dressed in her nightgown and yellow terry-cloth robe. She didn't know who looked more surprised.

With a drink in one hand, he stood there in all his dark, male splendor wearing only the bottom half of a pair of navy pajamas that hung low on his hips.

Rachel couldn't help but stare at the hard, powerful body she'd clung to only a few hours earlier. Her mouth had gone too dry to speak.

"You want my blessing in person, is that it?" Stasio demanded, his expression wintry.

"Hell, no!" Nikos bit out something untranslatable. "Rachel, would you please tell me what's going on?"

"Stop pretending you don't know!"

"Know *what?*"

"Today you told Stasio things that I revealed to you in total confidence last night." Tears smarted her eyes. She couldn't stop them. "Then you twisted the truth around for your own sick purposes. But you've done that once too often in your life. I'm sick of the lies, the jealousy, the cruelty. You're a thirty-three-year-old man. It's time to grow up! We're going to stay in this room and hammer this out once and for all, until everyone knows the truth about *everything*.''

Lines scored Nikos's handsome face. He wheeled around to face his older brother. ''Did you and I have a conversation at any time today, in which I revealed things she'd told me in secret last night?''

Rachel detected a nervous tic at the corner of Stasio's mouth. ''No.''

Nikos turned back to Rachel with a satisfied smile. ''Unlike me, my brother never lies. If he said I didn't do it, then I didn't do it. I rest my case.''

By now Rachel was confused and feared she just might be standing on shaky ground. Lifting her head, she stared at Stasio. ''If that's true, then how did you know Nikos came to my bedroom last night?''

''I was waiting for him to come home so we could talk. But when he entered the house, he went right upstairs. I followed him to call him back, but he disappeared inside your room.

''I didn't think he'd be long, so I waited in his bedroom. Half an hour later, I realized Eleni had been right. I left the house.''

Nikos eyed his brother shrewdly. ''What exactly did Eleni say?''

''That Rachel had always been in love with you.''

''I flattered myself into thinking the same thing. But my visit to Rachel's room soon opened my eyes to the truth.''

''What truth?'' Stasio thundered, his body taut.

Suddenly Rachel saw Nikos break into his famous smile. ''That's for me to know and you to find out. Tonight when Rachel slammed into my bedroom, demanding that we come to see you, I knew she was a woman in love. So I'll tell you what—I'm going to let you two sort this out for yourselves. But before I go, may I give you both *my* blessing?''

He made it as far as the door, then looked back at them over his shoulder.

''Rachel? Besides Stasio, who can speak for himself, Ari and Stella are already your most ardent admirers. For the record, you can now add me to your collection.

''Welcome to the family, *cherie*.'' He grinned. ''I know you want me to leave, but I have a couple more things to say.''

He turned to Rachel. ''One day I'm going to prove to you that I'm not the no-account ski bum you think I am. When Stasio decides to bring you back from your honeymoon, I'd like to pick your brains. In fact, I may hire you to become my business manager…help me get those ski schools organized.

''Stasio? I can't undo what damage I've done in the past. I had no right to interfere with you and Eleni. But from here on out, I'd like to promise I'll never undermine you again. I'd also like to help shoulder some of the responsibility around here, particularly with the nephew I'm crazy about.

''You were right. Ari belongs with our sister. His kindness reminds me of Mother.'' His voice grew husky. ''No wonder you wouldn't give up on him.''

He cleared his throat. ''As Rachel pointed out, it's time I acted like a man. With her help, I'm beginning to think it's possible. *Kulinichtu.*'' He flashed them a devilish grin. ''May all your problems be little ones. I won't mind if you name your first boy after me.''

The only sound Rachel heard after the click of the door was the relentless pounding of her heart. When she looked across the room, Stasio's eyes were like pinpoints of black fire. He put down his drink and started toward her.

"No, Stasio!" She backed away. "Don't come any closer! There's something I have to tell you first."

His mouth curved in a half smile. "You're right. I have to hear from your own lips that you're as in love with me as I am with you."

"You already know how I feel about you." She gave a deep trembling sigh. "I fell in love with you that first day in your office. But you don't know the real reason I came to see you. When you hear the truth, you'll ask me to leave Andros and never come back."

"What is this terrible thing?" he asked in the same gentle voice he used with Ari. By now he'd reached her and put his hands on her shoulders.

"Please, Stasio," she cried. "Don't touch me. This is serious."

"I have to touch you," he muttered as his hands caressed her arms. "But I'm listening."

"I—I can't talk when you're this close to me."

"I can't be in the same room and not touch you." He kissed her cheek. "I'm in love with you, Rachel." His lips made a trail to her eyes. "It happened in my office, just the way you described. Why else do you think I asked you to sail to Greece with me? I couldn't let you go without knowing I'd see you again before the day was out," he admitted in a husky voice.

But when he would have captured her mouth with his own, she wrenched herself free from his embrace and backed all the way to the door.

"I'm an evil person, Stasio."

"How evil?" he teased, coming closer. She couldn't breathe, let alone think.

Averting her eyes, she confessed, "My reason for

coming to your office was based on a lie. I had this plan to use your family to get what I wanted. I specifically targeted *you* to gain entrée. Carl Gordon helped me.''

Her pronouncement created a subtle shift in his mood. ''Go on.''

This was it.

Rachel now had a full understanding of why the Bible counseled that revenge be left to God. The consequences of her actions were almost too great to bear. When Stasio heard the truth, she would lose him forever.

She moistened her lips nervously. ''After my father was murdered, I was so frightened of Scan, I called my doctor in Pennsylvania for help. He didn't know the reason for my terror, but he did prescribe some sleeping pills. When they didn't help, I asked for something stronger.''

Stasio's chest rose and fell. ''Are you trying to tell me you got into drugs?''

''No.'' She shook her head. ''Dr. Rich realized I was on the verge of a nervous breakdown. He told me about a private clinic for women in Philadelphia called the Michelangelo Institute that might be able to help me.

''Even though I'd gone to university in Philadelphia for four years, I'd never heard of it. He said that was the whole point. It's an exclusive institute. It doesn't advertise. You couldn't even get in without a referral from someone they knew, and approved of. It was also very expensive.

''Dr. Rich said he'd refer me and gave me an application. At first I thought it was just some sort of glorified diet clinic or health spa. But when I read the instructions on the form, I realized it was much more than that.

"It said to write down the one goal in life I wanted to achieve above all else. It didn't matter how ludicrous, outrageous or farfetched it might sound. Michelangelo's would help me attain it."

She inhaled a deep breath, still backed against the door for support. "I didn't take it all that seriously, but I was so frightened, I didn't know where else to turn. The idea of enrolling in a secret place where no one could find me was like a godsend. So I wrote down this perfectly absurd goal."

"What was that?" Stasio prompted her.

"'By the year 2000, I plan to become Mrs. Nikos Athas.'"

After a slight pause, he asked, "You loved my brother all that time?" His voice was dispassionate.

"No! I never loved Nikos. It's true I had a girlhood crush on him. But after what he did to me, the things he said about me, I carried the hurt like a stone around my neck for years after. I don't think I even realized how deep that wound was until I found myself writing out that goal.

"Obviously there was a part of me that wanted revenge against him for hurting me and Stella. What better way to make him take back all those unkind words than to get him to fall in love with me? What better person to choose than a foreigner who had the kind of money and social backing to protect me from Sean?

"In fairness to Carl, my assigned counselor, he did warn me that if I ended up with Nikos, I'd be unhappy because I didn't love him."

Even as she spoke, she could feel Stasio's distaste.

It wasn't anything he said or did, but she could feel it all the same.

"Carl was the psychologist who would help me achieve my goal. Simply stated, he told me that when I was physically and mentally ready, I would leave Michelangelo's and renew my friendship with Stella. In the process, Nikos would find me, and the rest would be history.

"I told Carl I didn't know how to contact Stella. He said that part was easy. A-all I needed to do was approach y-you, the head of the Athas family, and tell you what Nikos had done to m-me." Her voice faltered. "Based on his research, Carl had nothing but praise for you and assured me I would be given a fair hearing and the chance to see Stella again."

She took another shuddering breath. Stasio was so quiet.

"I—I arrived at your office in a kind of daze, ready to carry out my agenda. But it had all been theory, and suddenly there you were in the flesh. Stasio Athas, the big brother Stella adored."

With her head bent, she admitted, "You weren't anything like Nikos had made you out to be. I think I loved you on sight." She had to swallow several times before she could speak again.

"As soon as we started talking about Stella, I seemed to wake out of this strange daze I'd been in. I realized that my fear of Sean had driven me to use your family, something I've never done in my life! It was evil.

"In that instant, I knew I didn't want any part of what I'd been planning. But I'd set the wheels in motion, and I truly did want to see Stella again. I'd missed her so much. And I wanted to explain why I'd been forced to end our friendship. I needed to do that to rid myself of the guilt.

"But even before you asked me to sail with you, I'd made up my mind that if you told me where I could find Stella, I'd talk to her and then fly straight to California. While you and I sat talking, I was already planning to visit Manny and then start a new life someplace where Sean would have trouble finding me.

"Stasio—you have to believe me when I tell you the only reason I went on the ship was that I wanted to be near you. Otherwise, I would've flown to Athens to see Stella before leaving for California."

The silence was excruciating.

"Last night I told Nikos the whole truth. That's why he was in my room so long. Now you know the whole truth, too," she whispered. "I still have to tell Stella.

"I—I don't expect any of you to forgive me, but I'm in love with you, Stasio…. I don't know how I could go on living if I thought you didn't believe me. Now that there's total honesty between us, I'll be able to get through the wedding before I fly back to the States."

She heard a sharp intake of breath. His face had darkened. "You think we have *total* honesty between us?"

What?

Her heart thudded hard. "I don't understand."

"Do you honestly believe I invited you to sail with me for any other reason than to get my hands on you and make love to you?" His voice shook. "Have you any conception of how I despised myself for wanting *you*, desiring *you*, instead of my own fiancée?"

Rachel almost fainted with joy. She'd never expected to hear these words.

"When Eleni phoned me on the ship and said she wasn't coming, I actually rejoiced because it meant I'd have you all to myself for seven days and nights. You sensed how I felt about you. Admit that's why you avoided me as much as possible and used Ari as a shield.''

"It was because I was afraid of my *own* feelings!" she cried out. "I was afraid that if you touched me, I wouldn't be able to control myself. I didn't dare add that to my conscience, not when I knew you were engaged to someone else."

"Obviously my engagement to Eleni didn't bother me enough to do the decent thing and leave you alone. By the time we reached Piraeus, I knew I was in love with you and I already had my own secret plan to make you marry me.

"I didn't particularly care how I did it as long as you became my wife. I had my own Carl in the form of Costas. I'm not proud of the fact that I used Ari to accomplish my objective. But I'd use him again if I had to...because I'm so desperately in love with you. Come here to me, Rachel."

Unable to contain such overpowering emotion, she ran into his arms. "Stasio, I need you so badly, I'm actually in pain."

"I've been in that condition much longer than you."

He swept her up in his arms and carried her to the bed. "Let me take it away for both of us. It's what I've been longing to do, my sweet, wonderful love. Give me your mouth, *agape mou*. Let me lie with you. Let me taste you, feel you."

Crying his name, she turned to him so their bodies lay side by side. He traced her trembling lips with his finger, then covered her mouth with his own.

She moaned in ecstasy. To be in Stasio's bed, in his arms, to feel his strong legs entwined with hers sent a voluptuous warmth through her body that had her calling his name over and over again.

His hands, his mouth, aroused a fever inside her that made it impossible not to give him everything in return. There was no other experience a man and a woman could share that brought this degree of rapture.

She heard him groan deep in his throat. "I love you, Rachel. You came into my life and filled the empty places so completely. I've become an entirely different person."

"I feel the same way," she whispered feverishly against his lips. "When I'm with you, I feel greater than I am. Immortal. But most of all, I'm so grateful I'm the woman who was privileged enough to love and be loved by you. If I could be granted one wish, I'd ask to spend all my days and nights right here with you, just like this. I adore you."

"Rachel—" he cried before pulling her on top of him, covering her in kisses. "You're so beautiful. There's nothing I want more than for this night to go on forever. But I need to know one more thing."

Rachel hid her face in his neck. "The answer is no. I've never slept with another man, because I've never been in love until now. I've never felt this way before."

On a moan, he buried his face in her hair. "I don't know how I was lucky enough to be the man you love, but I'd like to be worthy of you. So I'm going to ask you to leave my bed now. Don't come near it until our wedding night. After that, I'll never let you go."

"Stasio, I don't *want* to leave! Now that I've found you, I never want to be out of your sight. Can't I just lie next to you and…and face the other way?"

"No, my love, you cannot."

"But what if I just sit in a chair by the bed and hold your hand for the rest of the night."

"It wouldn't work. You *would* end up in my bed. All my good intentions would go up in smoke."

"I'll bring you some chocolates and tell you UFO stories."

"That might have worked with Ari. I happen to have other plans for us."

"Is there nothing I can do to tempt you?" she murmured against his lips.

"You do that by simply existing. That's why you have to go back to your room. Please, darling."

His voice sounded desperate.

"All right." She sat up. "I'm going." She slid off the bed and stood on unsteady legs. "But you'll be sorry."

"You think I don't know that?"

"Maybe we should have a rule that we won't see each other until I meet you at the altar the day after tomorrow. That's the only way I'm going to be able to stay away from you."

"Don't be ridiculous!"

She started to laugh and ran out of the room. He called her name but she refused to answer.

As soon as it was morning, she'd go to the *taverna* and ask for a room. The poor patron. He would know for a certainty that the soon-to-be-bride of Kyrie Athas wasn't running on a full tank.

"YOU LOOK BEAUTIFUL, Rachel!"

She leaned down and gave Ari a kiss. He and his mother were going to walk down the aisle first, hand in hand.

"You look so handsome in that tuxedo."

Then her glance flicked to Stella, who was lovely in the pale pink chiffon dress Rachel had chosen for her. "One day you'll walk down this same aisle with your husband and be as happy as I am."

Stella's brown eyes filled with tears. "I hope so, because I've never seen two people more in love than you and my brother." They hugged each other.

"Maybe. But I think he's mad at me right now."

"Frustrated is the word. Your idea of staying away from him didn't sit too well. He used to be easy to live with. Thank heaven your wedding day's finally arrived." Stella grinned. "Of course, he'll appreciate you all the more tonight. In fact, when he sees you in that wedding dress, all will be forgiven."

"You can say that again!"

"Nikos!" Rachel cried as he walked through the doors at the back of the church, resplendent in a black tux.

"How do I look?"

Ari stared up at his uncle. "You look just like me!" His comment made everyone laugh.

Stella signaled to Rachel. "The music has started."

"Is everybody ready?" Nikos wanted to know.

There was a collective yes.

He whispered in Rachel's ear, "I'll bet your stomach feels like mine when I'm at the top of a mountain waiting to start down the course."

"That's exactly how it feels," Rachel whispered back with a nervous excitement she could scarcely contain.

"Then let's take off and enjoy the ride. My brother will be waiting at the bottom to give you the victory kiss."

"I love you, Nikos."

"I love you, too." He kissed her lips gently, then put her hand on his arm.

Rachel watched Ari and Stella start down the aisle. When they were six feet ahead, she and Nikos began their walk. The tiny church was packed with well-wishers.

As they passed each pew, friends and neighbors stood up and smiled. Anna and Giorgio nodded to her. Ari couldn't have been raised by more charming people. According to Stella, they were planning to move to Greece, perhaps open a new restaurant on Andros. Everything was going to work out.

She saw Yannis and Melina. Their faces beamed.

"Carl!" she gasped softly when she saw him and his wife get to their feet. This was Stasio's doing. How Rachel loved her husband-to-be.

Carl looked at her, then Nikos, before he winked and a broad smile broke out on his kind face.

They continued their walk. Hal Rich and his wife had come, too, and their obvious happiness for her warmed Rachel's heart.

When they neared the front, she caught sight of a wheelchair. It was Manny! He nodded and blinked in recognition. She faltered, but Nikos was there to give her the support she needed.

By the time they reached Stasio, dressed in an elegant black suit, tears had blurred her vision. Then he turned to her with that beautiful smile meant only for her. She felt her soul leap to join his.

There was so much love in her heart, so much she had to tell him, so much she had to say—and all she could do was stand there and feast her eyes on him.

When he extended his hand, she clasped it eagerly. The priest began, "Dearly beloved…"

You are my beloved. She mouthed the words to Stasio.

As for Stasio, he couldn't take his eyes off his bride. Her red hair against all that silk and lace took his breath. Throughout the Mass, her blue eyes were talking to him, pouring out her love. She was letting him know everything she thought and felt.

He and Rachel had always been able to communicate without words. Today was no different. He knew her heart. She knew his.

When it was time to give her the ring Nikos had carried for him, Stasio slid it home next to her diamond. Then the priest pronounced the benediction and told Stasio to kiss his bride.

Rachel lifted her mouth to his. It seemed a lifetime since he'd known the wonder of her passionate embrace.

"Mommy?" Stasio heard Ari say aloud, "How come it's taking such a long time for Uncle Stasi to kiss Rachel?"

"Because they love each other very much," a gentle voice whispered back.

"They're married now, huh?"

"Yes, darling."

"You're my mommy now, huh?"

"Yes, and you're my little boy forever."

"Goody!"

"Goody is right," Stasio whispered against his wife's lips. "Goody for your plan of revenge. It backfired in my favor. I adore you...."

"I love you so much I can't wait until we're alone to show you."

"The things you say, Mrs. Athas. And the times you pick to say them..."

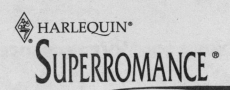

HARLEQUIN®
SUPERROMANCE®

From July to September 1999—three special
Superromance® novels about people whose
New Millennium resolution is

By the Year 2000: CELEBRATE!

JULY 1999—*A Cop's Good Name* by Linda Markowiak
Joe Latham's only hope of saving his badge and his reputation is
to persuade lawyer Maggie Hannan to take his case. Only Maggie—
his ex-wife—knows him well enough to believe him.

AUGUST 1999—*Mr. Miracle* by Carolyn McSparren
Scotsman Jamey McLachlan's come to Tennessee to keep the
promise he made to his stepfather. But Victoria Jamerson stands
between him and his goal, and hurting Vic is the last thing he wants
to do.

SEPTEMBER 1999—*Talk to Me* by Jan Freed
To save her grandmother's business, Kara Taylor has to co-host a
TV show with her ex about the differing points of view between men
and women. A topic Kara and Travis know plenty about.

By the end of the year,
everyone will have something to celebrate!

HARLEQUIN®
Makes any time special ™

HARLEQUIN CELEBRATES

FIVE DECADES OF ROMANCE

In July 1999 Harlequin Superromance®
brings you *The Lyon Legacy*—a
brand-new 3-in-1 book from popular
authors Peg Sutherland, Roz Denny Fox
& Ruth Jean Dale

3 stories for the price of 1!

Join us as we celebrate Harlequin's 50th Anniversary!

Look for these other
Harlequin Superromance®
titles wherever books are sold July 1999:

A COP'S GOOD NAME (#846)
by Linda Markowiak

THE MAN FROM HIGH MOUNTAIN (#848)
by Kay David

HER OWN RANGER (#849)
by Anne Marie Duquette

SAFE HAVEN (#850)
by Evelyn A. Crowe

JESSIE'S FATHER (#851)
by C. J. Carmichael

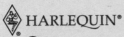

Harlequin is proud to introduce:

HEART OF THE WEST

...Where Every Man Has His Price!

Lost Springs Ranch was famous for turning young mavericks into good men. Word that the ranch was in financial trouble sent a herd of loyal bachelors stampeding back to Wyoming to put themselves on the auction block.

This is a brand-new 12-book continuity, which includes some of Harlequin's most talented authors.

Don't miss the first book,
Husband for Hire by Susan Wiggs.
It will be at your favorite retail outlet in July 1999.

HARLEQUIN®
Makes any time special ™

Look us up on-line at: http://www.romance.net · PHHOW